I0638936

The Movie Murders

a J.T. Ryan Thriller

A Novel
By

Lee Gimenez

RRP

River Ridge Press

The Movie Murders
by

Lee Gimenez

This is a work of fiction. The names, characters, places, incidents, and dialogues are products of the author's imagination and are not to be construed as real. Any resemblance to actual persons, living or dead, is entirely coincidental.

Printed in the United States of America.

Published by:

River Ridge Press

P.O. Box 501173

Atlanta, Georgia 31150

Cover photos: Franck Camhi and Gorodenkoff

Used under license from Shutterstock, Inc.

Cover design: Judith Gimenez

ISBN-13: 979-8-218-66748-1

Novels by Lee Gimenez

The Movie Murders

The Art of the Kill

The FBI Murders

Killshot

Tripwire

Blacksnow Zero

The Sigma Conspiracy

Crossfire

Fireball

FBI Code Red

The Media Murders

Skyflash

Killing West

The Washington Ultimatum

The Nanotech Murders

Death on Zanath

Virtual Thoughtstream

Azul 7

Terralus 4

The Tomorrow Solution

The Movie Murders

a J.T. Ryan Thriller

Chapter 1

Rome, Italy

"It's a beautiful day," Ann said, smiling. "Don't you think?"

Carl Parnell looked up at the blue sky and the shining sun. Then he glanced back at his wife. "I agree, Annie. It is."

The couple were strolling through the Roman Forum, the ancient city square built during the Roman Empire two thousand years ago. Rome's most famous tourist attraction, the Forum comprised the remnants of the ancient walls and monuments.

Ann grinned. "Thank you for bringing me here on vacation."

"It's my pleasure."

His wife looked as gorgeous as ever. Her long blonde hair cascaded down her back, and her azure eyes sparkled, part of the reason she had become such a famous actress.

She took his hand, and they continued along, passing the Arch of Titus and the Temple of Saturn. It was a cool, fall day, the summer tourist season was over, so the area was not crowded.

"Filming will start next month," she said. "Can you come? Please?"

"You know I have meetings scheduled in L.A."

"I know … I know …." Her eyes were pleading, her mouth quavering a bit. "It's just … I get so nervous when I start a new movie."

Parnell adored his wife and hated disappointing her. "All right, Annie. I'll be here."

Her face lit up. "Really?"

"Yes. I'll be here for the first few days when the filming starts. Okay?"

Ann went up on her tiptoes and hugged him tightly. "I love you! I love you so much."

Parnell hugged her back. "I love you too, Annie."

They continued strolling past the ancient ruins, walking over the worn cobblestone road, holding each other's hand.

He felt like today was a perfect day. In fact, the whole vacation had been great.

They neared the Basilica of Constantine, the imposing structure that was the largest building in the Forum.

Ann glanced up at him and pointed at the building. "Take my picture," she said sweetly, her smile radiant. "I want to remember this day for the rest of my life."

Parnell pulled his cell phone from a pocket and his wife strode under the archway of the ancient building.

She posed and grinned. She looked glorious in her short, white dress, her long blonde hair flowing well past her shoulders.

Parnell framed her with his phone and focused the lens.

Then, it all happened in a split-second.

He heard two muffled thuds.

Suddenly Ann screamed and clutched her chest, as bright red blotches appeared on the front of her white dress.

Her eyes widened, her knees buckled, and she collapsed on the cobblestone road.

Blood began to pool under her lifeless body.

Chapter 2

Atlanta, Georgia

John (J.T.) Ryan was driving north on I-75, heading toward his office in midtown Atlanta.

It was 8 a.m., the city's brutal traffic clogging the highway.

A semi in the next lane edged close to his Chevy Tahoe and Ryan leaned on the horn and jerked the wheel to avoid collision.

Just then Ryan's cell phone buzzed, and he picked it up from the center console. "Ryan here."

"It's Robert McKenzie."

"Colonel," Ryan said. "Good to hear from you. What's up?"

"I've got a new case, and I'd like you to work on it."

Colonel Robert McKenzie owned RMK Security, a large private security company. Ryan had completed several assignments for them over the last couple of years.

"That's great, Colonel. What's it about?"

"We've been hired by the GBI to help them investigate a murder related to a movie studio here in the Atlanta area. You'll be working with the lead agent assigned to the case. Special Agent Kelly O'Hara."

"Okay," Ryan said. "Do you want me to go to the GBI offices in town?"

"No. She'll come to you. I gave her your office address."

"All right. I'm headed that way now."

"That's good, J.T."

They said goodbye and hung up.

Ryan navigated his way through the heavy traffic and was in his office by 9 a.m.

He made coffee, booted up his laptop and scanned his email. That done, he started reviewing his pending cases.

Just then he heard a knock at his door.

Ryan opened a desk drawer and placed his hand on the handgun inside. In his line of work, it was good to be cautious. "Come in," he said.

His office door opened and a woman in a gray business suit came in. She was an attractive redhead with piercing green eyes. She appeared to be in her mid-thirties.

"I'm Special Agent O'Hara," she said, handing him her badge wallet. "You're John Ryan?"

"I am."

Ryan stood, and they shook hands. He glanced at her badge and returned it to her.

"Please have a seat," he said.

His visitor sat on one of the client chairs facing the desk.

"Colonel McKenzie called me this morning," he said, "and told me the GBI had retained his company to work on a case."

"That's right," she said. "I'm the lead agent on the case. The sign on your door says, *J.T. Ryan Investigations*. What's the T. stand for?"

Ryan smiled. "Terrific."

She frowned. "McKenzie told me you were a great investigator, but also a wiseass."

Ryan chuckled. "Guilty as charged." Then he said, "My full name is John Taylor Ryan, but everyone calls me J.T."

She nodded. "Okay."

"Would you like some coffee? I made a fresh pot this morning."

"Sure."

Ryan got up, went to the coffee maker on top of his filing cabinet, poured her a cup and handed it to her.

She sipped it and made a face. "How can you drink this crap? It tastes like motor oil." She placed the cup on his desk and pushed it away.

Ryan shrugged. "I'm used to it."

"So," O'Hara said, "do you know what we do at the GBI?"

He smiled. "The Georgia Bureau of Investigation. You're just like the FBI, just more convenient."

She frowned and shook her head slowly. "I'm not a big fan of the humor."

"I'm beginning to realize that."

"Let's cut the crap, okay?"

Turning serious, he said, "Yes, ma'am."

"Like I told McKenzie, we're investigating threats made to a movie studio here in the Atlanta area. As you probably know, several film companies have left California over the last ten years and set up shop here in Georgia. One of those companies is Genesis Worldwide Films."

"What kind of threats?" he asked.

"At first, they weren't threats. They were offers to buy out the company. When the company owner refused, the offers turned ominous. That's when we at the GBI were called in."

"I get the picture."

The GBI agent ran her hand over her long red hair, which was pulled into a ponytail. "Then things went from bad to worse," she said. "Recently a movie actress who was scheduled to star in a new movie for this studio was murdered."

Ryan began jotting down notes on a legal pad. "When and where?"

"The actress and her husband were vacationing in Rome, Italy a week ago. She was shot. Died at the scene."

"What about the husband?" he asked.

"He was unhurt."

"Any clues on who did it?"

She shook her head. "None. The Italian police found nothing at the scene. No clues of any kind. It appeared to them that it was not a random murder. They think it was a professional hit."

Ryan wrote all this down. "Can you give me the particulars of the film company and the owner?"

O'Hara spent the next half hour giving him the details of the case.

"How soon can you start working on this?" she asked.

"Right away. RMK is one of my best clients, so I'll rearrange my other work around this case."

"Good." She reached into her handbag, took out a business card and handed it to him. "You can contact me at my office number," she said, "or my cell."

Ryan glanced at the card. "Okay."

"McKenzie told me you were one of the best investigators he's ever worked with."

He smiled. "The best in Atlanta."

O'Hara frowned. "Modesty isn't one of your qualities, Ryan."

Ryan laughed. "I guess not."

He looked down at her business card. "Now that we're going to be working together, why don't you call me J.T., and I'll call you Kelly."

"I prefer last names. Call me Agent O'Hara and I'll call you Ryan."

He shook his head slowly and grinned. It was clear he wasn't going to melt her ice anytime soon.

"Works for me," he said.

Chapter 3

Tokyo, Japan

Nikita strode into the Operations Center and glanced around. The twenty people in the room, men and women, were at their computer workstations, focused on their respective assignments.

The large room featured one wall covered with a massive flat-screen TV, with several smaller TV screens to the side of it.

Nikita approached one of the workstations and the man there glanced up from his computer screen.

"Good job on the Rome assignment," she said, sitting at the chair next to the workstation.

"Thanks," Kruger replied, in heavily accented English. The German man, like all the workers in the room, communicated in English.

"I watched the news reports," she said. "They mentioned the Italian police have no clues as to the identity of the shooter."

Kruger nodded and crossed his arms in front of him. Kruger was a brawny, hard-faced man in his late forties.

"Do you have another project for me?" he asked.

"Not today, Kruger. But soon." She gave him a tight smile. "Our work is never done."

Nikita stood and strode around the room, stopping at several more workstations to get progress reports from other operatives. As the director of the operations center, it was her job to make sure everyone was working at peak performance. Staffed by people from many countries, the center had assembled highly skilled operatives with a wide range of skills. They were all paid extremely well to ensure their allegiance and confidentiality.

Nikita stopped at another workstation, this one staffed by a young French woman. Like all the other female operatives, this one was gorgeous.

"How is your current assignment going?" Nikita asked.

Marie shook her head. "Not well. Not well at all."

"You need to finish it," Nikita said, her voice low and harsh. "I pay you for results."

"Yes, Nikita."

"Have you fucked the man yet?"

The young French woman shook her head again.

Nikita glared. "What are you waiting for? You know the drill. Fuck him, film it, then blackmail him to get what we want."

"And it that doesn't work?"

"Then you kill him, Marie."

Nikita stood, and after talking with several more operatives, left the room. The Operations Center was located in the basement of the skyscraper, and she took the elevator to the top floor of the building.

She owned a penthouse suite, a lavishly decorated three-bedroom apartment that overlooked the Sumida River. The massive living room had a splendid view of Tokyo.

Nikita went to the teak cabinet, and poured out a large tumbler of *sake*, her favorite drink. Japan's most popular alcoholic beverage, *sake* was a rice-based wine. She took a sip and nibbled on *Himemaru* crackers.

As she stared out the floor-to-ceiling windows at the river below and the multitude of skyscrapers, she mulled over the progress on the ongoing projects. It was dusk now and the rows and rows of high-rise buildings were a riot of colorful lights.

A native of Japan, Nikita loved the city, loved the energy and excitement of living in a thriving, fast-moving metropolis of 37 million people. From her vantage point on the 70th floor of the building, everything below seemed orderly and perfect.

She sipped more of the *sake*, pleased with the current progress of the operations center.

Nikita was a beautiful and slender Japanese woman, with an alluring face. She could have been in her late twenties or in her forties, it was hard to determine. With piercing black eyes, long black hair, and flawless skin, she was the epitome of Asian beauty. But in addition to her beauty, she radiated confidence, high intelligence and determination, qualities that had always served her well. Once an operative herself, she had risen in the ranks until she became the operations director.

Like on most days, Nikita was dressed in traditional Japanese clothing. Today she was wearing a black kimono, with a red and gold sash, known as an *obi*. Although most Japanese businesswomen wore modern clothing, she preferred the traditional look of the kimono.

Nikita took another sip of the *sake* as she continued watching the riot of colorful lights below. Overall, today had been a good day, she mused.

A productive day. Her boss would be pleased.

Chapter 4

Atlanta, Georgia

J.T. Ryan was in his apartment, getting ready for his first appointment of the day, when he heard a knock at his door.

Striding to the foyer, he peered through the spyhole and saw no one there.

He went back to his bedroom, holstered his Desert Eagle pistol at his waist, and shrugged on his navy blazer. That done, he picked up his keys and left the apartment. Just as he was about to lock the door, he spotted two big, swarthy men in the corridor rush toward him. One was carrying a tire iron and the other a baseball bat.

With his heart pounding, he faced the two men. Going into a fighting stance, he threw a punch, hitting one of the thugs in the face. The guy groaned, dropped the tire iron and staggered back.

The other thug swung the bat and Ryan edged away from it, but not enough and the bat hit his ear, drawing blood.

Enraged, Ryan kicked the guy in the groin and the thug howled, clutched his groin and collapsed to the corridor floor.

Then Ryan turned toward the other thug, but by then the guy was racing toward the stairwell.

With his adrenaline pumping, Ryan took out his handkerchief and used it to stanch the blood dripping from his ear.

Then he turned to the criminal that was groaning on the floor. Taking out plastic cuffs, he rolled the guy on his front and tied his hands behind his back.

That done, he pulled out his cell phone and called 911.

When he was finished with the call, he shook his head slowly, aggravated that robberies and home invasions were on the rise in Atlanta. That was something the city's Chamber of Commerce conveniently left out of their brochures.

***

Several hours later, Ryan pulled into the parking lot of the Genesis Films headquarters building. Located in Sandy Springs, a suburb of Atlanta, the Genesis studios were a sprawling complex of several structures in a parklike setting.

He went into the building and approached the receptionist's desk. "I'm J.T. Ryan," he said to the woman. "I have an appointment with Mr. Atkins."

The woman looked over her half-glasses at him, then scanned a notebook in front of her.

"You're late, Mr. Ryan," she said in a stiff voice. She was a frumpy-looking woman in her mid-fifties.

Ryan smiled to disarm her haughty attitude. "Sorry about that. I was detained."

She frowned and shook her head slowly. She picked up the handset of her desk phone and spoke into it. Then she said, "Have a seat. Someone will be out in a moment."

A few minutes later he was shown into the large, impressive office of the studio owner, Matthew Atkins. The man stood, came around his desk and shook hands with Ryan. Atkins was tall, but Ryan was 6'4" and heavily muscled and towered over him.

"Please have a seat, Mr. Ryan."

"Thanks." Ryan took one of the plush visitor's chairs facing the desk.

"Agent O'Hara from the GBI called me," Atkins said. "She told me you were working with them on our case." The company owner was a distinguished-looking man in his sixties with silver hair and a silver mustache. He wore a dark gray three-piece business suit with a blue silk tie.

Ryan showed him his PI license and handed him one of his business cards. "That's right. The GBI has hired me to assist."

"What happened to your ear?" Atkins asked.

Ryan gingerly touched the bandage there. "That's the reason I was late. A couple of thugs tried to rob me this morning."

Atkins frowned. "Atlanta's not as safe as it used to be years ago."

"That's a fact."

"So, what happened? Did the police stop them?"

Ryan shook his head. "No. I took care of the thugs on my own."

Atkins nodded, then steepled his hands on his desk. "Did Agent O'Hara tell you what's been happening?"

"She did, sir. But it would be helpful if you could tell me everything. Start at the beginning."

"Okay, Mr. Ryan."

"Call me J.T. Everybody does."

"All right, J.T. About six months ago, we were contacted by a law firm here in Atlanta. They made an offer to buy my company. I have no interest in selling and I declined."

"This law firm," Ryan said, "were they representing a third party?"

"They were. But they wouldn't tell me who that was."

"What happened then?"

"A month later they came back and offered me more money to sell," Atkins said.

"And?"

"And I said no again. I told them I had no interest in selling."

Ryan rubbed his jaw. "What happened then?"

"The legal people made a third offer, even more money than the first two. And they also gave me a veiled threat. To sell, or else."

"Or else what?"

"It was clear to me, J.T., that these people would not take no for an answer. I threw them out of my office and called the Georgia Bureau of Investigation."

Ryan inclined his head. "Okay. Can you tell me about your business. What kind of movies you make?"

Atkins steepled his hands on his desk. "We at Genesis Worldwide Films make faith-based movies. It's a fast-growing market. It's a market shunned by Hollywood studios."

"All right. What happened after you turned down their third offer to buy you out?"

"Nothing at first, J.T. We continued making faith-based films. Then the unthinkable happened. A young actress we had signed for an upcoming film was murdered. I'm sure it's connected to the buyout offers."

"This actress was murdered in Rome."

"That's right. That's the location where our movie was going to be filmed."

Ryan mulled this over for a moment. "I agree, Mr. Atkins. It has to be connected. The murder was not a robbery gone bad, or a random killing. It was a professional hit."

Chapter 5

GBI Headquarters
Decatur, Georgia

J.T. Ryan concluded his meeting at Genesis Films and had just arrived at the main offices of the GBI, which were located in Decatur, a city adjacent to Atlanta. He was in their spacious lobby, waiting to see Agent Kelly O'Hara.

Established in 1937, the Georgia Bureau of Investigation was originally named the Department of Public Safety. It was the first statewide law enforcement agency in Georgia. The GBI has two main divisions, the Georgia State Patrol, and the 'plainclothes' division, officially designated the Division of Criminal Investigation. Currently this division has 350 agents. Their main function is to investigate crimes in the state of Georgia. They coordinate with local law-enforcement and with the FBI. The GBI also has a CSI department which performs forensic laboratory work. Another part of the GBI is its GCIC unit, the Georgia Crime Information Center, which mirrors the FBI's National Crime Information Center (NCIC).

Ryan had not assisted the GBI before and was looking forward to this case. He had helped with many FBI investigations, working closely with Erin Welch, the Assistant Director who ran the FBI's Atlanta office.

After waiting in the GBI lobby, he was escorted to Agent Kelly O'Hara's office on the second floor of the multi-story building.

The two shook hands and she handed him a day pass for the building. Then she sat behind her desk as he took a chair in front of it.

Today the attractive redhead was wearing a white blouse, a navy-blue skirt and navy flats. Her long mane of red hair was combed over one shoulder. She had piercing green eyes that flashed intelligence and determination. Her GBI badge was clipped to her belt, and she had a Glock 19 holstered on her hip.

"Before I hired you," she said, "I checked you out with someone you know well. Erin Welch. She gave you a glowing recommendation."

Ryan grinned. "And here I thought you hired me because of my charm and good looks."

O'Hara shook her head slowly. "Erin also told me you were a smartass."

He chuckled. "Guilty as charged." Then he turned serious. "I miss Erin. She was great to work with as the Atlanta ADIC."

"I agree, Ryan. But she got a big promotion to be the FBI Director. That was a big step up for her."

"True. But I know for a fact she hated leaving this city. She loved living here."

O'Hara pointed to his bandaged ear. "I read the Atlanta PD blotter this morning. Your name popped up, as an attempted robbery." She smiled. "I also read the thugs got the worst of it."

"Hopefully they'll think twice before pulling that crap on someone else."

The agent frowned. "I doubt it. In my experience, most crooks are stupid, or lazy or both."

Ryan gave the attractive woman a long look. "Did anyone tell you that you look more like a model than a law-enforcement officer?"

Her face flushed. "Are you hitting on me?"

"No. I was paying you a compliment."

She grimaced, trying to ascertain his motives. "Well, cut it out, Ryan. I want our relationship to remain strictly professional."

He gave her a half salute. "Yes, ma'am."

"Matthew Atkins from Genesis Films called me," she said. "Told me you two had met and that he filled you in on the case."

"Yes, he did. My next move is to fly to Rome and talk to the police there about the murder."

"Okay, Ryan. I was going to suggest the same thing."

Ryan grinned. "Great minds think alike."

The woman frowned. "Is this another one of your jokes?"

He shook his head. "Absolutely not. It's obvious you're highly intelligent. Otherwise, you wouldn't have gotten to where you are now. I did some research on you also – you've been promoted three times at the GBI and received several commendations."

O'Hara cocked her head. "Good research. All of that is true." She paused and then said, "I may have underestimated you."

"A lot of people do."

"How soon can you leave for Rome?"

"Right away," he said. "Delta has flights into there daily. There's just one thing."

"What?"

"I need to fly business class. I don't fit in those cramped coach seats."

"Bullshit. You'll fly coach, just like I do."

"You're not 6'4"."

She crossed her arms over her chest. "Nevertheless, I'm not going to let you upgrade to business class. Understood?"

Ryan shook his head slowly, then grinned. "You're a hardass, you know that?"

O'Hare tried to suppress a smile and failed. "I've been called worse."

Chapter 6

Rome, Italy

J.T. Ryan had been to Rome many times before and loved the city. It's a historic and beautiful place, with ancient monuments from the time of the Roman Empire. The city is also a vibrant, bustling metropolis with a population of over four million people.

He glanced out the window of the Delta jet as it went into final approach over the airport. They had just flown over several popular landmarks, the Colosseum and Saint Peter's Basilica, and were now over the main runway of Fiumicino, Rome's airport.

They landed soon after.

Ryan got up from his cramped coach seat and, along with hundreds of other passengers, made his way through the airport concourse. He grabbed his backpack from the baggage carousel, went through customs, and headed toward the Hertz rental location.

Unfortunately, all they had available at the moment were tiny Fiats and even smaller Smart cars, so he opted for a Ducati, a powerful Italian motorcycle.

He tied down his rucksack at the back of the motorcycle, donned a helmet, and turned on the motor. The large engine roared to life, and he drove out of the busy airport, dodging around cars, and trucks, and buses.

Soon he was in the bustling city center, and he made his way to the Cicerone, a hotel he had previously stayed at several times. The place was convenient to the center of Rome and close to the Piazza Navona, a popular dining and shopping district.

Ryan checked into the hotel, grabbed a meal at the hotel's restaurant, and went up to his room. Flights from Atlanta into Rome were overnight, and now it was 9 a.m. local time.

He showered, donned fresh clothes and headed out of his room.

An hour later, he went into the Carabinieri police building on Via di S. Vitale Avenue. He showed his ID to the desk sergeant on duty and asked to see Detective Maria Rosetti, the officer in charge of the Parnell murder.

Ryan was shown into a small conference room by the lobby and asked to wait.

When Rosetti walked in, Ryan stood and handed her his cred wallet.

"I'm John Ryan," he said in Italian. "I understand you've been assigned to the Parnell case."

The woman examined his credentials, handed them back and they sat across each other at a scarred wooden table.

"Yes, that is right, Mr. Ryan. I am working on the murder of the American actress." She gave him a hard look. "What is your interest in this case?"

The police detective was a matronly, heavyset woman in her forties. She wore a simple black suit, and her raven hair was pulled back into a tight bun.

"I've been hired by the Georgia Bureau of Investigation to help them investigate."

She nodded. "I see."

Ryan smiled. "I'm hoping you and I can pool our resources and solve the case faster that way."

Rosetti frowned. "I am not in the habit of sharing case information with civilians."

Ryan grinned. "I'm not just any civilian. I'm the best PI in Atlanta, and possibly in the USA."

Her frown deepened, then an amused expression crossed her face. "Is that a joke you are making?"

Ryan laughed. "It is."

She gave him a long look and eventually said, "All right. Maybe we can share information. But you first."

"Of course, Detective. We believe the murder of Ann Parnell here in Rome is part of a larger criminal conspiracy. A conspiracy intended to intimidate Genesis Films, a movie studio in Georgia."

"Who is behind the conspiracy, Ryan?"

"That's what I intend to find out. The criminals are trying to buy this movie studio and threatened the owner if he didn't sell it. He refused and Ann Parnell appears to be the first casualty."

"Okay," she said. "I understand. The young actress was murdered at the Forum, a popular tourist attraction here in Rome. The mayor of the city is very upset, as are all our city leaders. Tourism generates a lot of revenue for Rome. Our politicians want this murder solved fast and off the front pages."

Ryan tilted his head. "From the police reports I've read, there were no clues as to the identity of the killer."

"That is right. It appears to be a professional hit."

"It would be helpful, Detective Rosetti, if I you could show me the scene of the crime."

"That I can do. I will drive us over there."

***

Half an hour later, Rosetti and Ryan were striding through the Roman Forum, the ancient city square built during the Roman Empire two thousand years ago. They approached a large structure and Rosetti pointed toward it.

"That is the Basilica of Constantine," she said. "The actress was posing in front of that building and her husband was taking her photo when it happened."

The two of them walked over the worn cobblestone street and stood under one of the archways.

Ryan studied the scene for a few minutes. Then he glanced across the street at the ancient ruins of another building. "I'm guessing the shooter fired from over there. He used the building for cover."

"That is what I think also."

"What caliber rounds were used?" he asked.

"We found no shell casings, so the killer cleaned up his brass. But from the remnants we found in the body, we estimate it was a 9-millimeter round."

"Okay."

They spent the next half hour surveying the scene, and Rosetti filled him in on the scant details they had.

When she was done, Ryan said, "Where's the body now?"

"At the main morgue here in Rome. The woman's husband wants to take it back for a funeral, but we have not released it yet."

"I'd like to see it."

"The corpse?"

"Yes."

She gave him a quizzical look. "Why?"

"Sometimes I can generate clues from seeing the body."

She shrugged. "I think you are wasting your time."

"Humor me, Detective."

They left the Forum, and she drove them in her police car to the Municipal Morgue, which is located in the Piazzale del Verano.

They went inside and the technician on duty led them through the building into an extremely cold and bright room filled with metal lockers all along the walls. The place, like every other morgue Ryan had been to, smelled of bleach and disinfectant, which almost masked the underlying stench of human decomp.

After consulting a computer, the technician went to one of the metal lockers, opened it, and pulled out a metal tray.

The man pulled down the sheet that was covering the cadaver. Ryan recalled photos he had seen of Ann Parnell before her murder. She had been a young, beautiful blonde woman, vibrant and full of life. According to the things he had read, she had also been a talented actress with a bright future.

Now her nude body was so pale it looked grayish white. The Y incision of the autopsy was evident on her torso as were the two bullet holes in her chest.

Ryan examined the body for a long moment, then pulled the sheet over it. After saying a silent prayer for the young woman, he turned to Rosetti.

"I'm done," he said.

Rosetti nodded. "Learn anything?"

Ryan felt a surge of anger. "Yes. Ann Parnell was an innocent victim and should be alive. And I'm going to find the bastard who did it."

The two of them left the morgue and Rosetti drove them back to the police station. She parked her sedan in the lot fronting the building.

Before they went inside, Ryan said, "I'd like to buy you dinner. For sharing all the information with me."

The woman frowned. "Visits to the morgue kill my appetite, no pun intended. But I could use a drink. There is a tavern across the street."

"That would be great. I could use a drink myself."

They got out of the unmarked car and strode to the bar and walked inside. They sat across from each other at a booth at the back.

The waitress came over and Rosetti ordered a Campari and soda, while Ryan ordered a Peroni, his favorite Italian beer.

When the drinks came, he lifted his glass and said, "To finding the killer."

"I will drink to that," she said, taking a sip of her Campari.

He gave her an appraising look. "Tell me, Detective Rosetti, how did a gorgeous woman like you get into law-enforcement?"

She frowned, then her expression softened, and she chuckled. "Thank you for the compliment. But you are bullshitting me now. I'm no beauty. I'm far, far from it. I'm an overweight, frumpy woman with a plain face."

Ryan smiled. "Don't sell yourself short. Every woman is beautiful in her own way."

She gave him a lengthy gaze, as if trying to determine his veracity. "I'm not a fan of Americans. Most are rude, pushy tourists. But you seem different. You are a nice man."

Ryan nodded. "Thanks."

They both had another drink and Rosetti said, "What are your plans now?"

"I go back to the U.S. and keep working the case."

"I would appreciate it if you could keep me up to date on your progress, Mr. Ryan. The chief of police is pushing me hard to solve this damn thing."

"I'd be glad to," he said. "But on one condition."

"What is that?"

"Call me J.T. from now on."

Rosetti smiled. "Okay, J.T." Then she glanced at her watch. "I better get back to work."

"Of course." He handed her his business card, and she gave him hers.

Ryan pulled out his wallet and dropped Euros on the table to pay for the drinks.

Then they shook hands and left the bar.

Chapter 7

Tokyo, Japan

Nikita strode into the Operations Center and glanced around. The twenty people in the room were at their computer workstations, all focused on their respective assignments.

Nikita approached one of the workstations and the man there glanced up from his computer screen.

"I have another job for you," she said, sitting at the chair next to the workstation.

"Good," Kruger replied, in heavily accented English. The German man, like all the workers in the room, communicated in English. "I prefer being in the field. I hate sitting around staring at a computer all day." Kruger was a stone-faced, forbidding looking man with cold eyes.

Nikita handed him a file folder and they spent the next hour going over the details of the job.

"Should I try to change his mind before I terminate him?" Kruger asked.

She mulled this over for a moment. "You can try. I don't think it'll work, but go ahead. See if you can change his mind."

"How soon do you need this done, Nikita?"

"Right away."

"I know Japan Air has several flights to there every day," he said. "I'll book one of them."

She gave him a tight smile and lowered her voice to a whisper. "Before you go, I need something else from you."

"What's that?"

"I need a good, hard fuck, Kruger."

His face lit up in anticipation. "When?"

She smiled fiercely. "I'll go back up to my penthouse now. Come up in fifteen minutes."

Kruger grinned. "You're the boss, Nikita."

She stood. "That I am. And never forget that."

Chapter 8

Savannah, Georgia

Kruger had been in Savannah for the last three days, scouting out the city and the movie set. Genesis Films had been on location for the last month, filming throughout the city. Currently they were filming on Savannah's waterfront, on East River Street by Factor's Walk and The Waving Girl statue.

Genesis had set up their overnight operation nearby, with an assortment of travel trailers, RVs, trucks, and temporary storage buildings grouped together.

Filming had ended a few hours ago and Kruger had observed the film director go into his trailer. A catering truck had driven through the area a little while ago and dropped off dinners to the large group of people who were involved in the making of the movie. There were probably a hundred people in total, which included the actors, cameramen, stagehands, grips, sound engineers, and assistants.

Kruger, thanks to his forged press pass, had been able to easily wander around the filming location.

It was nighttime now and many of the travel trailers and RVs showed lights inside.

Figuring the timing was right, Kruger walked to the film director's trailer and knocked on the door.

A moment later the man opened it. "Can I help you?" he said.

Kruger's press pass has dangling from his neck, and he held it up for the other man to see. "I'm with the Savannah Morning News, sir. If possible, I'd like to interview you for our newspaper."

The film director inspected the press credentials and smiled. "Of course. Come in, please. I'm always glad to get publicity for our movie."

Kruger went into the trailer, and they sat across each other at the small table by the diminutive kitchen. He glanced around to confirm no one else was in the trailer.

"Thank you for taking the time to talk to me, Mr. Morris," Kruger said.

"Not a problem," the other man replied. "I'll be glad to answer any of your questions."

"Actually, I'm not a reporter, sir."

Morris's eyebrows shot up. "You're not?"

"No, I'm not. I'm here to give you a chance to drop your project."

The film director glared. "Stop filming? Why the hell should I? That's a crazy idea. Who the hell are you anyway?"

"I represent people who want you to stop making this movie."

Morris shook his head slowly. "Now I understand. You're part of the group who's been threatening our company president."

"That's right."

The film director pointed toward the door. "Get out. This conversation is over. Atkins told you no, and I'm telling you no. We are not going to stop making this film or any others. Understood?"

"Is that your final answer?"

Morris scowled. "Out! Now! If you don't, I'm calling the cops."

Kruger stood. "All right. I'm leaving."

He turned and left the trailer, then strode about one hundred feet away, to a parking area where he had left his rental car.

He glanced around the area, saw no one, and got in his vehicle. From his vantage point, the film director's trailer was still clearly visible.

Taking out the detonator from his pocket, he stared at the travel trailer intently. Last night he had attached a bomb underneath the trailer.

Kruger turned on the detonator. He took a deep breath and let it out slowly. Then he pressed the red button.

Instantly the travel trailer exploded, the bright red and orange flames shooting up into the nighttime sky. Shredded metal pieces rained over the area. A deafening *boom* echoed several times, then died away.

Kruger put away the detonator, then started up his rental car. He drove out of the parking lot and headed away from the scene, keeping the car well under the speed limit.

Chapter 9

Atlanta, Georgia

J.T. Ryan was in his apartment, getting dinner ready. From the fridge he took out the leftover lasagna he had prepared for himself a few days ago. After microwaving the lasagna and grabbing a Coors beer, he sat down at his dinette to eat.

Just then he heard a knock at his door.

He tensed immediately, recalling the last time someone had visited his apartment. He had dispatched the two thugs who attacked him, but the memory of it was still vivid.

Pulling his pistol from his waist holster, he went to the door and peered through the spyhole. Seeing who was there, he opened the door widely.

"What a welcome surprise," he said with a grin. "Come in, Kelly."

Kelly O'Hara strode in, and Ryan closed the door behind her.

"You can put the gun away," she said, pointing to it. "Unless you plan on shooting me."

Ryan holstered his weapon. "Not today," he said with a chuckle.

The GBI agent did not appear amused by his joke. The redhead was wearing a gray business suit with a white blouse. Her long reddish hair was pulled into a ponytail.

"I was just sitting down for dinner," he said. "I have plenty for both of us. Would you like to join me?"

"This isn't a social call, Ryan."

He smiled. "Too bad."

The woman glanced around Ryan's living room. "Let's sit. There's been another murder. I want to fill you in."

He nodded, and they sat across from each other.

"A man named Sam Morris was killed today," she said. "He was on location in Savannah doing filming for a new movie."

"How did he die?"

"The travel trailer he was in was blown up."

"Is this connected to the Genesis Films case, Kelly?"

"I'm sure it is. Morris was a film director for Genesis."

"I see. When did this happen?"

"An hour ago. The local cops called the GBI right away and we have technicians there already processing the scene."

Ryan rubbed his jaw. "Tell me more about this Morris guy. His name sounds familiar."

"It should. He's a famous movie director. He won an Academy Award a few years ago."

"Okay. I'll call Atkins at Genesis and get his take on this."

"I already did that, Ryan, before I came here. The studio was making a faith-based film in Savannah. He and Morris had already received threats not to make this film. It's clear this murder is related to the murder of the actress in Rome."

Ryan inclined his head. "I'll head to Savannah right away."

"Correction. We'll both be heading to Savannah."

"I prefer working alone, Kelly. I get better results that way."

She folded her arms across her chest. "I'm the GBI agent. I have jurisdiction in the state of Georgia."

Ryan frowned. "I'm not going to change your mind, am I."

"No."

"All right. I think it'll be faster if we drive there as opposed to flying. I can drive us there in my Tahoe."

She shook her head. "No. We'll take my Explorer, it's a law-enforcement vehicle. And I'll drive."

Ryan shook his head slowly, then smiled. "I bet you like to be on top, too."

Kelly's cheeks flushed, then her whole face turned beet red. "I can't believe you just said that! My sexual preferences are none of your damn business."

Ryan held up his palms, realizing he'd gone too far. "Sorry. I was just making a joke."

She grimaced. "Well, damn it, cut it out! I told you before, our relationship is, and will remain, strictly business."

"That's fine with me."

He glanced at his watch. "Before we leave, I need to have my dinner. It's the only food I've had all day. Like I said before, I have enough for both of us, if you'd care to join me."

"Okay. I'm hungry too."

They left the living room and went into the kitchen of his apartment. She took a seat at the dinette table.

He said, "Would you like a drink? I've got beer, bottled water, and milk. I don't have any wine, though."

"Actually, I prefer beer to wine."

He grinned. "That's refreshing. Most of the women I know are wine or vodka drinkers."

Ryan opened the refrigerator and peered inside. "I've got Coors, Sierra Nevada Pale Ale, and Guinness. Which would you like?"

She smiled. "Guinness? My parents are from Ireland, so I love Guinness."

"I love Guinness too. They make the best stout beer."

She cocked her head. "There's hope for you yet, Ryan."

He laughed, pulled out two bottles of the Irish beer from the fridge, opened them and placed them on the table, along with two glasses. Then he proceeded to reheat the lasagna. He also warmed up a loaf of French bread.

He spooned the lasagna into two bowls and set them on the table, along with the loaf of bread and butter and cutlery.

Kelly took a bite of the lasagna. "Mmm, this is good. Really good. What restaurant do you get your takeout from?"

He shook his head. "No takeout. I made this myself."

She looked skeptical. "Bullshit. You did not."

He raised three fingers of his right hand. "Scout's Honor. I cooked this myself."

Kelly gave him a long look. "Okay. I believe you. You're the first man I've known who could cook. I'm a crappy cook myself. Most of my meals are takeout Chinese or Mexican." She pursed her lips. "I may have underestimated you."

Ryan laughed. "Most people do. They think all I'm good for is kicking down doors and beating up thugs."

Kelly smiled.

Then they began to eat dinner and continued talking about the case.

When they were done an hour later, she glanced at her watch. "If we leave now for Savannah, we'll be there by morning. But if you're too tired, we can leave first thing tomorrow."

"We can leave now, Kelly. In the Army, I was in Special Forces. I'm used to little or no sleep."

"Good. I'd like to get going then. I've always found that the sooner you get to a crime scene the better."

"I agree."

Kelly studied him for a long moment. "Since you fed me such a tasty meal, I'll let you drive to Savannah, if you prefer."

He grinned. "We're making progress."

She returned the smile. "But don't let it go to your head. I'm still your boss. Understood?"

Ryan laughed and gave her a half salute. "Yes, ma'am."

Chapter 10

Savannah, Georgia

J.T. Ryan stared at the crime scene, which was encircled by yellow crime scene tape. The travel trailer, what was left of it, consisted of mangled and charred pieces of metal and plastic. Smoke still billowed from it, although the local fire department had extinguished the flames.

Nearby there were other travel trailers, and RVs, trucks, and temporary metal sheds which were used by the movie studio for the making of the film. Luckily, no one else besides Morris had been killed by the blast, although several people had suffered injuries.

CSI techs were at the crime scene also, collecting trace evidence.

Ryan turned toward Kelly, who was standing next to him.

"What kind of explosive was used?" he asked her.

"The techs told me they thought it was C-4 or Semtex."

"The hit was done by a professional, Kelly. Common criminals don't have access to sophisticated explosives like that. And whoever did it, wanted to send a message. This murder, like the one in Rome, was done in a very public way."

"I agree."

Ryan stepped back several feet and surveyed the scene for a few minutes.

"This blast zone looks familiar," he said.

Kelly turned towards him. "What do you mean?"

"You see how the trailer blew up? The detonation came from the center of it and the charred metal that's left is all around the scene."

"So?"

"I saw this same pattern during the war in Afghanistan," he said. "The Taliban would place explosives underneath Army Humvees and trucks at night when there was no one around. Then the Taliban would set off the bombs during the day, when the American soldiers were inside them. The blast pattern you see here is almost identical."

Kelly rubbed her chin. "So, what does that mean?"

"It means the killer most likely visited this area at night, taped the explosive to underneath the trailer, then remotely activated the bomb."

"Okay, Ryan. I follow what you're saying. But how does that help us find the perp?"

Ryan mulled this over for a moment. "The killer must have had access to this area. I saw private security guards when we arrived here. So, this film location area is restricted."

Kelly tilted her head. "I agree. I noticed the guards also." She pointed to a uniformed man who was nearby. "Let's ask him."

Ryan and Kelly approached the man, who was wearing a blue uniform and cap emblazoned with logos of a security company. He was carrying a clipboard and had a holstered pistol at his waist.

"I'm Agent O'Hara of the GBI," Kelly said. "We're investigating the murder and explosion. Can you tell us if this area is restricted, or can anyone just walk around?"

"It's restricted," the guard replied. "This area and all the areas where filming took place are restricted. The movie company didn't want people nosing around for safety reasons. That's why they hired our security company."

"Who was allowed in?" Ryan said.

"Anyone involved in the filming itself. The actors, and film crew, and the support staff, of course. But also food catering people."

"Anybody else?" Ryan asked.

The guard thought about that for a moment. "The press. Local TV station and newspaper people. They were very interested and visited the area frequently."

Ryan said, "Did these press people get passes?"

"That's right. They did. Our security company made badges for them."

"Tell me the process for that," Kelly said.

"It's simple, really," the guard replied. "The reporters came to me, showed me their ID and I would take their photo and make up a badge for them to wear when they were here."

Ryan nodded. "How many press passes did you issue?"

The guard checked his clipboard and flipped a few pages. "I made up 10 passes in total."

"Could you email me a list of these people?" Ryan said. "Their photos and which TV station or newspaper they worked for."

"Of course. No problem."

Ryan handed the guard his business card.

"Anything else you need?" the guard said.

"Just one last thing," Ryan replied. "How many security guards are involved?"

"There's three of us. I handle the day shift, since I'm the senior man. We have two other guards. They cover the rest of the day on 8-hour shifts."

"Thanks," Kelly said. "You've been very helpful."

The guard moved away.

Just then Kelly's cell phone rang, and she answered it. She spoke for several minutes, then hung up.

"That was my boss at the GBI," she said. "I've been assigned to an additional case. I have to get back to Atlanta."

"All right, Kelly. I'll stay in Savannah and keep working on this."

"We came in one car. How will you get back?"

Ryan grinned. "I'll hitchhike back."

She shook her head slowly. "Smartass."

"That would be me," he said, chuckling. Then he turned serious. "I'll catch a flight when I'm done here."

"Okay. I've got to get going." She began to walk away, then turned back toward him. "Looks like you got your wish after all, Ryan."

"How's that?"

"You get to work on your own."

"Looks that way," he said.

"But I want a written report of everything you find here."

He gave her a half salute. "Yes, ma'am. Will handwritten do, or do you want it typed?"

"You're insufferable."

"I'm also charming and good looking."

She glared at him. "Grrrrrr…."

"You have a beautiful face, Kelly. If you keep frowning like that, you'll get it wrinkled."

Kelly rolled her eyes, let out a long sigh, then stalked off.

Ryan grinned as she walked away.

Chapter 11

Savannah, Georgia

J.T. Ryan worked the rest of the day on the case, then checked into a hotel he had stayed at previously, the Marshall House. It was centrally located and close to the city's waterfront. He called Hertz, rented a sedan and had it delivered to the hotel. Then he had dinner at the Cotton Exchange, a nearby restaurant that served great gumbo, and went to bed early. Since he and Kelly had driven overnight from Atlanta, he was starved for sleep.

The next morning, he got up early, grabbed a coffee and a chocolate donut from the hotel's concession stand, then began his day.

Ryan spent the morning and early afternoon running down the leads he had received from the security guard. He drove his rented Mustang to the local television stations and newspapers around the city that had received press passes.

By 3 p.m. he only had one more to check out, a reporter for the Savannah Morning News. Since the other nine reporters had checked out, Ryan hoped this last guy was somehow connected with the bombing, otherwise his theory was a total bust.

Ryan entered the newspaper building, which was in downtown Savannah.

"I'm John Ryan," he said to the receptionist in the lobby. "I'm a private investigator working with the GBI. I need to see one of your reporters, Jim Hartlett." He handed the woman his card.

The woman, an elderly lady with coiffed white hair inspected his card closely. "A PI, huh," she said. "Like on TV." She gave him a long, up and down look. "You do look a bit like Magnum."

Ryan grinned. "I always thought I was better looking than him."

The receptionist smiled. "If you'll have a seat, Mr. Ryan, I'll find Jim for you."

Ryan thanked the woman and sat in the spacious lobby, which was designed in Georgian architecture style. The historic building had a Southern charm to it, like many of the structures in Savannah, one of the reasons Ryan liked the city so much.

Several minutes later a tall, lanky man wearing a seersucker suit came into the lobby, went to the receptionist desk and the woman pointed toward Ryan.

The guy in the seersucker suit approached him. "I'm Jim Hartlett," he said. "You wanted to see me?"

"I did," Ryan said, and the two shook hands. The PI studied the other man closely. "You look nothing like your photo, Mr. Hartlett."

Hartlett frowned. "I'm not sure what you mean."

Ryan took out a printout of the press pass he had received from the security guard, which included a photo. He handed the printout to Hartlett.

The reporter stared at the sheet, then shook his head. "What is this? It's clearly a press pass, with my name on it and my newspapers name, but this photo is not of me."

"You better sit down," Ryan said, "and I'll explain what I think is going on."

The reporter sat across from him.

"I'm investigating the explosion and murder that took place recently in Savannah," Ryan said. "I'm sure you've heard of it."

"Of course. Everyone has. Things like that never happen in Savannah."

"Someone obviously impersonated you," Ryan said, "to obtain press credentials to the movie filming. The killer used this access to the scene to commit the murder."

"This is crazy ... why me ... am I under suspicion?"

"Are you guilty, Mr. Hartlett?"

"Of course not!" the man said, raising his voice. "I've never been arrested! I've never even gotten a traffic ticket. You can check!"

"We will." Ryan studied the man's demeanor closely, trying to gauge his honesty. He'd been a PI for years and knew this guy was innocent.

"What happens now?" Hartlett said, his voice shaky.

"I'm working with the Georgia Bureau of Investigation. They'll do a deep dive into your background and financials. If you're clean, you have nothing to worry about."

Hartlett calmed down a bit. "Okay. Do I need to hire a lawyer?"

"I don't think that'll be necessary. But don't leave town."

"Of course. Of course."

Ryan handed the man his business card, then spent the next half hour talking with the man. When they were done, Ryan left the building, headed to the parking lot and got in his rented Mustang.

He took out his cell phone and punched in a number.

"It's Ryan," he said, when Kelly answered.

He described his day, recounting the reporters he questioned, and how nine of them had checked out. Then he told her about Jim Hartlett, the reporter from the Savannah Morning News.

"It's clear to me, Kelly, that someone impersonated Hartlett to get the press credentials."

"You think Hartlett is clean?" Kelly asked.

"I do. But I'll email you his info and you can check him out. I'll also email you the photo of the perp. Hopefully you'll be able to use facial recognition software to ID him."

"I'm glad you reminded me of that," she said, her voice dripping with sarcasm. "I would have never thought to do that."

They continued talking about the case for the next ten minutes, then he said. "I'll be catching a plane back to Atlanta soon. When I get back, I'll come see you at your office."

"Okay, Ryan."

He thought about something else and said, "Listen, Kelly. I know that I joke around, and that you don't appreciate it. But I want you to know I'm not trying to piss you off. It's just my nature."

38

She said nothing for a long moment. "Erin did warn me about you," she said. "But she also told me you're a good investigator. And your hunch about the bombing has already paid off. So, I guess I'll have to accept your wisecracks."

Ryan chuckled. "In that case, when I get back, I'll tell you a couple of jokes."

"Don't push it, Ryan," she replied, and hung up.

Chapter 12

Tokyo, Japan

Nikita strode into the Operations Center and glanced around. The men and women in the room were at their computer workstations.

Nikita approached one of the workstations and the young French woman there glanced up from her computer screen. Like all the other female operatives, Marie was attractive.

"How is your current assignment going?" Nikita asked.

"It's going well, Nikita."

"You followed my advice?"

"I did. I had sex with the man and filmed it. He's been cooperative since then. He doesn't want his wife to find out."

"I told you it would work, Marie. Keep me appraised of your progress."

"Yes, Nikita."

Nikita glanced around the Operations Center again. One of the workstations was vacant. "When Kruger returns from his trip," she said to Marie, "tell him I need to see him."

"Yes, ma'am."

Nikita stood and after talking with several more operatives, left the room. The Operations Center was located in the basement of the skyscraper, and she took the elevator to the top floor of the building.

She owned a penthouse suite, a lavishly decorated three-bedroom apartment that overlooked the Sumida River. The living room had a splendid view of Tokyo.

Nikita went to the teak cabinet and poured out a large tumbler of *sake*, her favorite drink. She took a sip and nibbled on her favorite snack, *Himemaru* crackers.

As she stared out the floor-to-ceiling windows at the river below and the multitude of skyscrapers, she mulled over the progress on the projects they were working on.

She sipped more of the *sake*, pleased with their current progress.

Like on most days, Nikita was dressed in traditional Japanese clothing. Today she was wearing a dark gray silk kimono, with a blue sash, known as an *obi*. Although most Japanese businesswomen wore dresses and pantsuits, Nikita favored the historic kimonos.

Nikita took another sip of the *sake* as she continued watching the scene outside. Then she turned away from the windows and approached the ornate *samurai* sword that was mounted on one wall of her living room. A present from her boss years ago, she always enjoyed the sight of the expertly crafted sword. The stainless-steel sword was sheathed in a steel scabbard engraved with ornate Japanese characters. She ran her hand gently over the steel, enjoying the feel of the cold metal. This particular *samurai* sword was known as a *Katana*, which was used by Japanese *samurai* warriors going back to the year 800 A.D. The *Katana* is characterised by a gently curved, single-edged upward-facing blade with a long grip for both hands. The upward-facing aspect of the blade is to allow the warrior to deal a fatal blow to the enemy in just one move. It is a slender, relatively lightweight sword with an extremely sharp edge, and is renowned for its deadly cutting ability.

Nikita then went back to her cabinet and poured herself another *sake*.

Just then her front door chime rang, and she went to the CCTV camera monitor by the door. Seeing who it was, she turned off the security alarm and let the man inside.

After closing the door behind him, she set the alarm.

"You needed to see me?" Kruger said.

"I did."

She noticed the brawny man was wearing a black shirt and black slacks, his usual attire.

"Let's talk in the living room," she said. "Would you like a drink?"

The man nodded and she led them into the room. After pouring out his drink and handing it to him, they sat on opposite leather couches.

"I saw the news reports of the explosion in Savannah," she said. "You did well. Any complications?"

Kruger shook his head. "None."

"Excellent. I'm very pleased with you. And my boss is pleased also."

"You have a boss? I didn't know that. I thought you ran the Operations Center."

She took a sip of the *sake*. "I do run the Center as I see fit. But I still have a boss. We all do."

"Who is it?"

"You don't need to know. All you need to know is that I'm your boss, and you need to keep me satisfied. Understood?"

"Perfectly. Do you have another assignment for me?"

Nikita nodded. "I'm working on that. I'll let you know soon." There was a remote control resting on the coffee table between them and she picked it up. Then she pressed several buttons on the device and the drapes to the floor-to-ceiling windows of the room closed.

Nikita took another sip of her drink. "Strip for me, Kruger. And do it slowly. You know the drill."

Kruger smiled and stood. Then he took off his shoes and shirt and pants and underwear.

She studied his muscular physique closely, enjoying the sight of his nude body. After gulping the rest of her *sake*, she rose, approached him and began running her hands slowly and sensually over every part of his body.

It feels good, she thought. *Very good.* Her silk panties were already wet. She enjoyed this part almost as much as what would follow.

Kruger's eyes shined with anticipation. He grinned and by his erection it was clear he was as ready as she was.

Nikita removed the blue sash around her waist, then slowly took off her gray silk kimono. Next, she took off her black silk underwear.

Taking his hand, she led him into the bedroom.

Chapter 13

Hartsfield-Jackson Airport
Atlanta, Georgia

J.T. Ryan's flight arrived from Savannah at 10 p.m., and after deplaning, he collected his bag from the luggage area.

Since he needed a cab ride home, he took the stairwell down to the taxi area. As soon as he began climbing down the steps, he heard muffled screams from the level below.

It was a woman's scream, and his heart began to pound. Dropping his bag, he raced down the steps and saw a young woman with torn clothes being held down by two swarthy men, while another guy, a leer on his face, was unzipping his pants.

Enraged at what was happening, Ryan raced to the standing guy and punched him savagely in the face. The guy toppled backward, while the other two thugs let go of the woman and attacked Ryan.

The PI kicked one of the guys in the balls, then punched the other in the gut.

Just then Ryan felt a blinding pain in the back of his head. He dropped to his knees and blacked out.

Chapter 14

Atlanta, Georgia

Kelly O'Hara knocked on the apartment door and waited.

J.T. Ryan opened it a moment later.

"Are you okay?" she said.

Ryan was holding a bag of ice to the back of his head. "I'll live."

She went inside and he closed the door behind them.

"I was in my office," Kelly said, "and I scanned the APD blotter. I saw your name pop up. The report said a woman was about to be raped and you stopped it."

Ryan nodded. "Yeah, that's right. I need to sit down."

"Sure."

He went to the couch and sat, still holding the bag of ice to the back of his head.

"One of the thugs got the drop on me," he said. "When I woke up, they were gone. Luckily the girl wasn't hurt, just shook up."

Kelly frowned. "Atlanta's crime is out of control. It's getting worse every damn day."

"I agree."

"Can I get you a drink, Ryan?"

"You bet. Grab whatever you want from the fridge."

She went into the kitchen, got two bottles of Guinness, popped the tops and came back into the living room. After handing him one, she took a sip from the other and sat across from him.

"That was a brave thing you did," she said. "Taking on three thugs on your own."

"Anybody would have done it."

"Not really," she said.

She sipped her beer and studied the handsome and rugged man. He was wearing a blue, button-down denim shirt and gray slacks. He had brown hair and brown eyes, a great smile and a charm that was hard to deny. She needed to be careful around him, she realized.

Kelly glanced around the living room, which was sparsely decorated with inexpensive furniture. The walls were mostly bare, except for an American flag on one wall and a small brass crucifix on another. There was a bookcase in the room, and she stood up and studied the contents. Most of the books were military: Special Forces, Ranger, and Green Beret manuals. There were also detective novels and a well-worn Bible.

She pointed to the Bible. "You must be religious, Ryan."

"I am."

She smiled. "You're a surprising man."

"Is that good or bad?"

"I'm not sure yet, Ryan."

"You know, you can call me J.T. Everybody does."

She gave him a long look. "I prefer calling you by your last name."

"Works for me."

He took a sip of the dark beer and set the bottle down. "Were you able to track down the guy from the photo I sent you? The man who was impersonating the Savannah reporter?"

Kelly shook her head. "No. I ran his photo through the GBI and the FBI facial rec databases and nothing popped."

"Okay." He picked up the Guinness and took another sip. "What about the reporter himself? Did Hartlett check out?"

"Yeah. The man is squeaky clean, just like you thought."

"All right. Once I get rid of this damn headache, I need to go on a trip."

She pursed her lips. "To where?"

"L.A. I need to interview the husband of the actress murdered in Rome. He may have information that'll help us solve this case."

Kelly tilted her head. "The man's a movie producer, right?"

"Yes. His name is Carl Parnell and he's a prominent figure in the film business."

"And I assume, Ryan, that you'd rather go out there on your own?"

Ryan grinned. "I'd prefer that."

She mulled that over for a moment, knew her case load was getting heavier. Her boss kept giving her additional investigations every day.

"Okay, Ryan."

"That's it? You're not going to fight me on this?"

"No."

He smiled. "My charm must be getting through to you."

"Don't flatter yourself."

Ryan's smile grew wider. "Not even a little bit?"

Kelly tried to frown but failed. After a long moment, she grinned. "Maybe a little. But don't let it go to your head, buster."

He laughed and gave her a half salute. "Yes, ma'am."

Chapter 15

Beverly Hills
Los Angeles, California

J.T. Ryan parked his rented Honda Accord on the circular driveway fronting the ultra-modern mansion. The lavish home was located in the exclusive Beverly Hills neighborhood of L.A.

Ryan climbed out of the sedan and strode up the flagstone steps to the impressive front door.

He pressed the bell and waited.

Moments later a Hispanic woman in a maid's uniform opened the door.

"I'm J.T. Ryan," he said. "I have an appointment with Mr. Parnell."

The maid opened the door wider. "Yes, he told me to expect you." She let Ryan inside and led him into a luxurious living room. The room was decorated all in white. It was furnished with sleek, white leather sofas, chairs, and chrome and glass coffee tables. Modernistic abstract paintings hung on the stark white walls.

A moment later a haggard-looking man in his seventies came into the room. He had thinning, gray hair, and wore a rumpled black suit, a wrinkled white shirt, and no tie. He had dark circles under his red-rimmed eyes. By his demeanor, it appeared he had not slept in a long time. Ryan had done research on Parnell and knew he was a famous movie producer. In the photos Ryan had seen of the man online, Parnell appeared vibrant and full of life, nothing like he was now.

"I'm Carl Parnell," the man said, extending his hand.

They shook and Ryan said, "Thank you for seeing me, sir."

Parnell motioned to the sleek white sofas, and they sat across from each other.

"I'm sorry for your loss, Mr. Parnell."

Parnell said nothing, then rubbed his face with both hands.

"I'm investigating the murder of your wife," Ryan began.

"Yes … yes … Agent O'Hara called and told me." The movie producer rubbed his unshaven face again. It was clear the man had not shaved in probably a week.

He stared at Ryan with a distraught look. "Can you bring her back to me, Ryan? Can you bring back my Annie?" he said, his voice breaking.

"I'm sorry, sir. That I can't do. But I will do everything I can to catch the criminal who did it and put him in prison."

Parnell let out a long sigh. "Yes … yes … that would be good …." He clenched his fists. "The killer has to pay …."

Just then Parnell bolted up from the sofa. "I need a drink. I need a fucking drink." He marched to a cabinet and poured himself a large glass of Chivas. He gulped it down, then refilled it.

He raised the glass and said, "Scotch. It's the only thing that's kept me going since …." His voice trailed off.

"You want a drink, Ryan?"

"It's only 9 a.m. I'll pass."

Parnell sat back down and sipped the scotch. "Annie was the love of my life. People always talked behind my back for marrying a woman forty years younger than me. But I loved her. More than life itself. And she loved me. She was vibrant … so full of life … so beautiful …." Tears rolled down his haggard face.

Ryan hated interviewing grief-stricken family members, but knew he had no choice.

"Mr. Parnell, can you think of anybody who wanted her dead?"

The man shook his head. "No … no one … she was a very popular actress … she had a huge following … fans adored her and flocked to all her movies."

"I understand some people criticized her for agreeing to star in a movie for Genesis Films, because it's a faith-based studio."

Parnell nodded. "That's true. You know how Hollywood people are. Very opinionated. But murder?" He shook his head. "No. No one would take it that far."

Then he stood up, refilled his glass of scotch again and sat back down.

"The only that's kept me going," Parnell said, "is a lot of Chivas and my work."

"I understand you're producing a new film, is that right?"

"I am."

"How is that going?"

The old man shrugged. "A lot of it is in place. We've got a dynamite script. The screenwriters did a fabulous job on it. And I've hired great actors and actresses for it. And a first-class director. But ...."

"There's a problem?"

"Yes."

"What is it, sir?"

"Financing. The movie is stalled over the financing."

"Why do you think that is?"

Parnell shook his head slowly. "I think a big part of it is the topic matter."

"What's the movie about?"

"It's a war movie. The heroes in it are American soldiers. It's a feel good, patriotic film, like *Maverick: Top Gun.*"

"I see. And you can't get it financed because of that?"

The man nodded. "I believe so. Patriotic movies are shunned by Hollywood."

"So, what are you going to do?" Ryan said.

"I've decided to finance it on my own. Using my own money."

"I see."

"It's a big risk," Parnell continued, "because I could lose it all. But after Annie's passing ... money doesn't seem that important any more ...."

Ryan spent the next hour talking with the movie producer, asking him questions that could lead to catching the killer who had murdered his wife.

When they were done, the men stood and shook hands.

Then Parnell's red-rimmed eyes welled up and tears ran down his cheeks. "Find the killer, Ryan. Find the bastard who did this … find the bastard who took my Annie away …."

"Yes, sir."

"And when you find him," the movie producer said, choking back tears, "don't arrest him. Kill him. Make him pay the ultimate price."

"Yes, sir."

Chapter 16

Tokyo, Japan

Nikita strode into the Operations Center and glanced around. Seeing Kruger at his workstation, she walked over and sat in the chair by the desk.

"I have a new assignment for you," she said.

"Who is it?"

She handed him a manila folder, which he opened and read. "All right. Do you want the man terminated?"

Nikita shook her head. "Not this time. I need you to kidnap him and bring him to me."

"To here, Tokyo?"

"Yes."

Kruger pursed his lips. "I can't do this on my own. To kidnap a high-profile man like him, I'll need help."

"I figured that. You'll need a good-looking female to pull it off. Take Marie."

"Yes, Nikita."

Nikita glanced toward Marie's workstation, which was about twenty feet away. She studied the attractive French woman, then lowered her voice. "One other thing, Kruger. I want you to stop fucking Marie."

Kruger's eyebrows shot up. "How did you know ...."

"I know everything that happens at the Center. Everything."

"But I like Marie, and she likes me."

Nikita stabbed her index finger on the man's chest. "I don't give a shit about that. You are not to fuck her again. Understood?"

He let out a long sigh and nodded. "Yes, I understand. Can I at least know why?"

Nikita gave him a cold grin. "Because I'm fucking you. As long as you work for me, you are mine. And mine alone. Are we clear on this?"

"Crystal."

Chapter 17

Sandy Springs, Georgia

J.T. Ryan pulled into the parking lot of the Genesis Films headquarters building. Located in Sandy Springs, a suburb of Atlanta, the Genesis studios were a sprawling complex of several structures, in a parklike setting.

He went into the building and approached the receptionist's desk. "I'm J.T. Ryan," he said to the woman. "I have an appointment with Mr. Atkins."

The woman looked over her half-glasses at him, then scanned a notebook in front of her.

"You're late, Mr. Ryan," she said in a stiff voice. She was a frumpy-looking woman in her mid-fifties. "If I remember correctly, you were late for your last appointment also."

Ryan smiled to disarm her haughty attitude. "Sorry about that. Traffic was terrible on I-85. There was a car accident."

She frowned and shook her head slowly. She picked up the handset of her desk phone and spoke into it. Then she said, "Have a seat. Someone will be out in a moment."

A few minutes later he was shown into the large, impressive office of the studio owner, Matthew Atkins. The man stood, came around his desk and shook hands with Ryan.

"Please have a seat, J.T."

"Thanks." Ryan took one of the plush visitor's chairs facing the desk. The company owner was a distinguished-looking man in his sixties with silver hair and silver mustache. He wore a dark blue business suit with a red silk tie.

"I wanted to fill you in on my progress," Ryan said. The PI then spent the next hour detailing his trip to Rome, and Savannah and then L.A.

When he was done, he said, "When we first met, Mr. Atkins, you told me about the offers to buy your company. Can you tell me more about that?"

"Of course. The offers were presented by a law firm from here in Atlanta. I got the feeling this law firm was not the buyer. They were representing the buyer."

Ryan took out a small notepad and a pen. "Tell me more about this legal firm."

"The name of the company is Grant and Mason Attorneys at Law. The main partner there is Howard Grant. He's the one who came to me and presented the offers."

Ryan wrote this down. "Where are they located?"

"Downtown Atlanta." Atkins consulted his laptop computer and read off the address.

"I'll go see them next."

Atkins frowned. "Good luck with that. But my impression of this Grant guy is not favorable. Especially when he gave me his last offer, which I also turned down. Then he gave me a veiled threat. Sell or else."

"Or else what?"

"He didn't specify, but I got the feeling they might resort to violence."

"And that's when Annie Parnell was murdered in Rome."

"That's right, J.T."

Ryan put away his notepad. "I think I have everything I need for now. I'll keep you up to date as I continue to work on the case." The PI stood, as did Atkins and they shook hands.

An hour later Ryan pulled into the underground parking lot of the Coastal States office building in downtown Atlanta. He got out of his Chevy Tahoe and took the elevator to the top floor.

The Grant and Mason legal firm occupied the whole of that floor, and from the lavish furnishings in the lobby, it was clear the company had wealthy clients.

Ryan approached the young woman at the front desk. He gave her his business card.

"I'm J.T. Ryan," he said. "I need to speak with Mr. Howard Grant."

The woman scanned the card. "Do you have an appointment?"

Ryan smiled. "Actually, no. But it's important that I speak with him today."

"I'm sorry, but Mr. Grant doesn't see anyone without an appointment."

Ryan dropped the smile and in a stern voice said, "Listen, I'm investigating a murder case for the GBI. Do you want to be charged for impeding an investigation? If not, I suggest you pick up that phone and let Mr. Grant know I'm here."

The young woman's eyebrows shot up and she picked up the handset of her desk phone. She talked into it for a moment and hung up. "Someone will show you into the conference room in a moment, Mr. Ryan. Please have a seat."

A few minutes later Ryan was shown into a massive conference room which contained a long, cherry wood table that could easily sit thirty people.

Moments later a tall and distinguished looking man walked in. He was in his mid-fifties and wore a charcoal gray business suit.

Without a word, Grant sat at the head of the table and glared at Ryan. "What's this about?" he said in a gruff voice.

Ryan stayed standing and looked down at the man. "I'm conducting a murder investigation for the GBI. That's what this is about."

"Are you a GBI agent, Ryan?"

"No, I'm not. I'm a private investigator helping the GBI on the case."

Grant scowled. "And which case is that?"

"The murder of an actress in Italy and the murder of a movie director in Savannah."

"And what the hell does that have to do with me?"

"Both of those people were working on movies for Genesis Films, a company here in Atlanta. Those murders happened right after your offers to buy Genesis were turned down."

Grant shook his head slowly and continued to glare. "And somehow you think I'm involved?"

Ryan, who already disliked the lawyer's arrogant attitude, placed both hands on the conference table and leaned down. "Maybe. Maybe not. But you have to admit, the timing of the offers and the murders are suspicious."

"I don't give a shit what you think, Ryan. All I did was to present an offer to buy Genesis Films. The offer came from one of my clients."

"Who's the client, Mr. Grant?"

The lawyer sneered. "You never heard of client attorney privilege?"

"I have. I also know two innocent people were murdered. And I'm not giving up on this investigation until the killers are brought to justice."

Grant pointed toward the conference room door. "Get out! Get out now, or I'll call security and have you thrown out!"

Ryan saw red, grabbed the man by his suit's lapels with both hands, and jerked him out of his chair.

"I'll leave! But I'm not done with you, Grant. Not by a long shot."

Then Ryan dropped the man back in the chair and marched out of the conference room, slamming the door shut behind him.

Chapter 18

Atlanta, Georgia

Several hours later, J.T. Ryan was in his midtown office, doing paperwork.

After finishing up a report, Ryan stood up from his desk and refilled his cup from the coffee maker. Then he took a donut from the Krispy Kreme box he had bought earlier.

Just then his cell phone buzzed, and he answered it. "Ryan here."

"What the hell were you thinking?" he heard Kelly O'Hara shout from the other end. He held the phone away from his ear.

"Calm down, Kelly. What are you talking about?"

"You threatened one of the most prominent attorneys in Atlanta! That's what I'm talking about."

"I didn't threaten Grant. I just –"

"Shut up, Ryan! Howard Grant is an important man. A very important man. After you left his office, he called the mayor of Atlanta, who then complained to the governor of Georgia, who then complained to the head of the GBI!"

"I'm sorry, Kelly. I really am."

"Are you trying to get my ass fired?"

"No, of course not. And you have a very cute ass, by the way."

"Ryan!" she yelled. "Stop joking around! This is serious."

"I'm really sorry. I guess I didn't think it through."

The woman said nothing for a long moment.

"Are you still there, Kelly?"

"Yes, I'm still here," she said, her voice a bit calmer now.

"I apologize, Kelly. This Grant guy just got under my skin. He's a slimy attorney. And I hate slimy attorneys."

"Look, I don't like them either, but you can't just barge into somebody's office and threaten them."

"I guess I got carried away …."

"You guess?"

"All right, Kelly. I promise. I'll try to be better in the future."

"Why don't I believe you?"

Ryan chuckled. "Okay. I will do my best to behave. And I do apologize."

Kelly let out a long sigh. "Apology accepted." She paused for a moment. "You think this Grant guy is dirty?"

"I do. I got this feeling in my gut that he knows a lot more than he's saying."

"I trust your instincts. But not your methods."

"Let me take you to dinner," he said. "To apologize for getting you in trouble. It's the least I can do."

"Absolutely not! That's out of the question! We need to keep this relationship strictly professional. I've told you that before."

"This would be a business dinner, Kelly. We would talk about the case. Anyway, you have to eat dinner, right?"

"Yes, I have to eat."

Ryan grinned. "There you go. I'll pick you up at your house at seven tonight and drive us to the restaurant."

"No. I'll drive myself and meet you there."

"Okay, Kelly." He gave her the name of the restaurant and directions, and they said goodbye.

Chapter 19

Alpharetta, Georgia

Kelly O'Hara parked her GBI issued Ford Explorer in the lot fronting the Village Tavern and went inside. The restaurant was located in Alpharetta, a suburb north of Atlanta.

She spotted John Ryan right away. The man was at the bar sipping a beer.

Ryan came over and the hostess seated them at a booth in the back of the restaurant.

"Do you come here often?" Kelly said.

"I do. They have great food, and I like the atmosphere."

The upscale place was decorated in dark woods and there was a roaring fireplace nearby.

She studied the good-looking man across from her. Ryan was wearing a blue blazer, a button-down white dress shirt and tan slacks.

"Would you like a drink, Kelly?" he said.

She shook her head. "No. This is a business dinner, remember?"

Ryan smiled that charming grin of his. "Of course."

He signaled the waitress, ordered a draft beer for himself and a glass of water for Kelly. The waitress handed them menus and moved away.

Kelly studied the menu closely. "What's good here, Ryan?"

"Everything. I prefer the pizza myself, but the steaks and seafood are good also."

She nodded and kept studying the menu.

"I'm sorry about earlier, Kelly. Getting you in trouble with your boss."

"Let's not talk about it, okay? I'd like to forget the whole thing."

"Good." He put down his menu and signaled the waitress. Ryan ordered pepperoni pizza, and Kelly ordered salmon with wild rice.

When the waitress moved away, Kelly said, "Let's go over the case."

They spent the next hour discussing the murder investigation as they ate their dinner, which was delicious.

When the waitress had cleared the plates, Ryan said, "Are you sure you don't want a drink?"

Kelly thought about that for a long moment. "I guess one glass of wine won't hurt."

He ordered the drinks and when they came, he raised his glass of beer. "To us solving the case."

She clinked glasses with him and took a sip of the merlot. "I'll drink to that."

"I'm not the first woman you've brought here, am I?" she said.

"That's true."

"I figured as much. I'm guessing you're a player."

"What do you mean, Kelly?"

"You're a handsome, charming guy. I bet you've bedded a lot of women in your time."

Ryan shook his head. "Actually, I'm a one woman at a time kind of man."

She stared at him for a long time, trying to gauge his truthfulness. She had been a GBI agent for years and had a good radar for truth telling. "I think that's true. Ever been married, Ryan?"

"No. I got close twice. But it never worked out in the end. And you?"

"I was married years ago," she said, her voice low and sad. "But I got divorced. I found out my husband was cheating on me. It was an ugly, ugly divorce. Ever since then, I've been gun shy about men."

"I figured something like that," he said. "You do seem ... kind of skittish ...."

She took a sip of her wine. "Let's change the subject. It makes me miserable every time I think of my failed marriage."

He grinned. "How about I tell you a couple of jokes? I've got some new material."

She frowned, then just shrugged her shoulders. "Okay."

"How did the tractor salesman find out his wife left him?" Ryan said. "He came home from work and found a John Deere letter."

Kelly groaned at the joke.

"I got a better one," he said with a grin. "I went to visit a psychic. When I knocked on the door, she yelled, 'Who is it?' So I left."

Kelly chuckled.

Ryan said, "Here's another one. 'You'll never believe who I bumped into on my way to the eye doctor. Everybody!'"

She laughed and so did he.

"Those aren't bad," Kelly said with a smile. "But don't quit your day job."

Chapter 20

Beverly Hills
Los Angeles, California

"I hate that bitch," Marie said.

Kruger, who was sitting in the driver's seat of the Suburban, glanced toward Marie, who was in the passenger seat. "Which bitch is that?"

Marie scowled. "Who do you think? Our boss, Nikita."

The Suburban was parked across the street from the ultra-modern mansion. The two operatives had been scouting the home for the last half hour.

"Let's focus on our assignment," Kruger said. "We've got a job to do."

"Screw the job. And screw Nikita. I hate her."

"We're paid extremely well for what we do," Kruger said.

Marie grimaced. "I've never liked Nikita, with her superior attitude. And this latest thing, telling us we can't have sex. It's none of her business what we do on our personal time."

"I'm not happy about it either, Marie. But she is our boss. She makes the rules."

Marie glared at him. "You like doing her, don't you? I bet you love screwing her. She's beautiful. I'll grant you that. But she's a Japanese whore, if you ask me."

"Calm down," he said. "We need to focus on this assignment. Okay?"

Marie let out a long breath. "Yes."

"Let's go over the plan again," Kruger said.

"We've gone over it a million times. I know what I need to do."

"Okay, Marie."

The young, attractive French woman was dressed in a stylish black dress with black flats. On her lap was a large manila envelope. She glanced down at herself. "Do I look okay?"

Kruger studied her appearance. "You look great."

Marie flashed a brilliant smile. "Thanks. You know, we can still do it. Nikita will never find out."

"We'll see."

"Don't be a wuss. Grow some balls, Kruger."

His face reddened and he gripped the steering wheel tightly.

"I'm sorry," she said. "I didn't mean it." She placed a hand on his cheek. "Forgive me?"

"Yes. But let's please focus on the assignment."

"Fine."

"You ready to do this?" he said.

"I am."

Kruger started up the Suburban, drove across the street and parked the SUV in the circular driveway of the mansion.

Marie grabbed her black shoulder purse and, carrying the manila envelope, got out of the vehicle. Then she strode to the front door and rang the bell.

A moment later a Hispanic woman in a maid's uniform opened it. "Can I help you?" she said.

"I'm from the studio," Marie said. "I need to deliver this package to Mr. Parnell."

"If you give it to me, I'll see he gets it."

"I'm sorry. But it's an important document. He has to sign for it himself."

"Of course. If you'll wait here in the foyer, I'll go get him." The maid opened the door fully and Marie stepped into the immense and lavish foyer. After closing the door behind them, the maid went deeper into the mansion.

Marie pulled her SIG Sauer P365 9-millimeter pistol from her purse and hid it under the package.

Moments later a haggard-looking old man walked into the foyer. He was wearing a rumpled suit and appeared as if he hadn't shaved in a week.

"You have a package for me from the studio?" he asked in a tired voice.

Marie smiled. "I do." She handed the envelope to him, then leveled the pistol at his face.

The man blanched and dropped the package to the floor. "What's … what's this about …."

"Shut up, old man," Marie yelled. "Do what I tell you or you die."

The maid was nearby, and she screamed.

Marie rushed to her and swung the pistol across the maid's face. Blood spurted and the maid sank to her knees and collapsed to the floor.

Marie pointed her gun at Parnell again. "Let's go to the garage. Now!"

Parnell's eyes were as big as saucers. "What … do you … want …."

Marie pressed the muzzle of the gun to the man's forehead. "Garage. Now!"

Parnell nodded, then turned and walked into a wide marble tiled corridor, which was decorated with large abstract paintings.

A few minutes later they reached the massive four car garage.

There was a Jaguar sedan in one of the bays and two Lexus SUVs in the other two.

"Open the empty bay garage door," Marie ordered, still pointing the gun at Parnell.

Parnell appeared bewildered and she yelled, "Do it, old man, or I'll blow your brains out!"

The movie producer went to a control panel on the wall and pressed a button. The garage door slowly opened.

Almost immediately the Suburban drove inside. Kruger climbed out of the SUV. He was also carrying a SIG Sauer pistol, which he leveled at Parnell.

The old man was shaking, and his eyes were wild with terror.

Marie went to the control panel on the wall and pressed a button and the garage door closed.

"Who else is in the house?" Kruger asked Marie.

"The maid. I knocked her out."

"I'll stay with Parnell," Kruger said. "Go back in the house and kill her."

Marie nodded.

"Also, check the rest of the mansion, make sure no one else is here. If you find anyone, kill them also. And wipe your prints from everything you touch inside the house."

"Got it," Marie said. She left the garage and moments later Kruger heard two muffled thuds from inside the home.

Kruger pointed his gun at Parnell's face. "Security cameras. You have a control room for those?"

"Yes ... yes ...." Parnell replied, his voice shaky.

"Let's go there. Now!"

Kruger followed the movie producer into a small room adjacent to the garage. There was a desk, and a variety of video monitors and computers.

Kruger, using the butt of his gun, smashed all the electronic components. That done, he said, "Parnell, get on the floor, on your stomach, and put your hands behind your back."

The old man complied, and Kruger tied the man's hands behind his back. Then Kruger removed a black hood from his pocket and put it on Parnell's head and cinched it tight at the neck.

Just then Marie came into the room.

"I took care of her," she said. "The maid is dead."

Kruger nodded. "Good. Anyone else in the house?"

"No."

"I'll load Parnell into the SUV," Kruger said, "and we can get the hell out of here."

Marie's eyes were bright with lust. "I found this great Jacuzzi in the master bathroom. Let's screw in there before we go."

Kruger shook his head. "You're crazy, you know that?"

She grinned. "I know. Let's do it."

"We don't have time for that, Marie. We need to get the hell out of here."

Marie looked crestfallen and she lowered her gaze to the floor.

Kruger lifted her chin with a hand. "When we get to a safe place, we'll do it. Okay?"

"You mean it?" she said.

"I do."

The young woman smiled. "I can't wait to rip your clothes off."

Chapter 21

Atlanta, Georgia

J.T. Ryan was in his midtown office, doing research on his laptop, when he heard a knock at his office door.

Ryan tensed, unholstered his Desert Eagle, and went to the spyhole on the door. Seeing who it was, he opened it.

"Well, if it isn't my favorite GBI agent," he said.

Kelly O'Hara walked inside, and he closed the door behind her. The attractive redhead was wearing a navy-blue business suit with a light gray blouse.

She pointed to his pistol. "You can put your cannon away. I promise I'm not dangerous."

Ryan re-holstered his gun.

"Tell me, Ryan, why do you carry such a big gun? Do you really need a .50 caliber weapon?"

"A few years ago, I used a Smith & Wesson .357 Magnum. But crime has gotten so bad, I felt I needed an upgrade."

She nodded.

"Is this a social call," he said, "or business?"

"What do you think?"

Ryan smiled. "I should know by now. You're all business, all the time."

She frowned. "Am I that bad?"

"Have a seat, Kelly. Can I get you a cup of coffee?"

"I've had your coffee. I'll pass."

"How about a donut? I picked up a dozen from Krispy Kreme this morning."

"You trying to make me fat?"

He gave her a long up and down look, taking in her slender and curvaceous figure. "I don't think you have anything to worry about."

"I'll pass on the donuts," she said, sitting on one of the visitors' chairs fronting his desk. Ryan sat on the other.

"I got a call from L.A.P.D.," she said. "There's been a development on our case. Remember the man you interviewed recently out there? The movie producer?"

"Sure. Carl Parnell."

"That's right. He's missing. And his maid was murdered."

Ryan shook his head slowly. "Damn."

"This just happened," Kelly said. "I wanted you to know right away."

"I need to go there ASAP."

"I figured you'd say that. When can you leave?"

"Today. I'll check the Delta flights to LA. Grab the first one I can get."

"Good," she said. Then she got a pensive look. "I've been thinking about what you asked for a while back. About how you're too big to fit in coach seats. If you like, you can upgrade to business class on this flight."

"And the GBI will pay for it?"

"Yes, we will."

Ryan grinned. "You're warming up to me, Kelly."

The attractive redhead frowned. "I didn't say that." Then her expression softened. "Well, maybe a little."

Chapter 22

Tokyo, Japan

Nikita was in her penthouse apartment, sipping *sake*, when her cell phone buzzed. Taking it out of the pocket of her kimono, she answered the call. "Yes?"

"It's Kruger," the man said. "I'm back from my trip."

"Where's the package?"

"I put him in the basement. He's drugged and tied up."

"Excellent work," she said. "Any complications?"

"None."

"You've done well," she replied. "Was Marie helpful to you on the trip?"

"She was."

"Good. I'll go see the man in a bit. I need to have a serious conversation with him."

"Will you need my help for that, Nikita?"

"No. I'll handle this part on my own."

Nikita hung up the phone.

She finished her glass of *sake* and went to her bedroom, where she changed out of her ornate kimono and into a sweatshirt and a pair of jeans. Then she pulled her long, raven hair into a ponytail.

That done, she left her penthouse suite and took the elevator to the level below the Operations Center. This basement level could only be accessed by herself and a few of her trusted operatives.

After using the retinal scan device and unlocking the door, she went inside the concrete walled room.

The place smelled dank and was illuminated harshly by overhead fluorescents.

The man was sitting on a metal chair, his hands tied behind his back. He was wearing a black hood.

His head was sagging on his chest, and it was clear he had passed out.

Nikita marched over and checked the bindings on his hands and legs, making sure they were secure. That done, she went to a metal cabinet in the room, pulled out leather gloves from a drawer and put them on.

Going back to the man, she pulled the black hood from his face.

"Wake up," she said, her voice harsh.

He didn't respond and she slapped him hard across the face. Nothing happened and she kept slapping him until he finally woke up.

He had an unfocused and bewildered look, and he blinked rapidly.

"Who ... are ... you ...." he muttered, his voice weak and raspy. "Why ... am ... I ... here ...."

"It's not important who I am, Parnell."

His eyes focused on her. "You've ... kidnapped me ... what do ... you want ... do you want money? I can ... give you money ...."

Nikita laughed. "No, that's not what I want."

"What ... what then ...."

"Some important people want you to stop making your film."

"My film ... what ... what are you talking ... about ... I don't understand ...."

"Yes, you idiot. The patriotic movie you're making." She paused and slapped him hard again. "We made it difficult for you to get financing. Unfortunately, you decided to fund it with your own money."

She slapped him again. "Big mistake, Parnell."

He recoiled from her, trying to avoid her hand.

She grabbed his face with both of her gloved hands. "My boss is very upset with you."

70

"You're ... crazy ... I'm just making a movie ... why do you care ...."

"If you agree to drop this movie, Parnell, we'll let you live."

"That's ... it ....?"

"Yes, that's right."

"Then yes, I'll do it ... I agree ...."

Nikita smiled, but it had no humor in it. "You agree. That's very good, Parnell."

"Will you ... untie me now ... and let me go ...."

Nikita laughed a harsh, cold laugh. "No, you idiot. I won't let you go. I'll let you live, but I'm not going to release you."

His eyes were wide with fear. "You're ... you're going to keep me ... imprisoned ...?"

"I am, Parnell. You may be useful to me in some way. Don't worry, you'll be fed. But you'll stay locked up here."

"Please ... please ... let me go," he said, his voice cracked and hoarse.

Nikita patted his cheek gently. "I'll stop by every once in a while, and see how you're doing."

Then she turned and headed toward the metal door.

She continued hearing his hoarse screams as she walked out of the room.

Chapter 23

Beverly Hills
Los Angeles, California

J.T. Ryan parked in the circular driveway of the sleek contemporary mansion. Getting out of his rented Toyota sedan, he surveyed the scene.

Yellow crime scene tape cordoned off the whole area, and police SUVs and sedans lined the streets and driveway.

He noticed uniformed cops and plainclothes detectives and CSI techs going into and out of the home.

Ryan approached one of the uniforms. "I'm J.T. Ryan," he said, "I'm looking for Detective Sargeant Malloy."

The cop pointed to a tall, black man wearing a business suit who was coming out of the mansion. "That's him over there."

Ryan approached the man. "I'm J.T. Ryan, Sargeant Malloy. I understand you're in charge of this investigation."

"I am," the sergeant said. "Agent O'Hara called me and told me you were coming out here." The cop frowned. "I'm not fond of PIs. Most of the guys in your line of work are 'know it all's'."

Ryan grinned, trying to disarm the man's negative attitude. "Then you're in luck, Sargeant. Because I know nothing."

The cop gave him a prolonged look, then his frown dissipated. "Okay."

"I'd like to help you solve this case," Ryan said. "Maybe if we pool our resources, you'll solve it faster and you'll get the promotion you're after."

Malloy's eyebrows shot up. "How did you know I was angling for a promotion?"

Ryan shrugged. "Everyone who's a sergeant wants to be a lieutenant, and every lieutenant wants to make captain, and so on."

The cop gave him a lengthy stare then a slight grin brightened his face. "Okay, Ryan. We can pool our resources."

"Great. What have you got so far?"

"I got a DB, the maid who was shot. Twice in the head."

"Where's the body now?"

"The M.E. just took her away."

"What caliber rounds?"

"The M.E. thought a 9 mil."

Ryan nodded. "And Parnell is missing?"

"That's right. We called his office at the studio, and no one knows where he is. He's missed several important meetings. We called his business associates and friends, and they haven't heard from him. Our assumption is he's been kidnapped."

"What about security cameras," Ryan said. "Do they have any footage?"

Malloy shook his head. "All of the equipment was smashed up. This murder and kidnapping were done by pros."

"Did the neighbors notice anything unusual?"

"Nothing."

"I'd like to see the inside of the house."

"Sure. Follow me and I'll show you around."

Ryan followed the man into the mansion, and they spent the next hour walking through the scene.

In the lavish foyer, tape on the floor outlined where the maid's body had been. Splotches of dark red stained the white marble floor.

Malloy led the PI through the rest of the mansion and eventually they reached a massive four car garage.

There was a Jaguar sedan in one of the bays and two Lexus SUVs in the other two.

"We think," Malloy said, "the perps brought their vehicle into the garage. They probably tied up Parnell here, put him in their vehicle, and drove out."

Ryan studied the scene for a minute. He noticed the garage door control panel on the wall. "I saw all the CSI people here. I'm assuming you dusted for prints."

"We have."

"Find anything?"

"A lot of the surfaces were wiped clean. The perps are pros."

Ryan pointed to the garage door control panel. "Any prints on that?"

Malloy nodded. "A few, yeah. But they're probably Parnell's, or the maid, or a worker servicing the equipment."

Ryan rubbed his jaw. "But maybe, if we're lucky, it'll be one of the perps. Can you send me the fingerprints?"

"I can."

"Thank you, Sergeant."

Then Ryan spent the next half hour filling the cop in on what he had found out during his trip to Italy and Savannah. Then Ryan said, "When I met with Parnell recently, he told me he was having trouble getting financing for his latest film, and he had decided to finance it on his own. Do you know anything about that?"

Malloy shook his head. "No."

"I think that Parnell's kidnapping and the murder of his wife, and the murder of the movie director, Sam Morris, are all connected."

"You'll keep me informed of your progress?" Malloy said.

"You bet."

Ryan held out his hand and the men shook.

"You're okay, Ryan. Even if you are a PI."

Ryan grinned. "I'll take that as a compliment."

The cop shook his head slowly. "I wouldn't go that far."

Chapter 24

Tokyo, Japan

Nikita was in the office of her penthouse suite, working at her laptop. She stopped typing and took a long pull from her glass of *sake*. Then she ate several *Himemaru* crackers, her favorite snack.

Just then her encrypted cell phone buzzed. Taking it out of her kimono's pocket, she glanced at the info screen. It was her boss, and she answered it immediately.

"How are you, Nikita," the man said.

"Excellent. I was just writing you an email. To give you an update."

"How did it go?"

"Parnell will not be a problem anymore," she said.

"Is he … still alive?"

"He is. But in a secure location."

"So, his movie …."

"That's done. There will be no filming. Without Parnell, the movie is dead."

"You have done well."

"Thank you."

"Nikita, now that you have solved that issue, I have another assignment for you. I will send you the details later today."

Nikita smiled, already eager to start working on it.

"When will you be coming to see me?" he asked. "It has been a while since we had a face-to-face meeting."

Nikita's enthusiasm dimmed. Although her boss paid her extremely well for managing the Operations Center, he needed other things from her, personal things she did not enjoy.

"Soon," she replied.

"Excellent, my dear Nikita."

There was a click on the line and Nikita realized the man had hung up.

Chapter 25

Atlanta, Georgia

J.T. Ryan was in his apartment in midtown when his cell phone rang. "Ryan here."

"It's Sargeant Malloy," the police detective said. "I've got some information for you. Something that might help both of us."

"Great."

"We were able to track down all the fingerprints from the scene of the crime. As I figured, they were Parnell's and workers and employees who worked for him. These people were local, all living in the Los Angeles area. But there was one print that we couldn't track down. I was hoping the GBI could help us identify who it is."

"You bet. Are you sending me the print?"

"I'll email it to you. You'll get back to me if you find anything?"

"Of course, Sargeant."

They talked for another minute, then they hung up.

Ryan was in his spare bedroom, which he had turned into a home office. Besides a desk and a couple of chairs, there was a whiteboard in it. He had been writing on it when the policeman had called.

Just then he heard a knock at his apartment door.

He went to it and glanced through the spyhole. Seeing who it was, he opened the door. "Come in, Kelly."

The attractive redhead barged in and slammed the door behind her. She was scowling and her hands were formed into fists.

"Are you okay?" Ryan said.

"No!" she yelled. "I'm so damn angry right now, I could scream!"

"Calm down," he said. "Tell me what's wrong."

The GBI agent, who was wearing a beige linen suit with a blue blouse, glared at Ryan. "The hell with that! I need a drink. What do you have?"

The woman didn't wait for an answer and simply stormed into the kitchen and flung open the refrigerator door. She snatched a Guinness beer bottle, uncapped it, and drained it in one long pull. She threw the empty bottle in the trash can by the fridge and grabbed another beer bottle, which she began to drink.

Ryan sat at the dinette table and watched as Kelly paced the kitchen, drinking her Guinness.

"Are you okay?" he said in a calm voice.

She glared at him, then stopped pacing, shrugged and sagged onto the chair opposite him.

"Care to share what's wrong?" he asked.

Kelly took a long pull of her beer. "It's my boss! My damn boss. Do you know what he did today?"

"No."

"He loaded me down with two new cases! And that's after he assigned me two new cases yesterday." She shook her head slowly. "There's no way I can solve them all."

Ryan nodded. "I'm sure he knows that. But you're probably his best agent, so he figures you're probably the one who can make the most progress on them."

She thought about that for a moment. "You think that's it? Or are you trying to make me feel better?"

"Both."

Kelly finished her beer, stood up and got two more from the fridge. She handed one to Ryan and began sipping hers.

"We've had budget cuts at the GBI recently," she said, "so we have less agents. And crime is up in Georgia. So, I guess it's not really my boss's fault."

She paused and then said, "Since my caseload is heavier now, you'll have to handle the movie murders on your own."

Ryan smiled. "That's a shame. I was enjoying being partnered with you."

"Bullshit! I know you like working solo."

"By the way," he said, "we may have caught a break on the case. The L.A. detective I met when I was out there just called me. He's sending me a fingerprint from the crime scene that they can't identify. It could be the perps. He's hoping the GBI can track it down."

"That's great, Ryan. I'll run it through the NCIC database."

She finished her beer, stood, and grabbed another one from the fridge. After opening it, she sat across from him again.

"Slow down," he said. "You've had a lot to drink already."

Her face flushed. "Screw you! Who do you think you are? My mother?"

"No. I'm just looking out for you."

She glared at him, then shrugged. "I know."

"Would you like something to eat?"

She raised the beer bottle. "No. The Guinness is fine."

They sat there for the next half hour, talking about the case, then went to the living room and continued the conversation. Kelly continued downing beers and after a while she began yawning.

Her eyelids closed and her head sagged on her chest.

Ryan heard her snoring lightly. Then her snoring deepened, and she slumped on the sofa, fast asleep.

Realizing she had passed out, he stood, picked her up off the sofa and carried her to his bedroom.

He threw off the covers, took off her shoes, and placed her on the bed. Then he covered her with the blanket, turned off the lights and left the room.

Glancing at his watch, he saw it was 11 p.m. Since he was tired also, he grabbed a blanket and a pillow from a closet and took them back to the living room. He turned off the lights, took off his shoes, and stretched out on the sofa. He was asleep in minutes.

***

Ryan awoke many hours later, startled by the sunlight streaming in through the windows. He got up, went to the kitchen and began brewing a pot of coffee.

Just then Kelly came into the room, her arms folded across her chest, a scowl on her face. "How the hell did I get in your bed?" she growled.

"I carried you there," he replied.

"Why the hell did you do that?"

"You passed out, remember?"

She shook her head in disbelief. "I did not!"

"You did. You had too much to drink last night."

She frowned, her face scrunched in concentration. Then she shrugged. "Well, maybe I did."

Then she stabbed a finger in his direction. "Did you take advantage of me last night?"

"Of course not, Kelly."

"I bet you did! I bet you had your way with me!"

Ryan shook his head. "I didn't. I swear."

She frowned, still processing what had happened last night. She glanced down at herself and saw she was fully dressed. "I believe you."

Then she shot him a stern look. "Why didn't you take advantage of me? Am I not pretty enough for you? Is that it?"

Ryan was at a loss for words.

First, she accused him of taking advantage of her. Now she was mad because he hadn't.

"Oh, my God," he said. "Are you kidding me? You're a gorgeous woman. I'd love to … you know …."

She glared at him, then turned around and marched out of the kitchen. A moment later he heard his apartment door open and then slam shut.

Ryan shook his head, not sure what had just happened. Women were so damn hard to figure out.

Chapter 26

Tokyo, Japan

Nikita glanced around the Operations Center and saw the man she was seeking. She strode over to his workstation and sat on the chair next to it.

"I have an assignment for you," she said.

"Good," the man said. He was a tall, muscled man with blond, close-cropped hair. His name was Shawn, and he was an American.

Nikita handed him a folder and spent the next hour describing the assignment. When she was done, she said, "Any questions?"

"No. I understand what needs to be done. How soon do you want me to do this?"

"Right away, Shawn. I need the subject to be terminated ASAP."

"Understood. The file says this is a two-person job. Who'll be working with me?"

"Kruger," she said. "I've already briefed him on it. He'll be the lead man."

"Okay."

Nikita stood. "But before you leave for your trip, I need you to come to my penthouse. I need a personal matter taken care of."

The blond man inclined his head, a grin on his face. "The same as last time?"

"That's right. Make your flight arrangements and then come see me."

"Yes, Nikita."

Then she stood and headed out of the Operations Center, already looking forward to her private time with Shawn. The muscled, blond American was one of her favorites.

Chapter 27

Beverly Hills
Los Angeles, California

Shawn glanced through his night vision binoculars at the scene below. He was sitting on the ground on a wooded hillside which overlooked the group of mansions, each bordered by high walls. It was 9 p.m. and the whole area was dark.

He put down the binoculars and picked up his Barrett Model 98B snipers' rifle and attached the bipod to it. Then he mounted a suppressor to the rifle.

After that, he lay on the ground and looked through the rifle's Pulsar N550 night vision scope. He adjusted the range and the mansion's front courtyard came into full view. The image was green tinted, but otherwise clearly visible. There was a Porsche SUV parked in the driveway. The mansion was well lit inside. From the research they had done, Shawn knew the man's wife and two children were in the house, along with a housekeeper.

Just then Shawn's cell phone buzzed, and he took the call.

"The target just left his office," he heard Kruger say. "I'll continue tailing him. I estimate he'll be home in about thirty minutes."

"Got it," Shawn said. "Is he using the same car as yesterday?"

"That's right. White Mercedes-Benz 500 sedan."

"Is he alone?"

"He is."

"Good. Anything else?"

"No, Shawn."

"Am I cleared to take the shot?"

"Yes."

They hung up the call and Shawn put the phone away. He glanced at his watch and noted the time. Then he adjusted the crosshairs on the scope and settled in to wait.

Thirty-five minutes later he saw headlights on the street in front of the mansion, then the imposing iron gate creaked open.

The Mercedes drove slowly onto the driveway and came to a stop in front of the mansion.

Shawn adjusted the crosshairs again and took a deep breath, which he let out slowly.

The man, dressed in a dark suit, climbed out of the sedan and took a briefcase out of the back seat.

Shawn's finger slid past the rifle's trigger guard to the trigger itself.

He took one final aim and pulled the trigger. The suppressed round made a thudding sound as the powerful rifle jolted up slightly.

The subject's head exploded. Brain matter and bone and blood gushed from the cracked skull.

The man's body collapsed to the ground.

Chapter 28

GBI Headquarters
Decatur, Georgia

"I'm sorry about the other day at your apartment," Agent Kelly O'Hara said. "I acted totally unprofessional."

J.T. Ryan waved that away. "Don't worry about it."

She shook her head. "No. I overreacted."

"You had too much to drink. It's understandable."

Ryan and Kelly were sitting in her office. She was at her desk, and he was in one of the visitors' chairs.

"Are we okay, then?" she said.

Ryan smiled. "You bet."

"Thanks, Ryan."

"You know you can call me J.T."

She gave him an appraising look, admiring his handsome features and rugged, muscular body. Today the man was wearing a navy blazer, a long-sleeve light blue button-down shirt, and gray slacks. "It's best that I don't."

"Works for me."

Kelly steepled her hands on her desk. "Now that we've got that out of the way," she said, "let's discuss the case. So far, you've gotten two leads. First is the photo of the man who was impersonating the Savannah reporter. He's the man who murdered the Genesis Films movie director."

"If I remember correctly, you hadn't been able to track him down using facial recognition software."

"That's right," she said. "I couldn't find a match using the GBI or the FBI databases. So, I broadened my search. I sent the photo to Interpol, the European police agency. They just got back to me today. They found a match."

"That's great, Kelly. Who is it?"

Kelly slid her laptop sideways so he could see the screen, then tapped on her keyboard.

A man's face appeared on the computer screen. He was a hard-faced man in his late forties. "This is our guy," she said.

"Who is he?"

"He's a German man. His name is Hans Kruger."

"Where does he live?"

"He was born in Berlin and his last known is an apartment there."

Ryan took out a small notepad and a pen. "Give me his address."

Kelly did so and he wrote it down.

"Does this guy have a rap sheet?" Ryan asked.

"Oh, yeah. A mile long. He's been arrested multiple times for robbery, assault, and murder, but never convicted. He always skated, the witnesses to the crimes always 'disappeared' before the trial."

Ryan rubbed his jaw. "Okay. Any recent arrests?"

"Interpol said no. Not for over a year. So, it's possible Kruger is not living in Germany anymore."

"All right, Kelly. You said you had something on the second lead? The unknown fingerprints from the kidnapping of Carl Parnell, the movie producer?"

"That's right. Once again, our friends at Interpol were helpful." Kelly tapped on her keyboard and a photo of a very attractive young woman with long, brunette hair appeared on the screen.

"This is her," Kelly said. "Her name is Marie Dubois. She's French. She lives in Paris. Or she did awhile back. I don't have a current address for her."

Ryan studied the photo for a minute.

"Don't say it, Ryan."

"Say what?"

"What you were thinking. That's she hot."

Ryan rubbed his jaw. "What makes you say that?"

Kelly shook her head slowly. "Because you're a man. And men think all attractive women are hot. A term that I find offensive."

Ryan chuckled. "I won't say that word. But she's a looker, that's for sure."

"I'll email you all the info I got from Interpol about Kruger and Dubois," she said. "Now that we have this, what are your next steps?"

"Most assassins are men," he replied. "So, I'll start tracking down the German guy first. After that, I'll start looking for Marie Dubois."

"I wish I could go with you. But I'm chained to my desk." She pointed to a large stack of case folders next to her laptop.

"Understood."

"When are you getting started?"

Ryan glanced at his watch. "I'll check the flights to Berlin. Hopefully I can book one for tonight."

Chapter 29

Berlin, Germany

J.T. Ryan took a Lufthansa overnight flight out of Atlanta, and by the next morning he was at Berlin's Brandenburg Airport. He rented a VW Jetta and headed toward Berlin's city center. During his Army service he had been to the city several times and was familiar with Berlin's layout. After checking into a small inn on Jagerstrabe Street close to the Brandenburg Gate, he showered, changed clothes, and ate a meal at the hotel restaurant.

That done, he drove toward Kruger's last known address, which turned out to be a five story, brick building on a busy street not far from the Berlin Wall, or what was left of it. The building was situated in the East Berlin area, which was not as prosperous looking as the west side of the city.

Ryan parked his sedan on the street and studied the rundown building. He felt uncomfortable being unarmed, but had no choice. Gun laws in Germany were extremely strict and since he didn't have a law-enforcement badge, if he was arrested for any reason, his weapon would be impounded. And Kelly would have to plead his case to get him out of jail. So, he had left his Desert Eagle at home and was relying on his tactical pen and his fists to get himself out of trouble.

Ryan zipped up his windbreaker and climbed out of the VW. It was a cold and blustery autumn day, and he wished now he'd worn an overcoat.

He strode to the building and went into the shabby lobby area. There was a large row of mailboxes on the right wall, and he scanned the names, looking for Hans Kruger. There was no name by the apartment number he'd gotten from Kelly, so he scanned the list again. One of the mailboxes listed Franz Muller, and it had superintendent under the name.

The apartment for Muller was on the first floor, so Ryan found the right place and knocked on the wooden door.

The door opened partway a moment later. "Can I help you?" the stooped, worn-looking older man said in German.

"Yes, sir," Ryan replied, in the same language. "I'm looking for Hans Kruger."

The super scowled. "Doesn't live here anymore. Hasn't for a long while." He began to close the apartment door, and Ryan stuck his shoe in, preventing it.

"I'll pay you a $100 for any information you have on him," Ryan said.

"Let's see the money first."

Ryan took out his wallet and pulled out five twenties. "I only have U.S. dollars."

The German man nodded. "I like dollars just fine." He opened the door fully and Ryan stepped inside.

"You're not police," Muller said, "otherwise you'd flashed your badge."

"I'm J.T. Ryan, private investigator." He handed the man his business card.

"How about the money?"

Ryan handed three of the twenties to the man.

"You said $100. This is only $60."

"Don't worry, Mr. Muller. You'll get the rest after we talk."

"Okay. I just made some coffee. Want some?"

"I would."

He followed the stooped man into the shabby kitchen. The German poured out two mugs and handed one to Ryan.

The old man sat at the worn and scratched wooden table and Ryan sat across from him.

Ryan sipped the strong and savory coffee. "You said Hans Kruger used to live here. How long ago?"

"He left about a year ago."

Ryan took out a photo and showed it to the old man. "Is this Kruger?"

The superintendent scrutinized the picture closely then scowled. "That's him. The son of a bitch. He was nothing but trouble."

"Why is that?"

"He was always involved with criminal activity. The police were always here, looking for him, arresting him. Then he'd bail out and be back. He had whores coming to his place too, at all times of the night. The other tenants complained about him. I was glad when the son of a bitch left."

Ryan put away the photo. "Do you remember the exact date of when he left?"

Muller thought about this for a long moment. "It was eleven or twelve months ago. I went to collect the rent, since he was always late with it. He didn't answer the door, so I left. I did this for three days in a row and got tired of it, so I used my keys and let myself into his apartment." He shook his head slowly. "The son of a bitch was gone. All his clothes and belongings were gone. He took off without a word."

"Any idea why he left and where he went?" Ryan said.

"I might, when I see the rest of the money you promised."

Ryan took out $40 and handed it to him.

Muller grabbed the money and pocketed it. "For the last couple of months before he left, Kruger was bragging about some big job he was lining up. He said it would pay him a lot more than he was making."

"What kind of job?"

The old man shrugged. "Something criminal, that's for sure."

"Was this job here in Berlin?"

Muller shook his head. "No."

"Where then?"

"My memory is hazy."

"How much to make it less hazy?"

"A hundred more."

Ryan nodded, took out $100 and handed it over. "Now tell me where."

"Kruger said this new job was in Japan."

"Where in Japan?"

"Don't know."

Ryan grabbed the old man by his lapels and lifted him off the seat. "You trying to shake me down for more money?"

Muller's eyes bulged. "No! No. I swear."

The PI let go of the other man. "Okay."

They talked for a while longer, Ryan asking questions about Kruger, trying to ascertain any details about the man that could help locate him.

Then Ryan said, "You have my business card, Muller. My phone number is on it. If you think of anything else, call me. All right?"

"Yes. I'll call you. You'll pay me?"

Ryan grimaced. "Yes. I'll pay you. But the info better be good. If it isn't, I won't be happy. And you don't want to see me when I'm not happy."

***

Ryan left the apartment building and using his cell phone, looked up the address of the main police station in Berlin.

It was located on Platz der Luftbrücke, and he drove there.

He spent the next couple of hours at the police station, trying to gather any additional information on Hans Kruger's current whereabouts. Kruger had a long rap sheet, going back many years. Unfortunately, all the data the cops had was from a year ago.

Realizing he would learn nothing new, he left the station and drove back to his hotel.

He was about to make flight reservations to Paris to hunt down Marie Dubois, when his cell phone buzzed.

"It's Sergeant Malloy, L.A.P.D.," he heard the man say.

"Hello Sergeant. What's up?"

"There's been another murder. And I think it's connected to the others."

"Who was it this time?"

"A well-known movie producer. James Carson."

"The name sounds familiar," Ryan said.

"It should. He produced over twenty hit films. He's been in the industry a long time. Headed up Warner Brothers, Paramount, and Columbia Pictures over the years. Recently he had set up his own studio, Carson Productions."

"How was he killed?"

"Shot from a long distance. We suspect a sniper rifle."

"Where did this happen?"

"At his home in Beverly Hills."

"Okay," Ryan said. "I'm in Germany right now. I'll book a flight to L.A. I'll call you when I get there."

Chapter 30

Tokyo, Japan

Nikita was in her penthouse, sweaty and exhausted from her hour-long exercise routine. It was a routine she maintained every day to keep herself physically and mentally sharp.

Although she was no longer an operative, but an administrator, she enjoyed keeping her body in top condition.

Nikita left her exercise room and went to her massive, luxurious bathroom. She stripped off her drenched sweatshirt and sweatpants and admired her lean and curvaceous body in the mirror, pleased with the image. Even though she was pushing forty, her gorgeous face and flawless body gave the impression she was closer to twenty years old.

Nikita was about to shower when her encrypted cell phone rang. She glanced at the info screen and saw it was her boss calling. Picking up the phone from the vanity, she took the call.

"Good evening, Nikita," the man said.

"Hello. It's good to hear from you." She sat on the edge of the hot tub.

"I'm calling to compliment you on the last assignment," he continued. "I read the news reports. Carson was taken care of very efficiently."

"My men did a good job," she said.

"You are too modest, Nikita. It was your creative and meticulous planning that made it happen."

"Thank you."

"You have done an extremely good job for me over the years. In fact, so good that I'm raising your salary, effective immediately."

"Thank you for that. I appreciate it."

Nikita grinned, delighted with the news. She was already very well off financially, but you can never have enough money.

Then she said, "Do you have a new assignment for me?"

"Not yet, but I will soon. However, I think we need have a face-to-face meeting."

Nikita's enthusiasm dimmed. Although her boss paid her extremely well for management of the Operations Center, he wanted other things from her, sexual things she did not enjoy.

"When do want me to come see you?" she asked.

"This week, Nikita."

"But I have other commitments —"

"This week, Nikita."

Then her boss hung up.

Chapter 31

Los Angeles, California

J.T. Ryan had flown from Berlin to L.A. and called Sargeant Malloy when he landed at LAX Airport. Although Ryan was tired from the long flight, he was eager to work on the case.

They arranged to meet in Beverly Hills, at the home of the murdered film producer.

Ryan parked his rented Mustang at the curb fronting the gated mansion and climbed out of the vehicle. The gate was open, and Ryan saw a multitude of L.A.P.D. sedans and SUVs in the driveway. Yellow crime scene tape cordoned off the whole area.

Ryan showed his ID to one of the uniformed cops at the gate and was allowed in.

He spotted Sargeant Malloy coming out of the mansion's front entrance. Like the last time he had seen him, the tall, black man was wearing a suit, tie, and a starched white dress shirt.

Ryan strode over and they shook hands.

"Glad you're here," Malloy said. The policeman pointed to the taped area on the driveway, which outlined a body. It was noon L.A. time and the dark red stains covering the flagstone surface were clearly visible. "Carson died here. The M.E. already took the body to the morgue." Then he pointed toward the wooded hill to the left of the mansion. "We estimate the shot was taken from up there. It happened last night."

"What caliber round was used?" Ryan asked.

"The M.E. is an expert in ballistics. He believes it was a .338 Lapua Magnum round."

"I'm assuming your people have searched the hillside for trace evidence?"

Malloy nodded. "Yeah. The CSI guys went over it with a fine-tooth comb. They found nothing."

Ryan glanced up at the wooded hill and studied the whole area. "The shot was taken at night from a long distance, so the shooter must have used a sniper rifle. And he used a scope with night vision. The sniper was a professional. Just like in the other murders."

"I agree, J.T."

"Was anyone else hurt?"

"No. Carson's wife and children and the housekeeper were in the mansion when it happened. Carson's wife heard her husband's car pull into the driveway, but when he didn't come into the house, she came out. Found the body."

"How is she holding up?"

Malloy shook his head slowly. "Not well. She was hysterical when the uniforms showed up later. The family doctor was called, and he came, and he gave her a sedative."

"You told me Carson had set up his own movie studio recently?"

"That's right. Carson Productions."

"Where are they located?"

Malloy took out a notebook, flipped it open and read from it. "Culver City. It's a town in L.A. County where a lot of movie studios are located." He read off the address.

"Since this murder is likely connected to the other killings of movie people," Ryan said, "I think I'll go there now and talk to the executives of Carson Productions."

"Sounds good, J.T. But remember, you're not a cop."

Ryan grinned. "Worried I'll shoot somebody?"

"I talked with Agent Kelly O'Hara of the GBI. I know all about your lonewolf tactics." Then the sergeant smiled. "I'd hate to have to arrest you."

Ryan laughed. "Don't worry. I'll be on my best behavior."

Ryan left the crime scene and got back in his rented Mustang. Pulling out his phone, he did some quick research on Culver City and where it was located. It turned out that the town was not far away. In fact, it was surrounded by the city of Los Angeles. In the 1920s, Culver City became a center for film production. It was best known as the home of Metro Goldwyn Mayer studios. Many famous movies had been filmed there, including *The Wizard of Oz*, *Gone with the Wind*, and *King Kong*. Many television programs are filmed there also, including *Jeopardy!* and *Wheel of Fortune*. In addition to MGM, Sony Pictures has their headquarters there, along with other smaller film companies.

Ryan fired up the Mustang and took I-10 to Culver City. He found the Carson Productions headquarters building, which was located on Washington Boulevard. He parked and went into the impressive lobby.

After a long wait he was shown into the office of the company's vice president, Ben Taylor. He was a short, rotund man with gray hair and a gray beard. He was wearing an obviously expensive business suit that did a good job of camouflaging his excess weight.

"Thank you for seeing me," Ryan said, after they shook hands.

The executive's eyes were red-rimmed, and his expression was morose. It was clear the man had taken the death of his boss hard.

Taylor sat back down behind his desk. "This is a … a horrific day … for us."

"Of course," Ryan said, taking a chair fronting the desk. "I know it's a difficult time, but I need to ask you some questions. As I told your assistant, I'm working with LA.P.D. to solve this homicide."

The studio executive steepled his hands and leaned forward in his chair. "Go ahead."

"Do you have any idea why this would have happened? Did Carson have any enemies?"

Taylor grimaced. "No. James Carson was a legend in the industry. Before he started his own firm, he ran Warner Brothers, and Paramount, and Columbia Pictures."

"Do you know why he started Carson Productions?"

"He had a vision. A vision of creating films that are currently not being made in the U.S."

"And what are those?"

"Patriotic, feel-good movies. Some based on religion, others just pro-America. Hollywood now shuns those kinds of films."

Ryan recalled that in the other murders, he had been told the same thing. "How does your company finance your films? I understand that financing is one of the biggest hurdles in the movie making business."

"That's true. Jim Carson was wealthy, so some of the money was his own. We also use crowd funding."

"I see."

Ryan spent the next hour talking with the movie executive, trying to glean as much information about Carson and the film industry in general.

When they were done, Ryan thanked the man and left the headquarters building.

Then he checked into a Marriott off I-405 in L.A. and spent the next day working with Sargeant Malloy on the case.

Chapter 32

Beijing, China

The China Film Group is the largest and most influential film company in China. Based in Beijing, the country's capital, the China Film Group (CFG) is owned and operated by the Central Propaganda Department of the Chinese Communist Party.

The CFG is a state monopoly that not only makes films but also distributes them. It also owns all the movie theaters in China and many of the movie theaters around the world.

In addition to this, CFG controls which films American studios can show in the country of China. Since China is such a huge market, American film companies are eager to tailor their movies to satisfy the Chinese.

The chairman of the China Film Group is General Zhang Wei. After graduating from Beijing University many years ago, he went into the military as an officer and rose through the ranks of the People's Liberation Army. Eventually he reached the rank of general, and because of his high intelligence, cunning, and ruthless nature, was given control over the China Film Group.

General Zhang was in his spacious office now.

He glanced at his watch and noted the time. Soon he would be meeting with the top executives of Universal Pictures, one of the largest film companies in the USA. They wanted the China Film Group to finance one of their upcoming movies.

Chapter 33

GBI Headquarters
Decatur, Georgia

J.T. Ryan entered the GBI headquarters building and asked to see Agent Kelly O'Hara. Ryan was becoming a familiar face at the GBI, and the receptionist recognized him right away.

"Hello, Mr. Ryan," the young woman said. "Kelly is in the impound garage downstairs. She told me you were coming in today."

The receptionist gave him a visitor's badge and instructions on how to find the garage.

Ryan entered the massive, high-ceiling garage a few minutes later. The place was filled with vehicles of all types: cars, vans, SUVs, and trucks. From what the receptionist had told him, the place was the storage area for vehicles impounded during the commission of crimes in Georgia.

He spotted Kelly soon after. She was standing by a Ford F-150 truck, writing notes on a clipboard. The redhead was wearing a blue blouse and black slacks. Her Glock 19 was holstered on her hip.

He walked over and she stopped writing. "Welcome back, Ryan."

"It's good to be back. I emailed you a progress report on what I found out in Germany and L.A."

"Read it. Thanks for keeping me informed."

He glanced around the massive garage. "What are you doing here?"

"One of my new jobs," she said. "Running the impound garage." She made a face. "As if I didn't have enough to do already."

He smiled. "You're a woman with many talents."

A frown crossed her face. "Is that a joke?"

"No, I mean it. It's obvious you're smart and efficient. And in most organizations, those kinds of people are the busiest." He paused, then said, "And they get the most promotions also. I figure you'll be running the GBI in a couple of years."

She inclined her head, as if trying to decide if he was serious or not. Then her expression softened. "Thanks."

Ryan noticed a red Chevrolet Corvette next to the Ford truck. He pointed to it. "Is the Corvette impounded also?"

"Yes. We just got it in."

"What's going to happen to it?"

"It'll be sold at auction, just like every other vehicle here."

Ryan walked over to it and inspected it closely. It was a top-of-the-line Stingray Coupe 3LT model with a V8 engine. Ryan knew it could go from 0-60 MPH in under 3 seconds, and had a top speed of 200 MPH. The sports car was a 2025 model, almost brand new, although he could tell it had been driven hard. The tires were worn and there was some damage to the bodywork.

Ryan had been wanting to buy a red Corvette for years, but had always put it off, mostly because new ones cost about $100,000.

"This is a real beauty," he said. "I'll buy it, for the right price."

Kelly flipped a few pages on her clipboard. "It's almost new. In fact, it's this year's model, a 2025. I'll sell it to you for $80,000."

He got on one knee and inspected the undercarriage, then opened the mid-engine compartment and scrutinized the 495 HP motor. Then he sat inside the car and examined the tan leather interior of the sports coupe.

After he climbed out of it, he said, "Bullshit. It's been driven hard. It'll take some work to get it running well. I'll give you 40 grand for it."

She shook her head. "No way. 70 grand."

"You're crazy. I'll buy it for 50, and I'm doing you a favor."

Kelly mulled this over for a long moment. Then she nodded. "Okay. Fifty it is. But I'm only giving you a good deal because you're helping me on the case."

She extended her hand, and they shook.

She wrote something on her clipboard and then she looked up at him. "Tell me, Ryan. If I had been a real hardass, and stuck to my guns on the price, how much would you have paid for this Corvette?"

Ryan smiled. "You don't want to know."

Chapter 34

GBI Headquarters
Decatur, Georgia

After J.T. Ryan took the Corvette for a test drive, he signed a GBI purchase agreement for the car, and gave Kelly a deposit for it.

That done, they went to the GBI cafeteria on the building's first floor. It was three in the afternoon and the place was almost empty.

Kelly had black coffee, while Ryan, who was starved, got a steak sandwich, fries, and a large Pepsi. They sat in a booth by the windows.

Kelly took a sip of her coffee. "What's your next move?"

He pointed to the large platter of food in front of him and grinned. "To eat this."

She rolled her eyes. "I mean on the case."

Ryan laughed. "I know."

He took a bite of the sandwich, which was delicious. Then he washed it down with Pepsi.

"I'll be heading back to Europe. To Paris. I need to find out more about this Marie Dubois."

"I figured that's what you were going to do."

"I'm hoping to link Dubois and Kruger in some way, since both people were involved in the kidnapping of Carl Parnell and the murder of his housekeeper. I'm positive Kruger and Dubois are involved in the other murders also."

Kelly took another sip of coffee. "I agree."

"The man I met in Berlin, the super of Kruger's apartment building, told me Kruger bragged he was getting a high-paying job in Japan. I'm thinking that's where he went."

Kelly inclined her head. "I did some checking on that. The population of Japan is 123 million people. It's not going to be easy to find out where Kruger is, assuming he's even there."

"If it was easy," he said, "you wouldn't need me."

She rolled her eyes, then her expression softened, and she let out a long sigh. "I'm so focused on getting the job done, I still have trouble getting used to your joking around."

Ryan laughed. "I've got a couple of new jokes I can tell you."

She laughed also. "Thanks. But no. I've reached my limit of Ryan humor for today."

Chapter 35

Tokyo, Japan

Nikita felt dirty.

She always did, after meeting with her boss. She had already taken three scalding hot showers, trying to scrub off the way he made her feel.

Nikita hated the sexual way he used her, hated the vile things he made her do. But most of all she hated that he was in control. But she had no choice. Her luxurious lifestyle would end quickly without his financial support.

After soaping up her body one last time, she rinsed in the intensely hot water for another long moment.

Then she stepped out of the shower and dried herself. She slipped into a terrycloth robe and padded out of the bathroom, barefoot.

Going into the sumptuous living room of her penthouse, she went to the liquor cabinet and poured herself a large glass of *sake*. She sipped it slowly, the alcohol soothing her nerves.

She knew there was only way to solve her present dilemma. Being in control, she knew, was the only way to restore balance in her life.

Picking up her cell phone from the coffee table, she made a call.

When the man answered, she said, "I need you. Now." She listened for a moment. "I don't care what you're doing, Kruger. Come up now."

Nikita hung up and went to the floor-to-ceiling windows of the living room. After drawing the drapes, she poured herself another tall glass of *sake*.

A few minutes later there was a knock at her front door. After checking who it was in the security camera, she let Kruger inside and into the living room.

She noticed the muscular man was wearing a black shirt and black slacks. She took another sip of *sake*, as she gave him a long, up and down look, already anticipating the pleasure he would give her.

"Take off your clothes," she said. "And do it slowly."

"You should strip for me, for a change."

"That's not how this works," she replied, her voice firm.

The man took off his shoes and shirt and pants and underwear.

She studied his powerfully built physique, enjoying the sight of his nude body. After gulping the rest of her *sake*, she approached him and began running her hands slowly over every part of his body. She enjoyed this almost as much as what would follow.

It feels so good, she thought. *So damn good.* She felt herself getting wet already.

Kruger's eyes shined with anticipation. He grinned and by his erection it was clear he was as ready as she was.

Then she took hold of him and began stroking him slowly.

He let out a low moan.

"You remember the rules, don't you?" she whispered, still stroking him sensually. "You can't come until I say you can come. Understood?"

He closed his eyes and moaned again. "Yes ... yes ...." he said, gasping.

Grinning excitedly, she continued to stroke him slowly, knowing he was reaching a breaking point.

"Do you like this?" she whispered.

"You know ... that I do ...." he said, breathing heavily. "Please, Nikita ... let's do this ... before ... before ...."

"All right."

She let go of him and unfastened the sash of her robe, showing him everything.

Then she took his hand and led him into the bedroom.

Chapter 36

Paris, France

J.T. Ryan had taken an Air France flight out of Atlanta and landed at Charles de Gaulle Airport nine hours later.

He rented a Peugeot 308 sedan at the airport and drove to an inn he had stayed at last time he was in Paris. The small hotel was centrally located and close to the Champs-Élysées Avenue.

After showering, shaving, and changing into fresh clothes, he grabbed a quick meal at the hotel restaurant.

Then he drove the Peugeot to the Saint Blaise neighborhood in Paris's 20th arrondissement. This neighborhood, Ryan knew, was known as a haven for criminal elements.

The address he had for Marie Dubois turned out to be a five-story walk-up building that had seen better days. Its brick façade looked tired, and by the battered cars parked on the street, it was clear the residents were not affluent.

Ryan parked at the curb, climbed out, and zipped up his jacket. Although not as cold as Germany, it was still a cool and blustery day, and he was glad he had brought warmer clothes on this trip.

He strode into the building, and after consulting the mailboxes in the worn lobby, took the stairs to the fifth floor.

The corridor was dimly lit, and the carpet was shabby.

He found the right apartment a few minutes later. Like in Germany, gun laws in France were just as strict, so he had not been able to bring his weapon on this trip either.

Ryan knocked on the worn wooden door and waited.

It was opened by a big, swarthy looking guy in his forties. He was wearing a dirty T-shirt and jeans. He had a ragged beard and a crooked nose. A crude tattoo was on his neck, a prison tat, Ryan figured.

"My name is J.T. Ryan," he said in his rusty French. "I'm looking for Marie Dubois. I understand she lives here, or did live here. I'm willing to pay to find her whereabouts."

The swarthy man smirked, showing stained, crooked teeth. "Your French is lousy," he said in English. "Lucky for you I speak English."

"That's great. Is Ms. Dubois here?"

The Frenchman shook his head. "No. She left a long while ago."

"Do you know where she went?"

The swarthy man tilted his head. "You mentioned money?"

"I did."

"How much?"

"Two hundred dollars."

The man grimaced. "Not enough. And I prefer Euros, not dollars." Then he began to close the door.

Ryan stuck his foot in the doorway. "Five hundred, for good information."

"That's better. Come in then."

Ryan went inside and the man closed the door behind him. The living room was small and furnished with threadbare, mismatched pieces. From the impoverished looks of the place, it was clear this guy was not a very successful criminal.

"I didn't catch your name," Ryan said.

"Bastien. Louis Bastien. You mentioned money? I'd like to see it first. As you Americans say, 'money talks and bullshit walks'."

Ryan pulled out his wallet and took out two hundred U.S. dollars. He handed the man the cash.

Bastein frowned. "You said five hundred."

"You haven't told me anything yet."

The Frenchman gave him a crooked grin. "True." He pocketed the cash. "Marie did live here. We were together for two years." He smirked again. "She was the best sex I ever had."

"Good to know," Ryan said. "Where is she now?"

The man shrugged. "Gone with the wind. She told me she got this good job. Overseas, she said. Then she packed her bags and left."

Ryan shook his head slowly. "I need my money back, friend. You haven't told me anything I didn't know before."

"Fuck you. You get nothing back, you American bastard." Then the guy pulled out a switchblade and flicked it open. "Get the fuck out of here, Ryan. Or I'll gut you like a fish."

Ryan saw red, furious at the other man. "Bullshit! Give me my money back." He closed his fists and went into a fighting stance, eyeing the switchblade closely.

The Frenchman swung the knife and Ryan jumped back, the blade missing by an inch. He slashed the knife again and this time it found its mark, the blade cutting through Ryan's jacket and shirt and slashing his waist.

Ryan grunted from the pain, then he punched the French guy in the face, knocking him off his feet. Blood spurted from the Frenchman's nose and lips.

The pain in Ryan's waist was so intense that he clutched his midsection and went to one knee. Then everything went black, and he collapsed to the floor.

***

Ryan awoke sometime later.

He was still in the Frenchman's apartment, looking up at the ceiling. He sat up and noticed he was bleeding from the knife slash across his stomach. The pain was not as intense now, and he managed to get to his feet. He glanced around the living room, then went through the apartment's other rooms. Bastien was gone. It was clear the man was a criminal and probably wanted by the police, so taking off was his best option.

Going into the bathroom, Ryan found some gauze and tape and, after taking off his jacket and shirt, he cleaned his wound as best he could and bandaged it.

Then he searched the apartment thoroughly but found no info about Marie Dubois. He did find a burner phone in a drawer, which he took. In his hurry, Bastein had left it behind.

Ryan felt a stabbing pain and looked down at his bandaged midsection. Bright red blood had seeped through, and he realized he had to get medical attention, or he would bleed out.

He put on his shirt and jacket and left the apartment.

Once he got back to his rented Peugeot, he used his cell phone and looked up the address of the nearest hospital.

After driving there, Ryan spent the next six hours waiting in the emergency room to see a doctor. The place was a madhouse of activity, with obviously poor people in ragged clothes streaming in and out of the emergency room. It was so crowded that Ryan had to lean against a wall, because all the seats were taken.

Finally, at around 3 a.m., he was taken back to a small, triage room. There a doctor cleaned his wound, stitched it, and bandaged it. The doc also gave him a shot and some pills for the pain. The doctor was old and stooped, but good at his job, Ryan realized when he was being stitched up.

The emergency room visit was expensive, and when he went to pay the bill, Ryan realized all his cash was gone from his wallet. Bastien had cleaned him out. Luckily, he'd left the credit cards, and the emergency room nurse was more than willing to take plastic for payment.

After paying the bill, he drove to the inn, took the pain killers and went to sleep. When he awoke hours later, he showered, dressed, and ate once again in the hotel's restaurant.

That done, he took out his phone and made a call. When Kelly answered, he said, "It's me."

"Where are you, Ryan?"

"Still in Paris."

"How's it going?"

"Not bad, considering I got a knife wound in my gut and spent six hours in the emergency room."

"Are you okay?" she said, concern in her voice.

"I'll live. Listen, I found the man Marie Dubois was living with, before she left Paris. A Frenchman named Louis Bastien. We got into a fight, and he took off."

"What about Dubois. Anything on her?"

"No. But Bastein left a burner phone behind. I'll give it to you when I get back home. Maybe you can use your tech magic and get something from it."

"Sounds good, Ryan. When are you coming back?"

"I'll spend a couple of more days here, see if I can find Bastein. I'll also meet with the French police. See if the local cops have anything on Bastein or Dubois."

"Okay." The GBI agent paused, then said, "And try not to get killed, all right?"

Ryan chuckled. "Because you'll miss my wit and charm?"

There was no answer for a long moment, and Ryan could visualize the woman grinding her teeth.

"No, Ryan. Because I still need your help solving this damn case."

Chapter 37

Paris, France

Louis Bastien had purchased a new burner phone, and he dialed it now.

When the woman answered he said, "It's me. Louis."

The woman didn't answer for a long moment, and he thought she'd hung up on him.

"Are you there, Marie?"

"Yes. I'm here. What do you want?"

"I miss you."

"You miss the sex, is what you mean," she said, no humor in her voice.

"That too. But I really do miss you. I care for you. When are you coming back to France?"

"I don't know, Louis. Maybe never."

"Don't say that." He paused a moment, then said, "There's a man looking for you."

"What man?"

"An American. He's a private investigator of some sort. From the U.S."

"What did he want?"

"To find out where you were."

"What did you tell him?'

"Nothing. Because it's the truth. I don't know where you are. You never told me."

"It's better that way, Louis. Who was this American?"

"His name is John Ryan. He's from Atlanta, Georgia. His ID said he was a private investigator."

"I'll deal with him on my own. Thanks for calling me, Louis."

"Don't hang up. Please."

"Okay."

"If you can't come back, at least let me visit you. Or you can visit me here in Paris."

"That's not possible, Louis."

"But why? I miss you …."

Then the line went dead, and he realized she had hung up.

Chapter 38

Tokyo, Japan

Marie Dubois hung up the phone and put it away. The call had been disturbing, to say the least.

Why the hell was an American investigator looking for her? she thought, her mind churning.

Marie paced her apartment, which was on the 11th floor of the building. She glanced at her watch, knowing she had to tell Nikita about this. Her boss would be furious with her, but she had no choice but to tell her. If she hid what was happening and Nikita found out from another source, it would be even worse for her.

Marie took out her phone again and dialed Nikita's number.

Half an hour later she was in her boss's penthouse apartment. Unlike her own, Nikita's was lavish and massive in size.

Nikita was pacing the living room, her beautiful face contorted in anger. The woman was wearing a red and gold embroidered kimono with a black sash.

Marie was sitting on the leather couch.

Nikita stopped pacing and shot her a furious look. "Tell me again what happened, Marie. And this time leave nothing out."

"I just got a call. From the man I was living with in France. His name is Louis Bastein. An American man came to see him. He asked questions about me, trying to find out where I was."

"And? What did this Bastein character tell him?"

"Nothing. He told him nothing. Because Bastein never knew where I went."

Nikita glared at her. "Are you sure about that?"

"Yes! Yes. I never told him."

Her boss's expression softened somewhat. "That's good. Very good. Who was the American man?"

"A private investigator, Bastein said."

"From Atlanta, Georgia?"

"Yes."

"This American – his name is John Ryan?"

"Yes."

Nikita went quiet and began pacing again. Then she went to the cabinet in the room and pulled out a bottle of *sake*. She poured a large glass and sipped it slowly.

"Can I have a drink?" Marie asked.

Her boss glared at her. "No, you may not, you bitch!" She downed the whole glass and poured herself another. Then she began pacing again.

After a long moment, Marie said, "What do you want me to do?"

Nikita scowled at her. "Nothing on this. Go back to your regular assignments. I'll take care of this Ryan character. I'll get Krueger and Shawn involved. Maybe some of my other operatives."

"Yes, Nikita."

Nikita began pacing the living room, deep in thought.

She stopped a moment later and glared at Marie. "Why the hell are you still here? Get out of here and get back to work."

Chapter 39

Atlanta, Georgia

Kelly O'Hara knocked on the apartment door and waited. She was carrying a pastry box with her.

J.T. Ryan answered it a moment later, a grin on his handsome face. The man was wearing gray slacks and a blue button-down dress shirt.

"Well, well," he said. "My favorite GBI agent is here. Come in, Kelly."

She went inside and he closed the door behind him.

"I just came to see how you were doing," she said. "You told me on the phone you'd gotten stabbed in Paris."

"I'm okay. I flew in last night and slept for 12 hours. I'm feeling pretty good now."

Kelly handed him the box she was carrying. "I brought you donuts. Thought you'd enjoy them."

"You bet. Krispy Kreme donuts are the best." He pointed toward the kitchen. "In fact, I'm starved. Let's have some now."

She followed him into the kitchen, and he placed the box on the dinette table. He reached into the refrigerator and pulled out a gallon jug of milk. He winced and held his hand to his waist. Pain registered on his face.

"Are you okay?" she said.

He waved that away. "I'm fine. The cut wasn't too deep."

"Let me look at it," she said. "I've had some medical training."

"Really?"

"Yeah. When I went through the GBI academy, I also got EMT training."

"I guess the bandage should be changed."

"I'll change it for you," she said.

They went into the bathroom, and he unbuttoned his shirt and took it off.

She glanced at his bandage and then stared at his chiseled, muscular body. He had an amazing physique, and her face turned a bright shade of red. She averted her gaze.

"Are you okay?" he said.

"Yeah," she responded, pushing her lustful thoughts away. She went to the sink and began to wash her hands. "I need to wash up before I change your bandage."

When she was done, she glanced at the mirror, saw she was still blushing. Then thoughts of her abusive husband and their horrible marriage flooded her mind, and the lust evaporated.

Kelly approached him and carefully removed the bandages from his stomach. She inspected the large number of stitches, saw the doctor had done a superb job. She traced her hand gingerly over the cut.

"That's quite a gash, Ryan. You're lucky to be alive."

He grinned. "I told you lucky is my middle name."

She shook her head slowly. "You shouldn't kid around about this. You could have been killed."

"You're right," he said, his tone serious now. "I've got bandages and other stuff in the medicine cabinet."

She opened the cabinet, took out the items and wiped the cut with disinfectant. Then she applied gauze to the wound and bandaged it.

"All done," she said.

"Thanks, Kelly."

"Don't mention it."

Ryan put on his shirt and buttoned it. "I can cook up some dinner for us, if you want to stay."

She stared at his handsome face and rugged good looks. "I better not," she replied, not trusting herself. "I have to get back to the office."

"You sure? I got plenty of Guinness beer."

Kelly nodded. "As tempting as that sounds, I do need to get back to work."

"Before you go, let me give you something."

"What?"

Ryan reached into his pants pocket and removed a cell phone, which he handed to Kelly.

"I found this in Bastein's apartment in Paris," Ryan said. "It's a burner, but maybe your tech people can pull up some helpful info from it. We might get lucky and be able to track down where Dubois is located."

"Good work on getting this."

He grinned. "Do I get a bonus?"

She shook her slowly and smiled back. "No, buster, you don't get a bonus. I'm already paying you too much as it is."

Ryan laughed. "I was just kidding."

"I know. I'm starting to get used to your sense of humor."

Chapter 40

Beijing, China

Since General Zhang was the chairman of the China Film Group (CFG), the largest film company in China, his office was lavishly furnished. It was located on the top floor of the CFG's headquarters building. The office had a breathtaking view of Beijing's downtown skyline.

General Zhang Wei was in his office now. As usual, he was wearing his People's Liberation Army uniform.

He glanced at his watch and noted the time. Soon he would be meeting with the top executive of Universal Pictures, the largest film company in the USA. They wanted the China Film Group to finance one of their upcoming movies.

This would be their second meeting on the subject. The first meeting did not go well.

Just then there was a knock on his door, and it opened partway. His assistant, Colonel Liu stood there. "Your guest is here," she said, in Mandarin. Like himself, the young woman was dressed in her PLA military uniform.

"Show him in, please," he replied in Mandarin.

Zhang stood and went to the massive rectangular conference table in the room. He sat at the head of the table.

The American executive came in and he and Zhang shook hands.

"Please have a seat, Mr. Reynolds," Zhang said in flawless English.

The American took one of the plush, high-backed executive chairs.

"Would you like some coffee or tea? I can have my assistant serve us some," Zhang said.

"No, thanks. I'm good." The American was tall and distinguished looking, with longish gray hair and a closely trimmed gray mustache. He was wearing a perfectly tailored business suit, a white dress shirt, and a red paisley tie.

"Thank you for taking the time to meet with me again," Reynolds began. "I know our last meeting wasn't very productive."

"Maybe today will be different."

"Yes, General. I hope that also. As I mentioned last time, we at Universal are interested in having CFG finance our next film."

Zhang nodded, said nothing.

"It's a big-budget action film," the American said. "We estimate the movie will cost us approximately $500 million to produce."

"How much of that would you like for us to finance?"

Reynolds inclined his head. "Most of it, actually."

"I see. That is quite a large amount of money."

"Yes, that's true, General. But we expect the film to gross three times that amount, so the return on your investment would be excellent."

Zhang frowned. "The movie could also flop, and in that case, we would lose our whole investment."

"That's unlikely. We feel confident this will be a blockbuster."

The general opened a desk drawer and pulled out a thick binder and placed it on his desk. He tapped the cover of the binder. "I have the read the script you gave me."

"What did you think?"

"It is excellent."

Reynolds beamed.

"But for us to invest in it," Zhang continued, "we would need to make some changes in the script."

The American's eyebrows knitted. "Changes?"

"Yes. Changes to make it a better movie."

"What kind of changes?"

"First, the main character in the film now is an American superhero, who battles the forces of evil and tyranny."

"That's correct."

"You will need to change the main character to a Chinese man who is the superhero."

Reynolds shook his head slowly. "That's quite a big change. I'm not sure we can do that …."

Zhang rose from his chair. "In that case, Mr. Reynolds, I think this meeting is over."

"Please, General. Let's not be hasty. All right?"

Zhang sat back down.

"Maybe," Reynolds said, "we could rework the script with your idea."

"That is excellent. I just have one other alteration that needs to be made."

"More changes?"

"Yes. Currently the location of the film is in the United States. We would like to see the film made here in China. In fact, we want our capital city of Beijing to be the main focus of it. We want to showcase our city's beauty."

Reynolds blanched. "That's quite a leap, General. I hope you're not serious."

"But I am."

The American let out a long breath. "And If I agree to your terms, you'll finance our film?"

"Yes. I guarantee it. I've already spoken with my superiors at the Central Propaganda Department of the CCP. They have approved it, if these changes are made to the film."

Reynolds sat there for a long moment, mulling over the conversation. He had a tortured expression on his face, and he said nothing for several minutes.

Finally, the American held out his hand. "I agree, General. I accept your terms."

Zhang shook his hand. "Excellent. I knew we could come to an agreement."

Chapter 41

Tokyo, Japan

Ueno Park is a public park in the Taito district of Tokyo. The park covers an area of 133 acres and contains several museums, Buddhist temples, as well as Japan's oldest zoo. It also contains the Tokyo National Museum, the Great Buddhist Pagoda, and the Tosho-gu Shrine. The park is considered one of the most beautiful places in the bustling and crowded metropolis of Tokyo.

The park has over 8,800 trees, the most famous being the Japanese cherry trees, which line the main walkway.

In 1873, five years after the Battle of Ueno, when the last supporters of the Shogun were crushed by Imperial forces, the Japanese government designated the area a public park.

One of the most scenic and peaceful settings of the park is Shinobazu Pond.

Nikita was at Ueno Park now, strolling along the pathway that faced the Shinobazu Pond. Kruger was walking with her.

There was no one else nearby in the almost deserted setting.

"Why do you come here so much?" Kruger said. "I never understood your fascination with this place."

Nikita stopped and glanced at him. "There's 37 million people crammed into Tokyo. It's one of the most densely populated areas in the world. But here, in this park, with its lush beauty, you forget that. This place helps me think."

Kruger shrugged. "You said earlier you had a new assignment for me?"

"I do."

"Another movie murder?"

"Not this time."

"What then?"

"There's an American that needs to be taken care of. I just found out about it from Marie. This American is a private investigator by the name of Ryan. John Ryan." Nikita paused, then said, "This Ryan was in France recently, trying to find Marie's whereabouts. I'm worried Ryan could trace Marie to Tokyo and to my operation here."

"I see. Do you want me to terminate Ryan?"

Nikita's black eyes flashed. "Of course, you idiot. Why else would I tell you about him?"

Kruger's face flushed and she realized she'd insulted him.

She placed her palm on his cheek. "Sorry about that. I'm just wired today."

His expression softened. "It's okay."

"This private investigator lives in Atlanta, Georgia," she continued. "He has an office and an apartment there. I did some research on him, and he has a military background. Special Forces. So, he'll be hard to take down. You'll need to take Shawn with you and another one of our operatives. I'll let you decide which one."

"Yes, Nikita."

Nikita gazed at the placid pond and the lush landscape that bordered it. The view always calmed her nerves.

"I'll email you the details for the operation," she said. "I want you to start on it right away."

Chapter 42

Atlanta, Georgia

J.T. Ryan was driving his Chevy Tahoe on Peachtree Street, on his way to the Varsity for a late dinner. He had spent the day at his office, doing paperwork. Ever since he'd taken on the GBI case, his other cases had been put on hold. So, he had spent today catching up on those as best he could and asking for extensions from his other clients until he completed the GBI investigation.

Ryan glanced warily at his rearview mirror. For the last week he'd had the feeling he was being followed.

It was past 8 p.m. and traffic was light on Peachtree. He saw nothing suspicious behind him and he pushed aside the thoughts of being tailed.

A few minutes later he was on North Avenue, and he drove into the parking lot of the historic Varsity restaurant. An institution in Atlanta, the famed restaurant had been in business since 1928. Known for its tasty menu of chili dogs and onion rings, it was more of a drive-in than a fancy eatery. But its savory fare made it one of Ryan's favorite places to eat.

He parked the Tahoe, and after checking the load on his Desert Eagle, he zipped up his windbreaker and climbed out. He took a long look around the lot to make sure there were no suspicious characters nearby.

He went inside the Varsity and ordered his usual, two chili dogs, a large order of onion rings, and three containers of chocolate milk.

Since it was close to the restaurant's closing time, there were only a few patrons in the place. During their bustling lunch hour, the Varsity was packed with people.

He grabbed a table which overlooked I-75 and ate his food while watching the headlights and taillights of the nighttime traffic on the Interstate.

As usual, the food was excellent.

While he ate, he received a text message from Kelly O'Hara. It said,

I'm still working on the phone you gave me. Hope to have a list of calls made from it soon. Will let you know when I get something. K.O.

Ryan replied,

Thanks, Kelly. By the way, I'm at the Varsity now. I can buy you a chili dog and onion rings and bring them to the GBI office if you want. J.T.

She replied instantly,

How can you eat that greasy food? No thanks! K.O.

Ryan chuckled and put his phone away. He knew Kelly's answer before her reply, but he enjoyed bantering with the GBI agent.

He finished his meal and left the restaurant. There were only a few vehicles in the dim parking lot, since the Varsity was set to close minutes later.

Ryan headed for his Tahoe, then heard the squeal of tires from behind him.

Turning around, he spotted a black Ford Explorer racing towards him, its headlights blinding him.

He dove behind a parked Toyota Camry and pulled his Desert Eagle. Peering over the car's trunk, he saw three men jump out of the Explorer. The men were wearing black clothing and carrying short-barrel carbines with suppressors.

The men in black opened fire, the semiautomatic rifles targeting Ryan's location.

The numerous rounds clanged into the Camry's doors and roof, shredding the tires and exploding the windows. Shards of glass flew everywhere.

Ryan, his heart racing, fired back, the booms from his .50 caliber rounds echoing loudly. He saw one of the men clutch his chest, drop his rifle and slump to the ground.

But the other two continued firing, now on full auto, their bullets shredding the Toyota's bodywork.

Ryan knew the only safe place for him was behind the Toyota's engine block.

With his adrenaline pumping, he fired several more rounds. Then, still in a crouch, he edged his way to the front of the car. When he was behind the hood, he ejected the spent magazine in the Desert Eagle and slammed a full one into the handgun.

Incoming rounds pounded into the Toyota, the metal clanging sound echoing loudly. By this time the car was riddled with bullets, all its tires were flat, and the window glass was totally cracked or gone.

Ryan peered around the bumper, fired three more shots and saw another man in black drop to the ground.

Sirens wailed in the distance and Ryan knew the police were on their way.

Just then he heard the screeching of tires, and he glanced over the Toyota's hood.

The black Ford Explorer was speeding out of the parking lot. Seconds later it was gone.

Ryan, his heart pounding, sat on the concrete and gulped in air. He was exhausted from the firefight, but glad to be alive.

***

An hour later, the Varsity parking lot was a madhouse of activity. APD police cars and SUVs were everywhere, their flashing blue lights illuminating the nighttime. There were also firetrucks and EMT vans, and CSI vehicles. A coroner's van was there also.

The whole area was a beehive, with uniformed cops, plainclothes detectives, and CSI guys moving in and out of the scene. Yellow crime scene tape kept out the large crowd of looky-loos that always sprouted like weeds at crime scenes.

Ryan sat on the tailgate of the EMT van and watched the scene. He had already given his statement to the APD detectives, and he had been checked out by the EMT guys. Luckily the stitches in his stomach were intact, although he felt a hell of a lot of pain from his waist during the shootout.

Two of the men who had attacked Ryan were dead. Ryan watched as the two corpses, now in black body bags, were loaded into the coroner's van.

The police had found the criminal's weapons, which turned out to be Heckler & Koch USC .45 caliber rifles. Ryan knew these were highly sophisticated rifles, used by professionals. The rifles were also equipped with suppressors, another sign the thugs were pros.

Just then Ryan saw Kelly O'Hara's SUV pull into the Varsity parking lot. She climbed out, flashed her badge to a uniformed cop and was allowed inside the crime scene.

Kelly approached Ryan, a worried look on her face. "Are you okay?" she asked.

"I'm all right."

Then he pointed to the coroner's van. "I'm doing a hell of a lot better than the stiffs they just put in there."

"APD called me and told me what was going on," she said. "I was working a case in Macon, and I drove up here as fast as I could."

She paused, then said, "Tell me what happened."

"Three armed men jumped out of an SUV and started shooting at me. I fired back, hit two of them. The third guy took off."

"Any idea who they were?"

"Oh, yeah. I got a good look at the third guy, the one that got away. It was Kruger. Hans Kruger, the German man we've been after."

Kelly nodded. "How about the other two? The dead guys."

"APD ran their prints through NCIC. One of them is an American named Shawn Crais. Last known is an address in Los Angeles. But it looks like it's been a year since he lived there."

"And the other guy?"

"An Australian by the name of Bill Martin. No known address."

Kelly ran a hand over her long, reddish hair, which was pulled into a ponytail. "So, what happened tonight is connected to our movie murders case."

"Yeah. I'm sure of it. Either Kruger or the Frenchwoman Dubois found out I was looking for them and decided to stop me before I located them."

"We still don't have a motive," she said, "for all the murders. All we know is that they're connected to the movie industry."

Ryan felt a stabbing pain from the stitches in his waist and held his hand over it.

"Are you okay, Ryan?"

Ryan grinned, despite the pain. "Don't worry. I'm the man of steel. Bullets bounce off my chest. And I can leap over tall buildings in a single bound."

"Bullshit. You're just as human as the rest of us."

Suddenly her words sank in, and Ryan felt his mortality like a thousand-pound weight crushing down on his shoulders.

She's damn right, he thought. *I could have died tonight.*

Ryan glanced toward the coroner's van as it drove out of the parking lot, realizing it could have been him in a body bag tonight.

His thoughts churned and he turned back toward the GBI agent.

"I think I'm going to need a few days off," he said. "I need to take care of a personal matter."

"What is it?"

He shrugged. "It's personal. It's something I've put off for quite a while. After tonight, I realize I may not get the chance to do it."

"Okay," she replied. "How long will you need?"

"Just a few days. I'll be traveling overseas."

"Where to, Ryan?"

"Amsterdam."

Chapter 43

Tokyo, Japan

Nikita was in the bedroom of her penthouse apartment, sipping *sake* as she watched the nude man next to her sleep. He was snoring lightly.

The man on the bed, an operative at her center, was one of her favorites. Sexually he was almost as good as Kruger. Like Kruger, he knew what she wanted and what she needed, and he always gave it to her.

She finished her drink, covered her nude body with the sheet, then slapped the man on his ass.

"Get up," she said. "It's time for you to go."

He sat up and rubbed his eyes. "Let me stay the night," he said groggily. "I want more."

Nikita shook her head. "You don't get more. We're done."

"Please, Nikita."

She slapped him hard across his face. "Get the fuck out of here!"

He flinched, and his cheek was now bright red.

Scowling, his hands formed into fists.

"If you don't leave right now," she hissed, her voice ice cold, "I'll cut your balls off. And you know me well enough to know I'm not kidding."

His eyes went wide, the fear evident. He got off the bed and began dressing.

"I hate being a bitch," she said, now in a sweet tone. "But you know the rules. No overnight stays. You give me what I need and then we're done."

129

He nodded, but she could tell he was still angry at her.

"Come here," she said. "Sit next to me."

The man sat on the bed.

She leaned in and kissed him, hard on the mouth.

Then she pulled away and caressed his cheek.

"I promise," she said, "next time, we'll spend more time together."

"I'd like that, Nikita. I'd like that very much."

She smiled. "Okay. Now run along. I've got a phone call I need to make."

"Yes, Nikita."

He stood and left her bedroom. A moment later she heard her apartment door open and then close.

She opened a drawer of her nightstand and removed an encrypted cell phone. Then she punched in a number she had memorized long ago.

When Kruger answered a moment later, she said, "How did it go?"

"Not well, Nikita."

Her teeth clenched and she gripped the phone tightly. "I don't like bad news, Kruger."

"I know. I don't either."

"Talk to me, damn it!" she screeched. "Tell me what the hell happened."

"We tried killing Ryan, but he got away."

"You fucked up!"

"I'm sorry ... I'm really sorry, Nikita ...."

"You're sorry? That's all you can say, you piece of shit? You're supposed to be my best operative!" She gripped the phone tighter. "I want you to go after Ryan again. And this time, do it right!"

"That's going to be difficult, Nikita."

"Why the hell is that?"

"During the shootout, I lost two men."

"Tell me you're kidding."

"No."

"Shawn is dead?"

"Yes."

"And Martin also?"

"Yes."

Nikita rubbed her temple, feeling a massive headache forming. "Those two were good. Along with you, the best in my operation."

"I know."

She tried processing this new development, trying to recalibrate her options. She had just received a new target from her boss, a movie person who had to be dealt with. Even though she had lost two operatives, she still needed to get her job done.

"What do you want me to do now?" he asked.

"Come back to Japan. I have a new assignment for you."

"What about Ryan?"

"Forget him, for now. I'll come up with a new way to take care of that bastard."

"All right. Should I come back now?"

"Of course, you idiot! And don't forget, you're still on my shit list for fucking up my plan. I'll make you pay for this screwup."

"Yes, Nikita."

Then she hung up the call, still infuriated at Kruger.

Chapter 44

Amsterdam, Holland

The home was a gorgeous three-story house in a suburb of the city. It was ultra-modern in design, and constructed in steel, glass, and concrete. J.T. Ryan had been here once before, and he realized the home was just as impressive now as it had been a year ago.

Ryan parked his rented Audi in the driveway, and after zipping up his jacket, he climbed out and rang the buzzer at the front entrance.

Moments later the door opened partway, and Amanda Johansen stood there, shock registering on her face. She looked just as beautiful as when he had last seen her. Amanda was in her mid-thirties, had long, flowing blonde hair, piercing gray eyes, and a stunning face and figure. The woman was wearing a long-sleeve blue blouse and black slacks.

After a moment her look of shock wore off, replaced with a tentative smile. "You came back. Hopefully not to arrest me."

Ryan returned the grin. "No, not to arrest you."

She opened the door fully. "In that case, John, come in."

He entered the home, and she led him into an immense living room with sleek Danish-style furnishings. Hanging on one wall of the room was a large painting of a Viking long ship. At the helm of the ship was a gorgeous, but also fierce-looking Viking woman wearing animal skins and carrying a bow and arrows. Ryan recalled the painting and also remembered that Amanda's heritage was Nordic, dating back to the time of the Vikings.

"I want you to know, John, that ever since you saw me last time, I've been good. I left my criminal past behind. You've got to believe me."

Amanda had been an assassin for hire, and Ryan had almost arrested her a year ago. But since the woman had a young daughter, Ryan had decided not to arrest her, on the condition she renounce her criminal ways. Amanda had also helped Ryan solve the FBI case he had been working on at the time.

"I know you've been good, Amanda. I've been checking on you."

"You have?"

"Yes. I have a contact at Interpol and another one in the Amsterdam police. They both said you have a clean record. No arrests, not even a parking ticket."

"So why are you here, John?"

"I wanted to … I needed to see you again … you made a big impact on me."

He felt a lot of positive emotions about her, the reason he had come here. He loved her looks, and the vibrant sexual energy she exuded, but it was much more that. They had made an emotional connection, even though they never had sex. It was hard to describe, but he knew it was true, and he always sensed that she felt the same way.

Amanda smiled, and it was a shy smile. "You made a big impact on me too. I always hoped you would come back."

She motioned to one of the sleek white leather couches in the room. "Please sit. Would you like a drink, John? I know you like beer, but unfortunately, I don't keep any in the house. Would you like a vodka and tonic?"

"That would be great."

She served the drinks, and they sat next to each other on the couch.

She sipped the vodka, then in a low voice said, "I've missed you. I always hoped you'd come back, and we could be close."

He took her hand and squeezed it gently. "I've missed you too."

She looked down at the floor. "Ever since you left, I haven't been with any other men."

"Really?"

"Yes."

"I'm glad, Amanda."

She leaned close to him and rested her head on his chest. "I've been studying at the university here in Amsterdam."

"I know. You're taking classes."

"Yes. I hope to graduate with a degree in a couple of years."

"What will you do then?" he asked.

"I'm not sure." She looked up at him. "I'm taking classes in law-enforcement and legal issues. Maybe I'll take up PI work, like you."

Ryan chuckled. "Maybe I'll hire you, and you can assist me on cases."

"I'd like that."

Then in a whisper, she said, "Hold me, John. Please."

Ryan put his arm around her and held her close. It felt good. Really good.

"Do you have anyone in your life now, John?"

"What do you mean?"

"A woman."

"No. Nothing steady. As you know, I've been with several, but my luck with women has never been great."

She placed a hand on his chest and massaged it. "Maybe that's going to change." She paused and then said, "Do you remember what I said a year ago, before you left?"

"We talked about a lot of things. You promised to renounce your life of crime if I didn't arrest you. So you could raise your daughter."

"Yes. But we also talked about personal things. I told you I wanted to share my bed with you."

Ryan remembered that vividly. It had been incredibly difficult to say no then, since Amanda was the most beautiful and desirable woman he had ever met.

"I remember, Amanda."

"I still want to do that."

He smiled at her and caressed her face lightly. Then he leaned close and kissed her, gently on the lips. She returned the kiss hungrily and he held her tight.

It felt great holding her, kissing her, all his emotions from a year ago returning.

When they broke off the kiss later, they were both breathing heavy.

"How long can you stay?" she asked.

"A few days. Then I've got to go back. I'm working on a case for the GBI."

"Stay with me then. Here in my home."

"I'd like that very much."

He embraced her again. "How's Jade doing?"

Amanda laughed. "As precocious as ever. She's eight now, going on twenty-five."

"Is she here?"

"Yes. She's playing outside in the backyard. My housekeeper is with her."

"I'd like to say hello to your daughter," he said. "I big part of me not arresting you last year was so you could raise her."

"I know. She'd love to see you too."

She took his hand and led him through the lavish house and into the immense back yard. Ryan saw a matronly, heavyset woman in her fifties and a little girl by the swings.

"Come here, Jade," Amanda called out. "There's someone I want you to talk to."

The little girl got off the swing and ran towards her mother.

"Jade," Amanda said, "say hello to John Ryan."

The little girl gazed up at him with an excited expression. She looked like a miniature version of her mother, with long, blonde hair, striking gray eyes and a very pretty face. Jade was an adorable looking child.

Ryan went to one knee so that he was eye level with her.

Jade extended her hand. "It's good to see you again, Mr. Ryan."

He shook her hand. "Do you remember me?"

The girl nodded. "Yes, of course. You were here a year ago." Jade studied him carefully with her bright and intelligent gray eyes. She giggled. "My mommy needs a man in her life. Can you stay with us from now on?"

Amanda shook her slowly. "Stop that, Jade. Mr. Ryan is just visiting us for a few days."

Jade had an impish look on her face. "You should marry my mommy, Mr. Ryan. She needs a husband, and I need a father."

Ryan laughed. "Is that a fact?"

Jade nodded, her face earnest. "Yes."

"That's enough out of you, Jade," Amanda said, her voice firm. "Go back and play on the swings again."

"Yes, mommy." Then she smiled and waved to Ryan. "Goodbye, Mr. Ryan."

"Goodbye, Jade."

When the girl was by the swings again with the matronly woman, Ryan said, "She's an adorable kid."

"She's a handful, that's for sure. Like I said, she's eight, going in twenty-five. She's incredibly smart. And she's precious to me. Ever since she was born, she became the center of my life."

"Did she ever find out," he said, "how you are able to afford the lifestyle you have?"

Amanda shook her head. "No. I never told her about my criminal past. And I don't ever want her to know."

Ryan nodded. "She'll never find out from me."

"Thank you, John. That means a lot."

Ryan and Amanda walked back toward the house, holding hands. When they were inside, she said, "Are you hungry? I can't cook worth a damn, but I can order in. There are several great restaurants nearby that deliver."

"Actually," he said, "I'm hungry for something else."

"What?"

He embraced her tightly and held her close. "You."

Amanda laughed, and it was a throaty, sexy laugh he remembered from a year ago. "In that case, you're in luck. Because I want that too."

Chapter 45

Amsterdam, Holland

"Do you really have to go?" Amanda said softly. Her gray eyes were watering a bit.

J.T. Ryan was embracing her tightly, gazing at her gorgeous face. "Unfortunately, yes. I've got to get back to work."

The two of them were in the foyer of Amanda's home.

The last two days had gone by in a delicious blur, Ryan thought.

Their lovemaking had been amazing. Frantically fast at first, urgent and physical and aggressive, the pent-up lust strong in both of them. Then their lovemaking became slower and more loving after that.

Ryan sensed the connection with the beautiful Nordic woman wasn't just about sex. He felt a strong emotional bond with her, and sensed she felt exactly the same way.

They had also shared enjoyable mealtimes with Jade, the little girl's high intelligence and effervescent personality on display.

"Will you come back and see us?" Amanda asked.

"I will."

"You promise, John?"

"I do."

Then he leaned down and kissed her on the mouth, gently and lovingly. She returned the kiss hungrily, and they stayed like that for a long moment. He embraced her tightly with both arms.

When they separated a moment later, they were both breathless.

Amanda gave him a lusty grin. "Are you sure you want to go now? That bulge in your pants says no."

Ryan laughed. "I'd love to stay. But I really have to get back."

She caressed his face lovingly with her palm. "I know." Then she said, "I want to give you something. Something to keep you safe."

"What is it?"

Amanda reached into a pocket of her slacks and removed a small silver crucifix, which she handed to him.

Ryan smiled. "I didn't know you were a Christian."

"I never was, before. But after I turned my life around and left crime behind, I started reading the Bible. I know I'll never be able to fully atone for my sins, but Christianity is helping me raise Jade."

"I'm glad for you, Amanda."

Ryan put the crucifix in his pocket. "I should go now. My flight leaves soon."

"Okay, John."

They kissed one last time and held each other for another long moment.

Then he left her house and got back in his rented Audi.

An hour later he was at Schiphol airport.

And soon after that he was on an SAS flight heading back to Atlanta.

Chapter 46

Beijing, China

General Zhang Wei was in his office. As usual, he was wearing his People's Liberation Army military uniform.

He glanced at his watch. Soon he would be meeting with the top executive of Paramount Pictures, one the largest film companies in the USA. They wanted the China Film Group to finance their upcoming movie.

There was a knock on his door, and it opened partway. His assistant, Colonel Liu stood there. "Your guest is here," she said. Like himself, the young woman was dressed in her PLA uniform.

"Show him in, please," he replied.

Zhang stood and went to the rectangular conference table in the room. He sat at the head of the table.

The American executive came in and he and Zhang shook hands.

"Please have a seat, Mr. Connors," Zhang said.

The American took one of the plush, high-backed executive chairs.

"Would you like some tea or coffee or whiskey?" Zhang said.

"No, thank you." The American was a short man with thinning gray hair. He was wearing a black business suit, with a white dress shirt, open at the collar.

"From our phone conversation," Zhang said, "I understand that you are interested in having the China Film Group finance you next film."

"That's right, General. It's a big budget movie and we at Paramount won't be able to fund it on our own. We estimate this film will cost over $450 million."

"I read the script of the film you sent me. It is an intriguing premise."

"You liked it?"

"Very much, Mr. Connors. Tell me more about it."

"As you read in the script, the movie revolves around an American astronaut who is stranded on the planet Mars. The rest of the movie involves the rescue of the astronaut by ingenious American scientists at NASA."

General Zhang rubbed his jaw. "Yes, I think the concept is excellent. I believe it will be a blockbuster film for Paramount."

Connors grinned. "So, you'll finance it?"

"We will, with a few changes to the script."

"Changes?"

"Yes."

"What type of changes?"

"We like the concept of the stranded astronaut on Mars. However, his rescue needs to be altered."

Concern crossed the American's face. "Altered how?"

"Instead of American scientists figuring out how to rescue the astronaut, we want him to be rescued by Chinese astronauts using highly advanced rocket booster technology. The film needs to show that this technology is created by the country of China."

Conners shook his head slowly. "I don't know, General. That's a big change. I don't know if my board of directors will go for it."

Zhang smiled, but it was a cold grin with no humor in it. "Then this meeting is over." He stood.

The American executive's mouth dropped open. "But ... can't we ... discuss this ...."

"There is nothing for us to discuss, Mr. Connors." His cold grin was still on his face. "As you Americans say, 'It's our way, or the highway'."

Connors stood. "Alright, alright. If that's the only way to secure your financial support, I agree to your changes."

"Excellent."

Zhang extended his hand and the men shook.

Chapter 47

Tokyo, Japan

"I'm still furious with you!" Nikita spit out, as she paced the living room of her penthouse apartment.

Kruger was sitting on one of the leather couches in the room, watching silently during her angry tirade. He knew it was best to keep his mouth shut and let her fury burn out.

"Not only did you fuck up the assignment and let Ryan escape," she screeched, "but you also got two of my best operatives killed."

"I'm sorry, Nikita."

"You're sorry? You're fucking sorry? That's the only thing you have to say?"

"We underestimated Ryan."

She stabbed her index finger in his direction. "That's a fact!"

Nikita continued pacing the room like a caged tiger for another few minutes, her face red with rage.

Then she went to her liquor cabinet, poured herself a tall glass of *sake*, which she downed in one long gulp.

That done, she sat down on a couch opposite him.

"I have a new assignment for you," she said, her voice somewhat calmer now.

"What is it?"

Nikita spent the next half hour describing the target and the location. When she was done, she said, "Any questions?"

"Yes," Kruger said. "After I terminate the target, you said you wanted me to dump the body in a well-known place. Did you have one in mind?"

"I do."

Then Nikita told him.

Chapter 48

GBI Headquarters
Decatur, Georgia

"Ever since you got back from your trip," Kelly O'Hara said, "you've seemed very happy."

Ryan nodded. "I am."

"You never did tell me what you were doing in Amsterdam."

Ryan and Kelly were sitting in her office. She was at her desk, and he was in one of the visitors' chairs.

"Like I said before my trip, it was a personal matter."

Kelly tilted her head. "Did it involve a woman?"

He frowned. "Why are you so curious?"

The GBI agent blushed. "Sorry. I didn't mean to pry."

"No problem."

Kelly opened a desk drawer and pulled out a black cell phone, which she placed on her desk. "This is the burner," she said, "you found in Bastein's apartment in Paris. The man who was Marie Dubois's lover. Our GBI tech guys have been working on it and have traced several calls to Japan. I think those calls were to Marie Dubois."

"That's great, Kelly. So, it looks like both Kruger and Dubois are based in Japan."

"That's right."

"Where in Japan is Dubois located?"

Kelly shook her head. "We haven't been able to pinpoint a specific city yet. But our tech guys are good. I think they'll find it soon. Once we know the city, we can triangulate her location from the cell towers in her area."

Chapter 49

Los Angeles, California

Kruger had been tailing the movie executive for the last three days, learning his daily routine. Most of the executive's time was spent at his office and he would drive home late in the evening.

Kruger was following the man's BMW sedan now, as it navigated its way on Mulholland Drive. The famous and scenic two-lane road is a twisty 21-mile highway that offers views of the Los Angeles Basin, the San Fernando Valley, downtown Los Angeles and the Hollywood Sign. Mulholland Drive is featured in a significant number of films, songs, and novels. The highway also has some of the most exclusive and expensive homes in the world. Many Hollywood celebrities live there.

Kruger's target had left his office at 10 p.m., so traffic was light on the road. Although there were few light posts along the highway, there was a full moon out, so keeping track of the BMW's taillights was easy. Currently the movie executive's sedan was two cars ahead of Kruger's rental, a Honda Accord.

Kruger glanced at his watch, knowing he had to make his move soon. He sped up and passed one car, then sped up some more and passed the second vehicle, an SUV.

The BMW was now directly ahead of him.

Kruger had studied the whole length of Mulholland Drive and knew that the upcoming stretch was the ideal spot to make the stop.

He accelerated slightly, gaining on the BMW. When he was five feet behind the other car, he sped up again, his bumper lightly crashing into the BMW's taillights. He heard the scraping of metal and the breaking of glass and plastic. It was a minor crash, but enough, he hoped, to get the executive's attention.

Kruger braked and pulled over to the side of the road onto the wide shoulder.

As he had hoped, the BMW slowed and stopped also, just ahead of him.

Kruger waited in his car for a moment while the two cars that were following went past the scene.

Then he exited the Honda and walked toward the stopped BMW. The movie executive was out of his car also, inspecting the damage to the rear of his car.

"I am so sorry," Kruger said to the other man. "I was following too close. It's all my fault. I'll pay for all the damages."

The movie executive shook his head and scowled. "It's a brand-new car, damn it. I just bought it two weeks ago."

Kruger held up his open palms. "I'll pay for all the damages," he repeated. "I take full responsibility for the accident."

"All right. I'll get my insurance information." The man went back to his BMW, got in and began rummaging in his glovebox.

Kruger glanced around the scene and saw there were no cars coming or going. He sprinted to the BMW's passenger door, pulled out his Glock 43 handgun, and climbed inside the sedan.

Seeing the gun, the executive's eyes bulged.

Kruger fired three shots to the man's chest. The gun was suppressed, and the sounds it made were *thud, thud, thud.*

The guy clutched his heart with both hands, groaned, and slumped on the leather seats. Bright red blood began to stain the tan leather interior and tan carpet. Kruger felt for a pulse and found none.

Kruger then quickly climbed out of the car and took another long look around. He waited as an SUV went by, then he raced toward his Honda, got in, and drove it right behind the BMW.

Getting out, he once again scouted the area and saw no traffic on the road. He sprinted to the BMW, dragged the executive's body out of it, and then dragged it to the rear of the Honda. After that, he popped the trunk and pushed the dead body inside.

When he was done, he went back to the BMW, took out a handkerchief and wiped any fingerprints he might have left behind.

Then he sprinted back to his own car and drove off at a slow pace. The last thing he needed was to be stopped for speeding.

Chapter 50

Los Angeles, California

The Hollywood Sign is an American landmark and cultural icon overlooking Hollywood, a neighborhood of Los Angeles. The sign is situated on Mount Lee, above Beachwood Canyon in the Santa Monica Mountains. When it was originally put up in 1923, the sign spelled out the word *HollywoodLand*. It was erected as a temporary advertisement for a local real estate development. The last four letters of the sign were removed in 1949. Among the best-known landmarks in California and the United States, the *Hollywood* sign is made of 45-foot-tall steel letters on concrete footings. The area is often featured in films and television programs.

The sign is on the southern side of Mount Lee in Griffith Park, north of Mulholland Drive. Because it is such a popular spot with tourists, access to the sign is restricted. It is situated in rough, steep terrain, and there are barriers to keep people out. A walking trail at the edge of the canyon is the closest point most people get to the sign.

Kruger was on the trail now.

Since it was 2 a.m. there was no one else around. He silently cursed Nikita for picking this area to dump the executive's body. He had tied the body to the rolling cart he was pulling. Since the *Hollywood* sign was at an elevation of 1,578 feet of rough terrain, it was an exhausting effort. Even though Kruger was a strong man, he was grunting and sweating from the work.

149

Luckily the full moon provided enough light for him to spot the security measures put in place by the Los Angeles Police Department. From his research of the area, Kruger learned the L.A.P.D. had placed motion detectors and security cameras along the trail. This meant he had to take detours off the trail to avoid being spotted.

An hour later, totally exhausted from the effort, he reached the *Hollywood* sign. He was at the base of it now, and he glanced up at the huge 45-foot-tall letters, which were painted white.

He sat on the ground for several minutes to catch his breath, as he looked around the area. The whole place was desolate, with no one around.

Then he untied the executive's body from the cart and dragged it to the base of the letters. Per Nikita's instructions, he propped the cadaver at the foot of the 'H' letter.

During daylight hours, Kruger knew, tourists would spot the body immediately.

That done, he took out a handkerchief and wiped his prints from the body's clothes and skin.

When he was finished, he made his way down the steep hillside, pulling the empty cart behind him.

An hour later he was back in his Honda Accord.

Two hours after that, he was at LAX airport, boarding a Japan Airlines flight to Tokyo.

Chapter 51

Atlanta, Georgia

J.T. Ryan left his apartment and took the elevator to the building's underground lot. He climbed in his Chevy Tahoe and fired it up.

Just then his phone buzzed. He took it out and answered it. "Ryan here."

"This is Sargeant Malloy, L.A.P.D." he heard the man say.

"Yes, Sargeant."

"We've had a development on the case. Another murder."

"Who was it this time?"

"Ed Harris. He is, or was, the senior Vice President of DreamWorks Pictures. Ever heard of that company?"

Ryan recalled the name. Ever since he'd been assigned to the case, he had done background research on Hollywood's major studios. "Yeah. DreamWorks is one of the biggest film companies in the world. If I remember correctly, they produced *Transformers, Shrek, Gladiator, Saving Private Ryan,* and a bunch of other big hits."

"That's right. Anyway, this murder fits the pattern of the others. I wanted to let you know right away."

"Where did this happen, Sargeant?'

"Right here in L.A. We found Harris's car on Mulholland Drive. By the blood stains it's clear he was murdered there, then the killer took the body and dumped it in a very public place."

"Where's that?"

"The *Hollywood* sign. One of L.A.'s biggest attractions."

Ryan let out a low whistle. "The killer was making a statement."

"You bet. When can you get out here, J.T.?"

Ryan glanced at his watch. "I'll catch a flight to L.A. this morning. I'll call you when I get in."

They said goodbye and Ryan hung up. Then he punched in another number and when Kelly O'Hara picked up, he said, "Hey Kelly. It's J.T."

"Hi, Ryan. What's up?"

"There's been another murder, and it sounds like it's connected to our case." He spent the next couple of minutes giving her the details.

"I assume you're heading out there today?" she said.

"I am."

"Okay, Ryan." She paused, then said, "Be careful out there. I don't want you to get hurt ... or worse ...."

Ryan chuckled. "I know. You need me to solve this case."

"It's not what I meant," she said, her voice low. "I don't want to lose you ...."

He mulled that over a moment, her concern puzzling him a bit. Sometimes women confused him.

"I promise," he said, "I'll be careful in L.A."

"Thank you."

They said goodbye and he hung up. Then he got out of his Tahoe and went back up to his apartment to pack some clothes for the trip.

Chapter 52

Los Angeles, California

J.T. Ryan and Sergeant Malloy were standing at the base of the *Hollywood* sign. The whole hillside was a beehive of activity, with uniformed cops, plainclothes detectives, and CSI techs working the crime scene.

Yellow crime scene tape cordoned the steep, wooded mountainside, but in the distance, Ryan could see a horde of reporters, TV camera crews, and curious onlookers gathered at the base of the trail that led up to the sign. It was a sunny, cloudless day and the visibility was excellent. Ryan also noticed that parts of the wooded areas were charred, a reminder that sections of L.A. had burned during the horrific fires in 2025.

Sergeant Malloy pointed up to the 'H' letter that towered over them. "The body," he said, "was propped up against the concrete support under this letter. A tourist saw the body and called it in. A half hour later this whole area was a zoo of activity." The tall, black police detective was wearing a business suit, a white shirt and a gray tie.

"Have you been able to determine what kind of weapon was used?" Ryan asked.

"The M.E. thinks it was a 9 mil. Three slugs to the chest at close range."

"You said you found Harris's car not far from here?"

"That's right. It was on Mulholland Drive. From the blood on the seats, it's clear Harris was shot there and dumped here."

"The killer was making a statement."

Malloy nodded. "That's a fact."

Ryan took another look up at the huge sign and at the whole area. "This fits the pattern of the other murders. The killer is sending a signal."

"I agree, J.T."

"Have you had a chance to interview any of his business associates?"

"I've tried. I went to the DreamWorks headquarters, but all of the top people there have lawyered up. None of them are guilty, in my opinion, but the movie business is funny. The top people over there don't want to be tainted by this murder." The police sergeant paused, then said, "But I think there's one person that may open up to us."

"Who's that?" Ryan said.

"Harris's assistant. A woman named Kathy Richards. She was reluctant to talk to me at the DreamWorks office. But if you try her at home, she may open up."

"Give me her details and I'll go see her."

Chapter 53

Marina Del Ray
Los Angeles, California

J.T. Ryan had called and spoken to Kathy Richards, and she had agreed to meet him at her home after her workday ended.

Richards lived in Marina Del Ray, an exclusive seaside community in L.A. The upscale harbor is a major boating and water recreation area. It's also the U.S.'s largest small-craft marina, with over 5,000 boats. Located just south of Santa Monica, the zone is a haven for tourists and locals, who frequent the many restaurants and clubs located there.

Richards lived in one of the condo towers that overlooked the marina.

Ryan located the place, pressed the buzzer and waited.

Moments later a woman in her fifties with graying hair opened the door partway. She was wearing a black dress and black flats and was holding a handkerchief. By her red-rimmed eyes it was clear she had been crying.

"I'm J.T. Ryan," he said, handing her his business card. "We spoke on the phone earlier."

She took the card, opened the door fully and he went inside. She motioned to the suede couches that fronted the sliding glass door. The condo overlooked Marina Del Ray, and it was a spectacular view, with thousands of sail boats and motorboats docked on the cobalt blue waters.

"Please have a seat," she said. "Would you like some coffee?"

"No, thank you. I'm good."

They sat on opposite couches and Ryan watched as the woman dabbed her eyes with the handkerchief. It was clear she was grief stricken and devasted.

"I'm sorry to disturb you, Ms. Richards. I'll try to be as brief as possible."

The woman nodded, said nothing.

"Did you work for Mr. Harris for a long time?"

"I did. Over ten years."

"As his administrative assistant?"

"That's right."

"So, you knew a lot about his business dealings?"

"Yes. I set up all his meetings and took care of his travel schedule and did pretty much everything he needed."

"I'm working with Sargeant Malloy of the L.A.P.D.," Ryan said. "He told me the executives at DreamWorks have all lawyered up. But he thought you would be receptive to answering questions without an attorney present."

"That's right, Mr. Ryan."

"Why is that?"

Her expression hardened. "I want to get justice for his murder. The killer needs to be caught."

"That's my aim also. Can you think of anyone who could have done this?"

She shook her head.

"Is there anyone at DreamWorks who hated him enough to have him killed?"

She shook her head again. "No. I know Mr. Harris had disagreements with the other executives, but not to the extent of murder."

"What kind of disagreements?"

"My boss had a different vision for the company. He wanted to produce patriotic films."

"And the other executives didn't?"

"That's right."

"Why not?"

"Hollywood people are driven by the culture of social justice. Do you know what that means?"

Ryan, during his research of the movie industry, had learned that most of the film industry was that way. "Yes, I know what it means."

The woman shook her head slowly. "So, my boss clashed with the other executives. The other executives felt that it was difficult to obtain financing for patriotic films."

"I see."

Just then the woman's eyes watered and she dabbed her eyes with the handkerchief.

"Were you and Mr. Harris close?"

"Yes ... very close ...."

"I hate to ask this, but were you intimate with him?"

She shook her head. "I loved him. Very, very much. But he was married and faithful to his wife, which is rare in Hollywood. Still, I loved him, and he loved me. That was very clear. We had a close but platonic relationship."

Tears rolled down her cheeks and she lowered her head and covered her face with both hands.

He said nothing, gave her time to compose herself.

When she faced him moments later, she said, "Can I answer any other questions for you?"

"Not right now, Ms. Richards. You've been very helpful. You have my card, if you think of anything else, please call me."

"I will." She wiped her red-rimmed eyes with her handkerchief. "I have a favor to ask, Mr. Ryan."

"Of course. Name it."

The woman's face hardened. "Find the bastard who did this. Find him and make him pay."

"I will."

Chapter 54

Tokyo, Japan

Nikita sipped *sake* as she paced the living room of her penthouse apartment.

Kruger was sitting on one of the leather couches in the room.

"You did very well on the L.A. assignment," she said, continuing to pace. "My boss called and congratulated me."

"I'm glad. Does that mean you're not angry at me anymore?"

She stopped pacing and stared at him. "You're forgiven. For now. But don't fuck up again like you did on the Ryan assignment. I can be a very vindictive woman, as you know."

"I know, Nikita."

"Would you like a drink?"

"Yes."

She went to the teak liquor cabinet, poured out a large glass of *sake* and handed it to him.

He took a sip. "Do you have another assignment for me?"

"I do. But it can wait a bit. I need something else from you first."

There was a remote control resting on the coffee table between them and she picked it up. Then she pressed several buttons on the device and the drapes to the floor-to-ceiling windows of the room closed.

Nikita took another sip of her drink. "Strip for me, Kruger. And do it slowly."

Kruger smiled and stood. Then he took off his shoes and shirt and pants and underwear.

She studied his muscular physique closely, enjoying the sight of his nude body. After gulping the rest of her *sake*, she rose, approached him and began running her hands slowly over every part of his body.

It feels so good, she thought.

Kruger grinned fiercely and by his erection it was clear he was as ready as she was.

Nikita was wearing a dark gray kimono. She removed the yellow sash around her waist, then slowly took off her silk kimono. Next, she took off her black silk underwear.

Taking his hand, she led him into the bedroom.

She pulled off the covers from the king-size bed. Then she faced him. "You know what to do," she said.

Kruger climbed on the bed and lay on his back.

Nikita sat next to him and admired his naked, powerful physique. She began to stroke him slowly and gently.

He closed his eyes and groaned.

"You remember the rules, don't you?" she said in a throaty whisper.

"Yes ... yes ...." he gasped.

"You can't come," she whispered, "until I say so."

She continued stroking him slowly, enjoying this part of the game almost as much as what would follow.

"Please ... please Nikita ... I'm not sure how much more ... I can take ...."

She grinned excitedly, enjoying the moment. She was dripping wet, her own desire at a fever pitch.

"Don't you like this?" she said, stroking him with one hand while massaging his balls with the other.

"God ... yes!' he said, his voice hoarse. His eyes were wide open now, as well as his mouth. He was gasping for breath. It was clear he was ready to burst.

"Please ... Nikita ...."

She laughed. "All right, Kruger."

Then she straddled him, took hold of his hardness and put him inside of her, the feeling so delicious she almost orgasmed then.

But she held off and began rocking back and forth on top of him. Slowly at first, then faster. When she was ready, she whispered, "You can come now …."

And he did, exploding inside of her.

And so did she, in one long, delicious moment.

She collapsed on top of him, completely satiated.

Kruger put his arms around her and held her close.

When they separated moments later, she lay on her back, still breathing heavy.

Then she turned sideways and faced him. "It's time for you to go," she said.

"Let me stay the night, Nikita."

"You know the rules. No overnight stays. You give me what I need and then we're done."

"I don't like your rules," he said, his voice testy.

She massaged his muscular chest with her palm. "I know," she replied. "I wish it could be different, but it can't."

"But why?"

Nikita couldn't answer his question, because she didn't know the answer herself. She just knew she couldn't get emotionally close to this man, or any other. It was something that she had felt her whole life. It was a coldness that enveloped her to her core and could never overcome.

"Go please …." she whispered.

He nodded, sadness in his eyes. He got off the bed and left the room.

When she heard her apartment door open and then close, she lay on her back and began crying.

Chapter 55

Greenville, South Carolina

Kruger walked into the lobby of the impressive hotel and glanced around. The place was obviously high-end, with expensive furnishings and beautiful artwork on the walls. A blazing fire was burning in the huge fireplace. It was only 8 a.m. and only a few people were in the lobby.

He skipped the elevators and found the stairs, which he took to the third floor.

Kruger had spent several days in Greenville, scouting out the area and following his target at a distance. The famous actor was on vacation with his girlfriend.

Kruger reached the right floor and peered down the hallway. The actor's room was the fourth one on the right.

After glancing around to make sure no one else was in the corridor, Kruger took out his Glock 43 and held it at his side, pointing down. He was wearing a black business suit, and it was easy to conceal the black gun. In his other hand he was holding a bottle of champagne.

Then he strode toward Room 306.

When he reached it, he knocked on the door.

A moment later he heard a muffled voice from inside. "Can I help you?"

"I have a gift for you, Mr. Stuart," Kruger said, a bright smile on his face. He knew the man inside was probably looking at him through the spyhole. "Compliments of the hotel manager. A bottle of champagne."

Kruger held up the bottle so the actor could see it.

He heard the unclicking of locks, and the door opened partway. A tall, handsome man was there, wearing a white bathrobe. His jet-black hair was tousled. Kruger recognized him immediately, since the actor had appeared in many popular movies.

"This is unexpected," Stuart said.

Kruger smiled. "We're glad you're staying with us. The champagne is our way of saying thanks."

He handed the actor the bottle and the man inspected the label.

"Dom Perignon," Stuart said. "The best. I love this stuff."

"We thought you would like it."

Then Kruger slammed his body into the other man, knocking the actor off his feet and on the floor of the room. The bottle of champagne dropped on the carpet.

After shutting the door closed behind him, Kruger pointed the gun at the man's torso.

He fired three times. The gun was suppressed, and the sounds were muffled.

Blood spurted from the white bathrobe as the actor clutched his chest, his eyes wide. He groaned, his eyes rolled white, and his body sagged.

Kruger checked his pulse, confirmed the man was dead.

Kruger's adrenaline was racing, his heart thundering in his chest. He scanned the room, realized it was a suite, with a sitting area and a separate bedroom, its door closed.

Knowing the girlfriend was probably there, Kruger sprinted to the bedroom and opened the door.

A young woman was sprawled on the bed, nude. Her long, brunette hair was disheveled. Empty liquor bottles and glasses were on the night table.

She was fast asleep, snoring lightly.

Kruger approached the bed, admiring her beautiful body and face.

It's a shame she has to die, he thought.

Then he pressed the muzzle of the gun to her temple and fired twice.

Thud. Thud.

After checking the pulse on the woman to make sure she was dead, Kruger wiped his prints from the hotel room. He also picked up the brass from his rounds and pocketed them.

Then he holstered his pistol and picked up the unopened bottle of champagne from the floor.

No sense in letting it go to waste, Kruger mused. As Stuart had said, Dom Perignon was the best.

Chapter 56

Atlanta, Georgia

J.T. Ryan had just returned from his trip to L.A.

He was in his apartment now, unpacking his clothes. He was tired from the cross-country flight, the jetlag catching up to him. The flight is normally five hours long, but there had been several delays at LAX, and it had turned into an 8-hour event.

Ryan yawned, finished unpacking, and went into his kitchen to prepare lunch or dinner, he wasn't sure which. He glanced at his watch, saw it was 4 p.m.

Just then his phone buzzed, and he took it out of his pocket. "Ryan, here."

"It's Kelly," he heard the woman say.

"My favorite GBI agent," he said. "This brightens my day."

"I'm not calling with good news," she replied, her voice all business.

Ryan sat at his kitchen table. "What happened?"

"Another murder. This time in Greenville, South Carolina."

"Who was it?"

"A well-known actor. Brad Stuart."

Ryan recalled the name. He had seen him in several films. "When did this happen?"

"This morning. He was murdered in his hotel room along with his girlfriend. The two of them were shot to death. The maid found the bodies when she went to clean the room."

"Do the cops have any suspects?"

"None. But it looks like another professional hit. The killer cleaned up his brass and wiped his prints. The door handles were clean." She then gave him more details about the murders.

Ryan rubbed his jaw, felt the stubble there from not shaving today. "Okay, Kelly. I'll drive to Greenville. It'll be quicker than flying there."

Then he yawned. "But I'm beat from my flight from L.A. I need to get some sleep before I go." He paused, then said, "The stiffs won't mind. They're not going anywhere."

"Was that a joke?" she said, her voice stern.

"Sorry. I couldn't help myself."

She let out a long sigh. "Goodbye, Ryan."

Then she hung up.

And he didn't blame her. Sometimes he got carried away, he knew. Once again, he chided himself for making jokes at inopportune times.

Ryan prepared dinner for himself, then went into his living room and powered up his laptop.

He began doing an internet search on the actor, Brad Stuart. Ryan used IMDb for his search, which is the most comprehensive online database of information about films and television series. It includes personal biographies of the cast, crew, and production people. It also includes plot summaries and reviews of all films and TV shows produced.

As he had recalled, Stuart had been in many popular films, including several blockbusters. He had received two Academy Awards. Stuart had starred in such movies as *Fight Club, Inglorious Basterds, The Departed,* and *12 Years a Slave.*

The only thing Ryan found online that was odd was the fact that Stuart had been banned from visiting China after he starred in the film *Seven Years in Tibet.* That movie gives a positive portrayal of the Dalai Lama, and the Chinese soldiers in the film are portrayed as evil and brutal.

Ryan wasn't sure how all this was important, or how it factored into the murders, but he wrote it down in his notebook.

Then he yawned and went to bed.

Chapter 57

Greenville, South Carolina

J.T. Ryan awoke early the next day and drove his Chevy Tahoe to Greenville. He had been to the small city several times before and always enjoyed it.

With a scenic downtown and vibrant nighttime scene, the town of 71,000 is a haven for tourists. With its wide sidewalks, outdoor plazas, streetside dining, upscale nightclubs, and art galleries, the pedestrian-friendly atmosphere is often compared to European cities. There is a 10-block stretch of downtown that features 110 restaurants, bistros, and cafés.

Known also for its exceptional outdoor beauty, downtown Greenville is nestled next to Reedy River Falls. The architecturally noteworthy Liberty Bridge spans the Reedy River.

When he arrived in Greenville, Ryan had gone directly to the city's police station and spoken to a police captain he had worked with on a previous case. The police captain gave Ryan permission to work on this case on his own.

Ryan was in the Reedy River Falls area now. Nestled next to the forested setting of the river is the Grand Bohemian Lodge, Greensville's most exclusive and expensive hotel. The Grand Bohemian is a multi-story structure that towers over the river area. Ryan had never stayed at this hotel since it was so expensive but had always admired the upscale place. It was easy to understand why Brad Stuart had chosen the hotel for a vacation.

Ryan walked into the impressive lobby and glanced around. The lobby was dominated by a massive stone fireplace, which was blazing. Native American artwork hung on the walls and rich, deeply cushioned leather furniture and mahogany tables furnished the space.

There were no hotel guests in the lobby. Because of the murders, the police had closed the hotel yesterday and today, but it was scheduled to reopen tomorrow.

Ryan noticed several uniformed cops in the area along with CSI techs. After identifying himself with one of the cops, Ryan was shown to the security director's office on the hotel's first floor.

"I'm J.T. Ryan," he said, after shaking hands with the man. "Thank you for seeing me, Mr. Adams."

The security director was tall and lean, with a crew cut and a mustache.

"Good to meet you, Mr. Ryan. The police called me and told me you were coming over. I'm sure you want to see the scene of the crime first."

"I would."

Adams led Ryan up to the third floor and to Room 306. A uniformed cop was by the open door, which was secured with yellow crime scene tape.

Adams and Ryan went inside, and Ryan immediately saw dark red stains on the gray carpet. White tape on the carpet outlined the location of a body.

"We found Stuart's body here," Adams said. "He'd been shot at close range. Three shots to his chest. The M.E. believes the killer used 9-millimeter rounds."

"And no brass was found?"

"That's right. The killer cleaned it up. And the doorknobs and other surfaces had been wiped clean, so we found no prints except those of the deceased."

Ryan went to one knee and glanced toward the open door of the room. "How did the killer gain access to the room?"

"It appears Stuart opened the door. From the CCTV footage we got from the corridor, the killer was holding a bottle of champagne. It appears he used that as a ruse to gain entry."

"I'd like to get a copy of that video."

"After we're done here," Adams said, "I'll get that for you."

"Where was the other body found?"

Adams led Ryan into the bedroom, a large, upscale room with a magnificent view of the Reedy Falls River area below.

There was a king-size bed, which had been stripped of the pillows and bedsheets. Dark red stains covered the top of the plush mattress. White tape outlined where the body had been.

Adams pointed to the bed. "Stuart's girlfriend was murdered here. She was shot twice in the temple, at very close range. We found powder burns on her skin, so we suspect she was asleep when she was shot."

Ryan studied the scene for a long moment, his anger surging. Another senseless murder of an innocent victim. He clenched his fists, more determined than ever to catch the bastard who had committed this crime along with the many others.

After they were done in the hotel room, Adams took them back to his office on the first floor.

The security director went to his laptop and opened a video file. "I'll run the CCTV footage from the third-floor corridor," he said.

The video came on, which showed no movement in the hallway for several minutes. Then a man appeared striding down the corridor. He was wearing a black business suit and carrying a bottle of champagne. When the man's face appeared on the screen, Adams froze the video.

Ryan stared at the screen and realized who it was immediately.

It was Kruger.

The assassin who had committed several of the other murders.

Chapter 58

GBI Headquarters
Decatur, Georgia

"I've been thinking about the murder of Brad Stuart and his girlfriend," Agent Kelly O'Hara said. "And I can't figure out the motive."

"I agree," J.T. Ryan replied. "The motive for the other killings is clear. Those people were either involved in making or starring in movies that were patriotic, or faith based. These latest murders are different. Stuart didn't star in films that involved those topics."

Ryan and Kelly were sitting in her office. She was at her desk, and he was in one of the visitors' chairs.

Then Ryan remembered something. "Before I drove to Greenville, I did research on Stuart's background. He starred in a lot of hit films and received two Academy Awards. But he was also banned from visiting China after he starred in a movie called *Seven Years in Tibet.*"

"Yeah," Kelly said. "I recall that now. The Chinese government was angry because the Chinese soldiers were portrayed as being evil and brutal."

Ryan rubbed his jaw. "But I still don't see the connection. Everything we've found out so far is that the killers, Kruger and Dubois, are based in Japan, not China."

"That's true, Ryan."

They went quiet a moment, then she opened a desk drawer and pulled out a black cell phone which she placed on her desk.

"This is the burner," she said, "you found in Bastein's apartment in Paris. He's the man who was Marie Dubois's lover. Our GBI tech guys have been working on it and have traced several calls to Japan. We think those calls were to Marie Dubois."

"Where in Japan is Dubois located?"

Kelly frowned. "We're not entirely sure. It appears she's using some kind of high-tech masking device on her calls. We've traced it to the country of Japan, of that we're certain."

"Japan is a densely populated country," he said. "Over 124 million people live there."

The GBI agent nodded. "I know."

Ryan mulled this over for a long moment. "Right now, we have no other leads."

"I know that too."

"Looks to me like I'll be going to Japan."

"Do you speak Japanese?" she asked.

He shook his head. "I speak several languages, but not that one."

"So let me get this straight. You're going to Japan. But you have no clue in which city Dubois is located. And you don't speak Japanese."

Ryan smiled. "That's right."

Kelly cocked her head. "So, what's your plan?"

"What I always do. Go with Plan A."

"And what's that?"

"I look under rocks and see what crawls out from underneath."

She frowned. "And if that doesn't work?"

"Then I go with Plan B."

"Which is?"

Ryan grinned. "I kick down doors and blow shit up."

Chapter 59

Tokyo, Japan

J.T. Ryan's Japan Airlines flight landed at Narita Airport, and he deplaned. The airport, the country's busiest for international flights, was a madhouse of activity. The concourse was packed with tourists and businesspeople from all over the world, which was easy to discern since he heard many different languages spoken.

After going through customs and grabbing his bag from the luggage area, he made his way to the taxi stands. Since he had only been to Japan once before, he had decided not to drive until he got a better feel for Tokyo.

Before his trip, Kelly had called the Tokyo Police Department and had arranged for him to meet with one of their detectives.

So he grabbed a taxi and took it to their headquarters building on Kasamigaseki Avenue, in the Chiyoda-ku section of the city.

After paying the taxi fare, he went inside the large, multi-story building. On the flight over, Ryan had done some research and learned that the Tokyo Metropolitan Police Department (TMPD) had a staff of over 40,000 police officers.

Ryan identified himself and was asked to wait in the lobby. He took a seat and scrolled through the text messages on his phone.

After a few minutes, a very attractive Asian woman approached him. The woman was young looking. She was wearing black slacks, a black jacket and a white blouse.

"I am Detective Keiko Kanata," she said, with a small bow. "You are John Ryan?" She spoke flawless English with a Japanese accent.

Ryan stood up, and he towered over her. At most, she was 5 feet tall.

"Yes, I'm J.T. Ryan."

She held up her badge for him to inspect, and he handed her one of his cards.

"We can go into one of the conference rooms," she said, pointing to one side of the lobby. "Please follow me."

They went into one of the rooms and sat down at the table across from each other.

He looked at her closely. She had shoulder-length black hair parted down the middle and she seemed extremely young to be a detective.

"I have been assigned to assist you, Mr. Ryan."

Ryan smiled. "Please call me J.T."

"Okay."

"GBI agent Kelly O'Hara called your police chief and explained why I was here."

"Yes. I was given those details."

Ryan tilted his head. "You seem very young to be a detective."

She suppressed a smile. "I am older than I look. But I am the youngest detective in the TMPD. If it had been the FBI calling us, the police chief would have assigned our most experienced detective to help you. But since it was the GBI, you get me."

Ryan smiled. "I'm okay with it."

"So, how can I help you, Mr. Ryan?"

"I prefer J.T. or John."

"All right. John it is. And you can call me Keiko, if you like."

"Yes, I would like that."

"I understand you are trying to solve the murders of people associated with the movie business?"

"That's right." Ryan spent the next hour detailing each of the murders that had taken place. He began by telling her about the first murder, the killing of the actress in Rome, then the second murder, the film director in Savannah. He continued, telling her about the kidnapping of Carl Parnell, the movie producer. After that came the murders of James Carson, Ed Harris, and finally Brad Stuart.

When he was done, she was wide-eyed. "That is quite a list, John."

He leaned forward in his chair. "It is. And I'm determined to find the killers responsible."

"Do you have suspects?"

"We do."

He reached into a pocket of his navy blazer and took out two photographs which he placed on the table.

He pointed to one of the photos. "The woman in this picture is named Marie Dubois. She's one of the killers."

He then pointed to the other picture. "This man is named Hans Kruger. He was involved in several of the murders."

"And you have tracked down these people to Japan?"

"That's right. Marie Dubois received telephone calls from her lover. We traced those calls to Japan."

"Where in Japan?"

"We're not sure."

"Then why are you in Tokyo? Japan has many cities, Osaka and Kyoto and Hiroshima, to name a few."

"True. But I figured since Tokyo is the capital city, she probably would be here."

"If I can have these photos, I can scan them and load them into our TMPD database. We can run facial recognition on them. I can also try and locate these people if they have been arrested in our country."

Ryan handed her the photos and she left the conference room.

She came back fifteen minutes later, a glum expression on her face. She handed him the photos.

"Unfortunately, John, these two people are not in our database. I ran their images in our facial recognition program and did not find anything."

"And they have never been arrested either?"

"No."

He mulled this over a long moment. "I guess I'll have to find them a different way."

"And how is that?"

He grinned. "Turn over rocks and see what crawls out from underneath."

She cocked her head. "Is that a joke?"

"Yes."

She smiled. "You are a funny man, John Ryan."

"I'm glad you think so. A lot of people don't appreciate my humor."

Keiko laughed. "I am okay with it."

Then she glanced at her watch. "It is almost the end of my shift. We can work on this tomorrow, yes?"

"Of course."

"What hotel are you staying at?"

He shrugged. "I haven't checked into one yet. I came here directly from the airport."

"I know a good place close to here. The Wakana Hotel. It is a *ryokan* type inn, with its own small restaurant. Do you have a car?"

Ryan shook his head. "No."

She stood. "I will drive us over there then."

"Sounds good, Keiko."

They left the conference room and went to the building's underground lot. Her car was a tiny Suzuki sedan and his muscular, 6'4" body barely fit into the passenger seat.

Keiko drove them through a nightmare of evening traffic, the streets packed with cars, trucks, mopeds and motorcycles. Tokyo's massive population was clearly on display.

Half an hour later they pulled into the parking lot of the Wakana Hotel and soon after Ryan had checked in.

There was a restaurant in the inn's first floor and Ryan said, "I'm starved. Would you like to join me for dinner? I'm buying."

She glanced at her watch. "My apartment is almost an hour away. And I am hungry too. So, yes, I will join you."

"Great."

174

After they were seated at the restaurant, Keiko ordered *sake*, and he ordered a Sapporo beer.

When the drinks came, he sipped his beer, which was excellent. "I've heard of *sake*," he said. "What kind of liquor is it?"

"It is a very popular drink here in Japan. It is made from rice."

He nodded, then glanced at the menu, which was all in Japanese. "Maybe," he said, "you could order for both of us. My Japanese is rusty."

"Do you speak any Japanese?"

"I know the words *mizu*, and *kohi* and *biru*."

She laughed. "So, you can order water and coffee and beer."

He grinned. "That's about it."

"I will order for the both of us." Keiko signaled the waitress, and the elderly woman came over. Then Keiko spoke rapidly in Japanese and the waitress went toward the kitchen.

"What did you order for us?" he asked.

"Lots of healthy food. For an appetizer, rice and soybean crackers with seaweed, and for our meal, *yokimono*, which is grilled eel basted in a sweet sauce. I also ordered squid, ramen noodles, and *tempura*, which is a deep-battered vegetables with fish."

Ryan made a face.

"Do not worry, John. It is delicious."

Ryan shook his head slowly, not looking forward to the meal. "Yum, yum."

Keiko took a sip of her sake. "You will love it. I promise."

Ryan took a long pull from his Sapporo.

Soon after their dinner came.

Although the food looked suspicious to Ryan, it smelled great and to his surprise, was delicious. When he was done, he pushed aside the empty plate.

"That was good," he said.

"Told you."

The waitress came, took away their empty plates, and served them a new round of drinks.

The attractive young woman drank down her *sake* and ordered another.

Ryan studied her beautiful, doll-like face and she caught him staring at her. She blushed.

"Sorry," he said, realizing it had made her uncomfortable.

She looked down at the table. "It is okay. I do not mind, really." Then she looked up at him. "You are a nice man."

"Thanks. By the way, how did you get into police work? Looking at you, I'd figure you'd be model."

"My father was a policeman, and my grandfather was also. Since I was an only child, my parents encouraged me to go into law-enforcement."

"That explains it."

"How about you, John? How did you become a PI?"

"After college I went into the military. I was in the Army for years, mostly Special Forces. The Rangers and Green Berets. Then when I left the Army, I became a private investigator."

"With your military training, I'm surprised you did not become a police officer."

Ryan shook his head. "Too many rules to follow. I like being on my own."

She smiled. "Like Rambo?"

He smiled back. "Just like that. Only more handsome."

Keiko laughed. "You are funny too."

"I'm glad you like my jokes. A lot of people don't appreciate them."

She glanced at her watch. "It is late. I would love to stay and talk some more, but I have a long drive home."

"Of course."

Then she inclined her head. "Can you tell me one other thing, John, before I go?"

"Sure."

"Is there a Mrs. Ryan?"

He laughed. "Yes. But's she's my mother."

Keiko grinned. "That is good to know."

Chapter 60

Tokyo, Japan

J.T. Ryan waited on the sidewalk in front of the Wakana Hotel, and at exactly 7 a.m., Keiko Kanata's Suzuki sedan pulled to the curb in front of him.

Ryan climbed inside.

After saying good morning, she took off, shifting through the gears of the manual shift car rapidly. It was clear she was a good driver, which was a big plus considering the nightmare of traffic on the highly congested roads. It appeared the morning rush hour was just as bad as the evening one, and Keiko weaved around the heavy traffic effortlessly.

They got to the TMPD headquarters building forty minutes later, and soon after they were sitting across each other at the same conference room in the lobby.

"Before I left for Japan," Ryan said. "I researched your gun laws. I saw it's illegal to carry a gun here unless you are a police officer."

"That is correct, John. We have very strict weapons laws in my country."

Ryan smiled. "I feel naked without my gun. In the U.S., I always carry. Is there any way you could loan me one of yours during my stay here?"

"I could. But then I would have to arrest you."

"Is that a joke?"

She smiled. "Yes. I was making a joke." Then the smile vanished. "But it is true. You cannot carry a weapon here."

He shook his head slowly, not happy with her answer.

Then she pulled aside the jacket she was wearing, and he saw the holstered pistol at her waist. It was a SIG Sauer 9-millimeter. "You will have to depend on me to protect you," she said.

Ryan nodded. "Works for me."

Then he said, "Yesterday you used your facial recognition program to try to locate Marie Dubois."

"That is right. She did not show up in our database. And neither did the man you are looking for, Hans Kruger. Neither one has been arrested in Japan."

"I have an idea on how to find Dubois," he said.

"And what is that?"

"Do foreigners need work permits to be employed in Japan?"

"Yes, John. They do."

"So, Dubois had to get a work permit, and those would include her photograph."

"That is correct."

"Then all you have to do is run her photo through the database of work permits."

She shook her head. "I do not have access to those. Those records are separate from the ones at TMPD."

"So access them."

"That is not easy to do, John. I would have to get a court order to access them."

He shook his head. "You're kidding, right?"

"No."

He frowned. "I can see things in Japan are more complicated than in the U.S."

"That is true."

"How long would it take to get a court order?"

She scrunched her face in concentration. "About a week."

He slammed his hand on the conference table. "I can't wait a week, damn it! More innocent people could be murdered in the meantime."

She leaned back in her chair, wide-eyed.

"I'm sorry, Keiko. I didn't mean to be rude. But I still need to find Dubois, and fast."

The young detective pursed her lips and looked deep in thought. "There may be a way for me to access what you want."

"How is that?"

She looked down at the table. "I would have to hack into those records."

"You can do that?"

She faced him again. "Yes. But it is illegal. I could get into trouble if my boss found out."

"No guts, no glory."

She said nothing for a long moment, then said, "All right. I will do this for you."

"Thank you, Keiko. You won't regret it."

She shook her head. "I already do. But, since you are a nice man, I will do this for you."

He smiled. "I'll buy you dinner again, to repay you."

"I would like that, John. I would like that very much."

Then she stood. "I will go now and do this. I will be back soon."

She left the conference room and came back half an hour later. "I found her, John." She sat across from him again.

"Great."

Keiko placed a printout on the table. "Marie Dubois works at company here in Tokyo. This company is named Tokama Import Export Corporation. They own a high-rise building in the Chuo Ku district in central Tokyo. It overlooks the Sumida River."

"Is that far from here?" he asked.

"Not too far."

"Okay."

"From what the records indicate, Dubois lives in this building and also works there."

"Did you find out anything about this company?"

Keiko shook her head. "Tokama Import and Export is owned by another company, which has no employees. And this other

179

company is a subsidiary of another corporation that is just an address, without employees."

"These are cutouts, dummy corporations, that don't really exist. I've run into this before. Cutouts are used by criminal organizations."

"That is correct, John. I am aware of these types of fake companies."

"Did you get the exact address for Dubois?"

She pointed to the printout. "Yes. It is all here."

"Great."

"Do you think we should go there now?"

"Yes, Keiko. The sooner the better. But I need to do this on my own."

She appeared confused. "By yourself? What do you mean?"

"I need to confront Marie Dubois without you there."

"But why?"

"As soon as you flash your badge, she will lawyer up. Isn't that what all criminals do? It could be weeks or months before we can find out anything from her."

"Yes, that is true. But still. You have no arrest powers in Japan."

"I don't need arrest powers. I just need to ask her some questions."

She scrunched her face, then shook her head. "That is not true, John. You will threaten her and then interrogate her."

"You're right. That's why you can't be there. You have a bright future with the TMPD. You're a highly intelligent woman. If you follow all the regulations, you'll probably become the police chief one day."

She cocked her head. "That sounds like what you Americans call 'bullshit'."

He grinned. "Yeah. You're right. But I don't want you to get in trouble. It's one thing to hack into a database, but it's another to interrogate someone using force. You have a bright future here. I don't want you to screw it up."

Keiko went quiet for a long time. Then in a low voice, said, "What you say is right. What you plan to do is illegal. Still, I am worried about you, John. You do not even have a gun."

He closed one hand into a fist. "Don't worry. I'm good with this. I can take care of myself."

"Is this the Rambo thing we talked about yesterday?"

Ryan nodded. "Yes, this is the Rambo thing."

She mulled this over for another long moment. "I will let you do this on your own. But I do not like it."

She stared down at the table. "I do not want to see you get hurt."

He lifted her chin with his hand. "I promise. I won't get hurt."

She shook her head slowly and gave him a tentative smile. "You are such a bullshitter, John."

Ryan laughed. "I can't argue with that."

Then she reached into the pocket of her jacket and handed him one of her business cards. "Call me if you need me. Anytime of the day or night."

"Will do, Keiko."

"I will drive you over to this building."

He shook his head. "I'll take a cab over. It's better if you don't get involved with any of this."

"As you wish, John."

They said goodbye and he left the conference room.

Chapter 61

Tokyo, Japan

The Tokama Import building was exactly where Keiko had said. The skyscraper overlooked the Sumida River and was nestled among a row of other high-rise structures. It was located in the Chuo Ku district of central Tokyo.

After getting dropped by the taxi, J.T. Ryan scouted the location on foot, trying to get a feel for the area. It was a bustling business area, with throngs of Japanese businesspeople, men and women, crowding the sidewalks. And the streets were jammed with vehicles of all types. As Ryan had noticed during his whole stay in Japan, Tokyo was teeming with people.

After an hour of scouting the exterior areas, he went into the building's lobby. There was a coffee shop on one side of the area and a group of elevator banks on the opposite side.

There was a reader board also in the lobby and he went to it. The name of the company, Tokama Imports and Exports was listed at the top. There were offices with different names on them listed by the floor number. He noticed that the first three floors were not listed at all. Then, starting on the tenth floor, he saw initials by the room numbers. It was clear that these were apartment numbers.

He located Dubois's apartment on the reader board, which was on the eleventh floor of the building.

Glancing at his watch, he saw it was 10 a.m. Figuring she was probably at work and not at home, Ryan skipped the elevators and took the stairs up to the eleventh floor. He wanted to scout out the area before formulating a plan.

After reaching the right floor, he found Apartment 1107, which was located midway in the corridor. He noticed CCTV cameras by the elevators and at both ends of the hallway.

Ryan briefly considered breaking into her apartment and waiting for her to get home. But the risk was too great that the CCTV cameras would spot him. He was sure there was a security office in the building that monitored the video feed 24/7.

Knowing he had learned as much as possible from this visit, he took the stairs down to the lobby and out of the building.

He strode the crowded sidewalks for the next half hour, trying to come up with a plan on how to approach Dubois without arousing suspicion, and without alerting the security people at the Tokama building.

He finally settled on a plan and hailed a taxi.

***

Ryan returned to the Tokama building at 7 p.m. that same day, figuring that by then Marie Dubois would be home from work.

He was no longer wearing a navy blazer, a white dress shirt, and gray slacks. He had found a store in the city that sold employee uniforms. Although he had not been able to get an exact match, the purple and orange logoed uniform he was now wearing closely resembled what FedEx employees wore. He had even obtained a cap that looked like their hats. And he had stopped at a local FedEx store location and obtained a large overnight delivery box.

Ryan walked into the lobby of the Tokama building and headed for the stairs. It was a long climb to the 11th floor, but being trapped in an elevator for whatever reason was not worth the risk.

When he reached the right floor, he walked purposely toward the woman's apartment.

He pulled his cap lower to hide his face and held the FedEx box in front of him. Then he rang the buzzer and waited.

Ryan heard muffled steps and then a muffled voice from the other side of the door. There was a spyhole on the door, and he figured the woman was looking at him now.

"Can I help you?" the muffled woman's voice said.

"FedEx delivery," he said, holding the box higher. "For Marie Dubois."

"Leave it on my doorstep, please." She spoke English with a French accent.

"I can't do that, ma'am. You have to sign for it."

In an exasperated voice she said, "All right."

Then he heard the clicking of locks and the door opened partway. He recognized Marie Dubois immediately. She was an attractive woman in her mid-thirties, dressed in a dark gray pantsuit and a gray blouse.

Ryan handed her the box and she took it, and in that instant, he kicked open the door fully and rushed inside, knocking her off her feet.

He slammed the door shut behind him and locked it, then faced the French woman, who was scrambling to stand up.

Her face full of rage, she screamed, "You bastard! What the hell are you doing!"

"If you do what I say," he replied, "I won't hurt you."

"Screw you!" she screamed, jumping to her feet and pulling a knife from her pantsuit pocket. The blade's sharp edge glinted from the overhead light.

Ryan jumped back, recalling that the French woman was a trained killer. They circled each other cautiously in the apartment's living room, then she lunged at him, slashing the knife in front of her.

He jumped back again, the blade barely missing his chest. Then he rushed her and knocked her off her feet. They both crashed to the floor, and they wrestled for a moment, as he tried to take the knife away from her.

She was strong for a woman and a wily fighter, but his superior strength was too much, and he grabbed the knife from her and put it in his pocket.

She was flat on her back now, and he was straddling her, pinning her down with his thighs and hands.

Her nostrils flared and her eyes burned with hate.

"What do you want?" she spit out. "Who are you? You're not from FedEx, that's for damn sure!"

"If you do what I say," he replied, trying to calm her. "I won't hurt you."

"Do you want to screw me? Is that it? You're going to rape me?"

"No."

"Then let me go."

"No. Not until you calm down."

Her eyes flashed anger, then slowly softened.

"Okay," she said, her voice sultry now. "I'll calm down. We can have sex now, if you want …."

He realized now that the French woman was not just an assassin, but was also a seductress, which would make her even a more deadly killer.

Still, he didn't want to hit her or hurt her in any way. He despised hitting women and did everything possible to avoid it, even if they were vicious criminals.

"If I let you go," he said. "Will you cooperate?"

She gave him a sensual grin. "Sure. I'll do whatever you want. You can have me."

Ryan let go of her arms and got off her, standing up. He held out his hand and helped her to her feet.

Suddenly she spun around 360 degrees and hit him with a roundhouse kick to his solar plexus. The painful blow knocked the air out of his lungs, and he staggered back and went to one knee.

Dubois attacked him again, this time with a front kick toward his groin. He turned sideways, and the kick hit his thigh instead.

Ryan grabbed her extended leg and pulled her forward, sending her tumbling down to the floor.

Then he slammed his powerful body on top of her again, pinning her down to the floor with his thighs and arms.

Her face was full of rage again. "Damn you!"

"Do you give up?" he yelled. "I don't want to hurt you. But I will if you don't cooperate."

Dubois let out a long breath. "All right."

"Do you mean it?"

"Yes."

He let go of one of her arms and made a fist with his hand and pressed it to her cheek.

"You have a beautiful face, Dubois. I'd hate to bloody it."

Her eyes bulged and for the first time she seemed afraid. "Don't. Please. I'll do what you want."

Ryan let go of her and they both stood.

He pointed to one of the couches in the living room. "Sit."

To his surprise, she complied and sat on the sofa.

"Who are you?" she said, her eyes wary. "You're no delivery man, that's for damn sure."

"We'll get to that."

He took out a small roll of duct tape from one of his pockets and approached her.

"Put your hands out," he ordered.

"Why?"

"Just do it!"

She held her hands in front of her and he bound them together with the duct tape. Then he went to one knee and bound her legs together with the tape.

Then he stood. "Where's your gun?"

"I don't have a gun."

"Bullshit," he stated, his voice stern. "You're a trained killer. I know you have a gun."

She nodded toward one of the other rooms. "In the nightstand in the bedroom."

Ryan went there and found it inside the drawer of the nightstand. It was a SIG Sauer semiautomatic. He pocketed it. He also found a cell phone in the drawer, and he took that also.

Then he went back to the living room and pulled a chair in front of her and sat down.

"Who the hell are you?" she spit out. "And what the hell do you want? If this is a robbery, you'll be disappointed. I don't keep much cash." She paused, then said, "And it's obvious you're not here to rape me. Otherwise, you would have already done it."

"You don't recognize me, do you?" he said.

She shook her head. "No. We've never met. I would remember you."

"You're right, Miss Dubois. We've never met. But I know you. I've been trying to find you and your partners for a long while now."

Her face scrunched in concentration, obviously trying to place him. After a long moment, she whispered, "Yes, I remember now. I saw a photo of you once. You're the American. The private investigator."

Ryan nodded. "J.T. Ryan. It's good to meet you at last, Miss Dubois. Or can I call you by your first name, Marie."

"What do you want, Ryan?"

"Since I'm here, you know what I want."

She shook her head. "I don't know what you're talking about."

"Don't play stupid, Marie. You and your accomplice Hans Kruger kidnapped the movie producer Carl Parnell and killed his housekeeper. And I'm sure you're also involved with several other murders of movie people."

"You're crazy! I had nothing to do with that! I'm not a killer. I'm a clerk at an import export company."

Ryan had to smile at that. "You're too good with a knife and with martial arts to be a clerk. You almost took me down, which is hard to do."

She said nothing, her eyes blazing with anger.

"If you cooperate with me," he said, "and tell me everything about your operation, maybe I can help you. This operation you're involved with, the murders of numerous movie people around the world, took a lot of planning and manpower. You're beautiful and cunning, but I don't think you're the mastermind. If you tell me who your co-conspirators are, maybe I can help you."

"Help me how?"

"Maybe get you a lighter sentence. Maybe a better prison."

"Bullshit! I'm not saying anything. I want a lawyer."

Ryan shook his head slowly. "Wrong answer, Marie. Talk, or you'll regret it."

"Lawyer now!"

"I'm not a cop," he said. "I don't have any rules that I have to follow."

"Call the police, then. Have me arrested. I know Japanese law. It's just like American law. I don't have to say anything without my attorney present."

Ryan shook his head. "That's not going to happen. I'm not calling the police until you give me everything I want."

Her eyes narrowed and it was clear she was trying to figure out a way to get out of the situation.

"Here's the deal," she said, her voice soft and sultry now. "I tell you everything you want to know. Then we can have sex. I'll let you. It'll be fun – you're a handsome guy and I'm great in bed. After that you let me go, and I get the hell out of Japan."

She paused, then said, "We'll never see each other again. This way you get what you want, and I get what I want. It's a win-win deal for both of us. How's that sound?"

Ryan realized she was great at her job. A sexy seductress and a cold-blooded killer. A deadly combination she had employed many times before.

He shook his head. "As tempting as that sounds, the answer is still no. I can't let you go."

She grinned seductively. "Come on, let's do it. I promise, it'll be fun."

Ryan laughed, despite the tenseness of the situation. She was a great actress. "Under different circumstances, I'd love to do it. But the answer is still no."

She scowled, then her shoulders sagged. "Too bad. In that case, I'm not saying another word."

Ryan mulled this over, knowing he needed her to talk now, before other murders took place. Too many innocent people had already died. But he couldn't call detective Keiko Kanata now.

188

Marie would lawyer up and they would find out nothing for weeks, maybe months.

He considered this for another moment, trying to come up with a plan of action.

Then he decided on an approach he had used previously during other interrogations.

"Then you leave me no choice, Marie."

"What are you going to do?"

Ryan pulled out the knife from his pocket. It was the one he had taken from her earlier.

She eyed the blade suspiciously. "What are you going … to do with that …."

He held the knife an inch from her face. "You have a gorgeous face, Marie."

"You can't do that!" she gasped.

Ryan moved the sharp edge of the knife closer to her cheek. "I don't want to. I really, really don't, but…."

"Please Ryan! I'm begging you …."

He pressed the knifepoint to her cheek, now touching it lightly. If he pressed it a bit closer, it would cut her skin.

As a soldier in the Army, Ryan had interrogated enemy combatants in Afghanistan and knew that the fear of pain was worse than the pain itself. If he could convince her he was serious, he would win. But deep down he knew he couldn't really slash her face. It was a line he would never cross.

Her eyes bulged and beads of sweat rolled down her face. "Please … please Ryan …."

"Will you talk now?" he growled.

He slid the knife point slowly and carefully up her cheek and closer to her eye.

"YES! Yes … I'll talk …."

"You're sure, Marie? I don't have time to play games with you."

"Yes! I swear. I'll tell you everything you want to know." Her eyes were wild with terror.

Ryan pulled the knife away from her face.

She was breathing fast, and he gave her a long moment to catch her breath.

"Would you like a glass of water?" he said, his voice calm.

She nodded. "Yes … please yes …."

He went to the kitchen, filled a glass from the tap and went back to the living room. He brought the glass to her lips, and she drank it down.

He put the glass down on the coffee table and sat across from her again.

Her breathing was becoming normal again, and she said, "Thank you … for not … you know …."

Ryan nodded. "You have a very pretty face. I would have hated to cut you. The pain would have been horrible. And the scars would have been permanent."

"I know." Then she held out her bound hands in front of her. "Can you please untie me? They hurt."

Ryan shook his head. "No, I can't do that. Not yet. Not until you talk."

She shrugged. "Fine."

"You'll talk now and tell me everything I want to know?"

"Yes. And after? What happens to me?"

He mulled this over, trying to decide what to say. Dubois was a smart woman and would detect a lie, so he went with the truth.

"You'll be arrested by the Tokyo police. Then you'll be extradited to the U.S. There you'll face a trial for your crimes. After that you'll be sentenced to prison."

"For how long?"

"I don't know, Marie."

"Will you talk to the prosecutors and tell them I cooperated with you?"

"Yes."

"Are you lying to me?"

"No. I swear. I will try to do everything I can to help you. But first, you have to help me. All right?"

She nodded, a resigned look on her face. "Yes. I will help you."

"Then tell me everything. Start at the beginning."

"What do you want to know?"

"You and Hans Kruger kidnapped Carl Parnell in L.A. and killed his housekeeper. Is that right?"

"Yes."

"What did you do with Parnell?"

"We brought him back to Tokyo."

"Where in Tokyo?"

"This building. The one we're in now."

"Is Parnell still alive?"

She shook her head. "I don't know. We handed him off to our boss and I don't know what happened after that."

"Who's your boss?"

"Nikita."

"What's her last name?"

"I don't know."

Ryan made a fist with his hand and held it in front of the woman's face. "Bullshit!"

Marie shook her head forcefully. "It's true! I swear. I only know her by that name."

"Is this Nikita woman the mastermind behind this whole operation?"

"Yes. She assigns us to specific jobs."

"Where is Nikita located?"

"She lives in this building. On the top floor. She has a penthouse suite."

"Do you work here in this building?"

"Yes. We work in the Operations Center. All of us work there."

"Where is this Operations Center?"

"In the basement of this building."

"Okay, Marie. Does Kruger live here also?"

She nodded. "Yes. His apartment is on the 10th floor."

"What does Nikita assign you to do?"

"Because of my looks, my job is usually to seduce powerful men in the movie industry, film it, then blackmail them. Sometimes I have to seduce women also, but that's not much fun for me."

"Does the seduction always work?"

She shook her head. "Not always. Sometimes I can't seduce them."

"What happens then?"

"I kill them."

"Are all these people in the film industry?"

"Yes."

"What's the purpose of all this? Why is the movie industry being targeted?"

She shook her head. "I don't know. I just do my job. I make a lot of money here. Five times what I made in France. So, for me this is a good situation."

"But not so good for the victims. The people you kill," he said, his voice hard.

She frowned but said nothing.

"How big is this operation?" he asked.

"There's twenty of us. Mostly men, but a few women like me. Actually, there's less than twenty of us now. I think you killed a few of the operatives when they went to the U.S."

"Yeah. I know all about that. I was lucky to survive." Ryan mulled over something. "How is this operation funded? You don't really do import export, right?"

"That's right. The import export is just a cover."

"So, I ask you again – how is this operation funded? It costs a lot of money to fly your group all over the world to assassinate people."

Marie shrugged. "I don't know. Nikita handles all that."

"What else can you tell me about this operation?" he asked.

She scrunched her face in concentration. "Nikita sleeps with the men operatives."

"How do you know that?"

"Because she screws Kruger all the time. I hate that."

"Why is that?"

"Hans Kruger and I are lovers." She paused a moment, then said, "What will happen to Hans? Will you kill him?"

He shook his head. "Not if I don't have to. If he cooperates like you're doing, he'll be arrested."

"I'm glad you won't kill him. I like Hans a lot. By the way, what will happen to Nikita?" Her face contorted in anger. "I hate that bitch. I hope you kill her! It's what she deserves!"

"I'm guessing you're not good friends of hers."

Marie spit on the floor. "I hate that evil slut!"

Ryan considered everything the woman had told him about the operation. It was great information. With Marie testifying to the Tokyo police, he was sure they would be able to arrest Nikita and the other people in the operation.

Just then he felt Marie's phone vibrate in his pocket. He took it out and glanced at the screen. Marie had gotten three text messages from Kruger.

Ryan clicked on the text messages, which stated that he wanted to see her tonight, clearly for a hook up.

Ryan put the phone away but now realized that Kruger might show up at Marie's apartment anytime.

Just then he heard a loud knock on the apartment's front door.

Chapter 62

Tokyo, Japan

After knocking on the apartment's door several times and getting no answer, Kruger pressed the buzzer and waited.

He knew Marie was home, since they had talked about getting together tonight.

Kruger mashed the buzzer again, then went back to knocking on the door. But there was no answer.

Frustrated and angry, he stalked off and went back to his own apartment. But before he went inside, something occurred to him that gave him pause.

What if she's in trouble? What if she's hurt? he thought. *Should I break down her door?* Realizing that seemed drastic, he instead went to the security room on the third floor of the Tokama building.

He went inside the room and was greeted by the security guard on duty. The guy was a young Japanese man, and like everyone in the operation, spoke English.

Mounted on one wall of the room were over 40 flatscreen TVs, showing live video feeds of the building's lobby, the exterior sidewalk in front of the structure, and every corridor of every floor. The CCTV cameras ran and were monitored 24/7.

"Have you spotted any problems tonight?" Kruger asked the man.

"No. It's been quiet."

"Pull of the CCTV feed from the 11th floor corridor."

The security man tapped on his computer keyboard. "All right."

"I want to see what happened two hours ago," Kruger said.

The security guy nodded and tapped on the keyboard again. Then he pointed to one of the video screens on the wall. "The feed is on screen 23. It is time stamped on the lower right part of the screen."

The screen showed nothing happening on the 11th floor corridor. "Speed up the video," Kruger said.

The man did so, and Kruger watched as the time moved forward and people went into their apartments or left them. The people were operatives like himself, or support staff, and he recognized all of them. Everything seemed normal for the first hour, then Kruger spotted something different.

"Freeze the video," he ordered.

The security guard did so, and Kruger saw a FedEx delivery man knocking on Apartment 1107. The man was carrying a large package.

"Start up the video and run it in slow motion," Kruger said.

The CCTV footage started again, and it showed Marie's door opening. After a moment the FedEx man went inside the apartment and the door closed behind him.

"Do you want me to keep running the video feed?" the security guard said.

"Yes."

The video continued and after five minutes with nothing happening, Kruger knew something was wrong. "Back up the feed to when the delivery guy first gets to Apartment 1107."

"Yes, sir."

The images rewound and a moment later Kruger said, "Freeze it here and zoom in closer to the FedEx guy's face."

The security man did so, and Kruger's heart began to race.

Although the delivery guy was wearing a cap pulled low over his face, he recognized him immediately.

It was Ryan, the PI from Atlanta. The man he had almost killed.

Kruger's heart thundered in his chest and his hands formed into fists.

***

Kruger raced out of the security office, sprinted down the corridor and took the elevator to the penthouse floor of the building.

He knocked loudly on Nikita's door.

A moment later she opened it partway. She was wearing a white bathrobe and was holding a glass in her hand.

"What is it, Kruger?" she asked, her tone aggravated. "Why are you bothering me? I was getting ready to soak in the hot tub."

"We have a problem," he said. "A big problem."

She gave him an exasperated glare, gulped down the contents of her glass, then opened the door fully. "Come in then. But make it quick."

Kruger went inside the sumptuous foyer, and she closed the door behind him.

She set the glass down on the table in the foyer. "What's the problem?"

"He's here, Nikita."

"Who's here? What the hell are you talking about?"

"The American private investigator. John Ryan."

She scowled. "Are you insane? Have you been drinking?"

He shook his head forcefully. "No. I'm telling you the truth. I saw Ryan. Here, in our building."

"You're crazy. No way Ryan is here. How could he find us?"

"I don't know. But it's true. I saw the CCTV footage. He went into Marie's apartment a while ago. He was wearing a FedEx uniform and carrying a package. I'm sure he used this disguise to get into her apartment. Earlier tonight I went to see her and got suspicious when she didn't answer her door."

Nikita still looked skeptical, then concern clouded her face. "Let's take a look at the video. I want to see this for myself."

She strode toward one of the many rooms of her penthouse and he followed her. They went inside it, and she turned on the lights. This room was a smaller version of the security room downstairs.

There was a workstation with a computer and flatscreen TVs on the walls.

Nikita sat at the workstation and turned on the computer. Then she tapped on the keyboard and one of the video monitors on the wall came on.

"When did this happen?" Nikita said.

"Over an hour ago, on the 11th floor."

She worked at the keyboard again and the image of the 11th floor corridor came on the screen. The time stamp read 1 ½ hours earlier in the evening.

Nikita tapped the keyboard, speeding up the image until the delivery man came into the picture.

Kruger pointed. "There! That's him!"

She zoomed in closer and focused on the man's face.

Her hands formed into fists. "Damn it! That is Ryan! How the hell could this be happening?"

Kruger shook his head. "I don't know."

She glared at him. "How could you let this happen?"

"It isn't my fault – "

"Shut up! Let me think, damn it!"

Nikita went quiet for a minute, her face contorted with rage. Then the anger slowly dissipated and was replaced by a look of determination.

Kruger said nothing, knowing it was best to let his boss think things through. She was the brains of the operation, always had been. If anyone could process a way out of this, it was her.

Nikita finally spoke. "I may have figured out a solution. The only thing I'm not sure about is if Ryan is working alone, or if he's working with the Tokyo police. What do you think?"

"I don't know."

She grimaced. "You're a fucking idiot, you know that?"

His face turned red, but he said nothing.

Nikita stood up from the workstation. "We need to kill Ryan. Now. I want you to get 8 of our operatives together, arm them, and go into Marie's apartment. Break down her door and kill him. I want him dead ASAP."

"What about Marie?"

She glared at him. "What about her?"

"I don't want her to get hurt."

"I don't give a fuck what you want, Kruger! Kill Ryan. And kill Marie too. I hate that bitch. I have for a long time."

"Why does she have to die also?"

She sneered. "You're still fucking her, aren't you? Even after I forbid you to. Isn't that right?"

Her blazing black eyes bore into his and he lowered his gaze to the floor. He said nothing.

"What I said is true, isn't it?" she spat out. "You're still doing her."

He finally looked up at her. "Yes."

"Then she dies. Kill her and Ryan both. Understood?"

"Yes, Nikita."

"One last thing. If things go badly, you know where to go?"

He tilted his head. "You think your plan won't work?"

"It'll work. But it'll be loud, from the gunfire. If the police show up, we'll meet at the secondary location."

"Yes, I understand."

"Then get going, Kruger! Get the men together. Now! We don't have a second to waste."

Chapter 63

Tokyo, Japan

"That was probably Kruger who was knocking on your door, right?" J.T. Ryan said.

"Yes," Marie Dubois replied. "We were supposed to get together tonight."

The two people were sitting across from each other in the living room of her apartment.

He was holding her SIG Sauer pistol, and Marie's hands and feet were still bound with duct tape.

"He sent you three texts," Ryan said. "When you didn't respond, he came to your door. If you don't respond to his texts, he'll know something's wrong and come back."

"That's right. If you untie me, I'll send him a text telling him that I don't feel well and that we can't have sex tonight."

Ryan mulled that over a moment, didn't think that would work. Kruger didn't seem like the kind of man to take no for an answer.

Then Ryan remembered something else. The security camera at the end of the corridor on this floor. *Kruger knows what I look like.* Even disguised as a delivery man, the German assassin would spot me.

Realizing he needed help now, Ryan pocketed the gun and took out his phone. He punched in a number he had memorized.

"It's Ryan," he said.

"How is it going?" Detective Keiko Kanata replied.

"I'm in Dubois's apartment now. She's cooperated. She'll be a good witness. With her help we can take down this whole operation. But Kruger is also in this building. He's coming back to her apartment soon and will probably bring his men with him. From what I learned today, this operation has close to twenty people. No way I can fight all of them on my own. I need help. Now."

"Of course. I will coordinate with my boss and go there."

"Bring a SWAT team with you, Keiko. These people mean business."

"I will do that. Where are you exactly?"

"On the 11th floor, Apartment 1107."

"Okay, John."

"And hurry, Keiko."

Chapter 64

Tokyo, Japan

J.T. Ryan hung up the phone and put it away. Then he took out the SIG Sauer pistol.

"Was that the police you were talking with?" Marie said.

"Yeah."

"You remember our deal?"

"Yes, Marie. If you testify, I'll do everything I can to help you."

"Untie me then. At least my feet, please. When Kruger comes back, there's bound to be shooting. At least let me hide in the bathroom. I don't want to die."

Ryan considered this, knowing it was true. "All right. I'll untie your feet. But if you betray me, you die. Understand?"

"Yes."

Ryan pocketed the gun and took out Marie's knife. Then he cut the duct tape that was binding her legs together.

That done, he said, "Do you have more ammo for this pistol?"

"Yes. It's in my bedroom closet. I keep three loaded magazines in a box on the floor."

"Stay here. I'll go get the extra ammo."

He turned toward the bedroom, and in that instant, she executed a martial arts roundhouse kick, the heel of her shoe slamming his back. He felt the stab of pain but ignored it and whirled around to face her.

Marie's face was beet red in anger, and he realized she had betrayed him once again.

201

Ryan turned sideways and rushed her, knocking her off her feet and to the floor. On the way down, her head hit the arm of a chair, and she slumped, unconscious.

Realizing the woman could not be trusted, he bound her feet with duct tape again, then carried her limp body into the bathroom. Then he placed her inside the bathtub and left the bathroom, closing the door behind him. He didn't want her to get shot, since he needed her alive to testify.

Then he went to the bedroom, found the three extra magazines for the SIG Sauer, and pocketed them.

That done, he went into the living room, knowing Kruger and his crew could be back anytime.

A few minutes later, he heard muffled sounds from the corridor outside the apartment.

He went to the door and glanced through the spyhole to see what was happening.

There was a large group of men in the corridor, all armed with pistols. He spotted Kruger leading the group. He also saw that one of the men was carrying a battering ram.

It was clear what they intended to do. Break down the door and kill him.

Ryan's heart raced, knowing his odds were not good.

He counted at least 8 or 9 men in the corridor. He had faced bad odds before, during combat in Iraq and Afghanistan, and had survived. But he also knew that he wasn't Superman, and bullets didn't bounce off his chest.

Still, he had a SIG Sauer semiautomatic with three extra magazines. Maybe he could hold them off long enough until Keiko and her SWAT team arrived.

Ryan glanced around the living room, looking for the best way to shield himself when all hell broke loose.

He spotted a sturdy looking wooden cabinet at one side of the room and raced there and crouched behind it.

From this vantage point he had a clear view of the door but was away from the center of the room.

As he waited tensely for the fireworks to erupt, he recalled something Amanda had given him in Amsterdam a while ago. He took out the small silver crucifix from his pocket and said a silent prayer to Jesus Christ. He knew some people thought it was corny or stupid to have faith in God, but Ryan had always found that praying before a firefight calmed him.

Ryan put away the crucifix and trained his weapon on the apartment's front door. His heart was pounding and his thoughts raced.

Seconds later he heard it. The loud pounding of the battering ram on the door. The door held for several blows, then split apart in multiple pieces, the wood splinters flying into the room.

Then he heard the roar of gunfire, as the attackers opened fire, spraying the living room with rounds. The men were still outside the apartment, shooting in.

Luckily, he had chosen a spot off to one side, and the hail of bullets shredded the furniture and pockmarked the walls of the room. The sound of the gunfire was deafening.

Ryan waited before firing back, wanting them to be inside, so he could take them down as they entered.

The bullets kept flying in, literally shredding the room. His adrenaline spiked and his heart thundered in his chest.

Then two men rushed inside, their heads on a swivel, their pistols in front of them.

Ryan fired two rounds, and one of the men dropped to the floor. Ryan fired again and the second guy clutched his chest and collapsed.

There was a lull in the action and Ryan figured Kruger was assessing the situation before sending in more men.

Ryan ejected his half empty magazine and slapped in a fresh one. The technique was called a tactical reload, exchanging mags before they're empty. It was something he had learned in Afghanistan, something that had kept him alive during more than one combat mission.

Ryan heard whispering from the hallway, then two more men rushed inside the apartment. He fired instantly, his rounds hitting one guy in the face, blood and flesh spurting out. The bright red gore spattered the wall.

Another one of Ryan's bullets shattered the shooting hand of the other man. The man howled in pain and went to one knee and then collapsed.

The gunfire was deafening and the sound echoed throughout the apartment.

Ryan was gasping in ragged breaths, his pistol still pointed toward the smashed front door. He had taken down four of the attackers but knew there were at least four or more outside.

He'd been lucky so far, he knew. But he also knew the odds of his survival were still only 50/50 at best. The men in the hallway were trained assassins, and having lost some of their own, had a big score to settle.

Ryan did another combat reload and exchanged his half empty mag for a fresh one.

Then he heard it, in the far distance. The sound was low at first, then got progressively louder.

The wail of police sirens.

The sound got louder and louder and Ryan sensed the SWAT team was getting closer to the building.

For the first time in the last hour, he felt like he would make it out alive today.

Still, he was wary and kept his gun trained on the shattered door.

He heard the rustle of footsteps from the hallway, then everything went quiet.

But he stayed where he was, worried that the group of killers was still in the corridor. When nothing happened for several minutes, he stood up, and with his gun trained forward, he cautiously advanced toward the door.

Reaching it, he quickly glanced outside and saw nothing.

The attackers had fled.

He breathed a sigh of relief.

***

"I am glad you are not hurt," Detective Keiko Kanata said to Ryan, when she entered the shattered living room five minutes later. The Tokyo SWAT unit had come in five minutes before that and had searched the apartment. They found Ryan, the four dead attackers on the floor, and Marie Dubois, who was still tied up and lying in the bathtub. The SWAT team had read Dubois her rights, arrested her, and taken her away.

Ryan smiled at Keiko. "I'm glad also."

She looked around the shot-up room, with bullet holes on the walls and the shattered furniture.

Then she stared at the bloody corpses on the floor.

The gore covered much of the carpet.

Keiko made a retching sound and covered her mouth. She looked pale and Ryan took her hand and led her into the bathroom. She promptly kneeled in front of the toilet and retched, the vomit filling the bowl.

Then she wiped her mouth and sat on the floor, an embarrassed look on her face.

Ryan sat next to her on the floor of the bathroom. "Is that your first time? Seeing dead bodies covered in blood?"

She nodded, then looked away from him, clearly embarrassed.

"It's okay," he said calmly. "Everybody goes through that."

"Really?"

"Yes, Keiko. Really."

She still looked green, so he stood, moistened a towel in the sink and sat down next to her again. He used the towel to wipe her face for a couple of minutes.

She still looked ashen, but she managed to give him a small smile.

"Thank you, John."

"No problem. Would you like a glass of water?"

"Yes, please."

Ryan stood, went to the kitchen and filled a glass from the tap. A few of the SWAT team officers were still in the apartment, along with CSI people. The bodies, Ryan knew, would be bagged once the coroner finished with them.

Ryan went back to the bathroom, handed Keiko the glass of water and sat down next to her again.

She drank down the glass in one long pull, then placed it on the floor. She was starting to get her color back.

"I feel so stupid," she said. "I am a police detective. I need to be stronger. Tougher."

"Don't be so hard on yourself." He grinned, trying to cheer her up. "Listen, I've got a couple of new jokes I can tell you. Would you like to hear them? It might cheer you up."

She smiled and it lit up her pretty face. "No, thank you. But I do appreciate it."

"Of course." Then he squeezed her hand. "Feel better now?"

"Yes, John. I do feel better."

"When the SWAT teams came into the building," he said, "did they find anyone?"

She shook her head. "No. The lobby was empty, and there was no one in the corridors. We came up to the 11th floor right away. The SWAT teams are searching the rest of the building now."

"Good. I found out a lot about this operation from Dubois. She told me there is a Japanese woman who runs it. Her name is Nikita. She lives on the penthouse floor of this building."

"That is good information," Keiko said. "By the way, how were you able to fight off the men who attacked you?"

Ryan pulled out the SIG Sauer, which was in his jacket pocket.

"I used this," Ryan said. "I got it from Dubois."

She cocked her head. "I told you before, you are a foreigner in Japan. You are not allowed to have a gun."

He grinned. "Are you going to arrest me?"

She smiled back. "No, I am not going to arrest you. But please put it back in your pocket. I do not want another police officer seeing you with it. They will not be as understanding as I am."

"Nor as pretty."

She grinned, then blushed. "Stop that, please. You are embarrassing me, John Ryan."

"I'll act professionally from on."

She reached out with her small hand and squeezed his brawny hand. "You are a nice man."

"Thanks, Keiko. You're a sweet woman."

Just then one of the SWAT men came into the bathroom. He spoke rapidly in Japanese and Ryan understood none of it.

Keiko got to her feet quickly and so did Ryan.

"What did he say?" Ryan asked Keiko.

"They have searched the whole building and only found one person, an American."

"Who is it, Keiko?"

"He had a wallet on him, and it identified him as Carl Parnell."

"That's great news," Ryan said. "I was hoping he was still alive. When I interrogated Dubois, she told me she and Kruger had brought Parnell here after they kidnapped him. I was worried they had killed him."

"We should go see him," Keiko replied.

"Absolutely."

Keiko turned to the SWAT officer and spoke rapidly in Japanese. Then the three of them left the apartment and took the elevator down to an underground level of the building, the SWAT man leading the way.

A few minutes later they entered a dimly lit concrete walled room furnished with a cot, a metal chair, and two pails. From the foul odor in the room, it was clear what the pails were filled with: piss and excrement.

A disheveled-looking older man was laying on the cot. He was wearing a dirty T-shirt and dirty slacks and had an emaciated look.

Ryan recognized him right away. It was Carl Parnell, the famous movie producer.

There was an EMT team in the room and they were checking Parnell's vitals.

Ryan approached the cot and went to one knee, so he was eye level with Parnell. The old man's eyes were unfocused at first, then lit up.

"Ryan," Parnell said, his voice hoarse. "You found … me …."

"I did. How are you feeling?"

"Like … shit … I've been a prisoner here for … I don't know how long …."

"Don't worry. The Japanese police are here with me. They'll take care of you. And when you feel better, we'll take you back to the U.S."

"That's … that's great … I just want … to go home …."

"Tell me what happened," Ryan said, "after you were kidnapped in L.A. The woman kidnapper, Marie Dubois, told me they brought you here, to this building."

Parnell's face scrunched in concentration, then he said, "They put me here … in this room … I've never left it … I was questioned … a few times … by a Japanese woman …."

"Was her name Nikita?"

"I don't know … she never said …."

"Why did they kidnap you?"

"I was planning on making … a patriotic movie … she … didn't want me to … make it."

Ryan considered what Parnell had just said.

"This whole operation," Ryan said, "the people who kidnapped you and killed all the others, is expensive to run. Do you know how it's funded? The cover they use, an import export company, is all fake."

Parnell shook his head. "No … I don't know …." Then his eyes closed and stayed closed. It was clear the old man was exhausted.

Ryan stood and faced Keiko. "Will the EMT's take Parnell to a hospital?"

"Yes, John. He will be well taken care of."

"Good. Dubois told me there is an operations center in the basement of this building. Did the SWAT team find it?"

"Yes, John. They found it. But no one was there."

"Let's go there, Keiko."

Keiko spoke to the SWAT officer in Japanese and the three of them left the room.

They found the operations center right away, and as Keiko had said, the place was unoccupied. The large room featured one wall covered with a massive flatscreen TV, with several smaller TV screens to the side of it. There were twenty computer workstations in the room.

"According to Dubois," Ryan said, "this room is where it all happened. The operatives got their assignments here."

Keiko glanced around. "There is a lot of computer equipment and electronics here. As you said, this place would be very expensive to operate."

"That's true. Clearly, it's well funded. Can your tech people search these computers? And find out more about Nikita and this organization?"

"Yes, John. I will arrange it."

"Good. Let's go up to the penthouse floor. That's where Nikita lived."

Keiko spoke to the SWAT man again and the three left the room. They took the elevator to the top floor of the building.

There were two uniformed police officers posted on this floor, standing next to an impressive double door. The door was open, and it was clear the lock had been broken to access the room.

Ryan and Keiko and the SWAT man went inside the penthouse suite, a lavishly decorated three-bedroom apartment that overlooked the Sumida River. The massive living room had a splendid view of Tokyo. The floor-to-ceiling windows displayed the river below and the multitude of skyscrapers. It was dusk now and the rows and rows of high-rise buildings were a riot of colorful lights.

"Nikita lived very well," Ryan said, admiring the penthouse apartment. "This place smells of money. Big money."

"I agree," Keiko replied. Then she turned toward the SWAT man and spoke in Japanese, and he responded. As usual, Ryan understood none of it.

"The SWAT team," Keiko said to Ryan, "searched the whole apartment and found no computers or phones."

Ryan shook his head slowly. "That's too bad. We need to find Nikita. She's obviously the brains behind this operation. Did they find any written records? Files of any type?"

"Yes, John. But the files are cryptic and use some type of code."

"Can your tech people try to decipher it?"

"Yes. I will arrange it."

"Good. Let's go to Nikita's bedroom."

They went deeper into the lavish apartment and found a massive master bedroom with a king-size bed.

Ryan went into the huge walk-in closet. There were clothes and shoes strewn on the floor, and several empty hangers.

"Nikita packed in a hurry," Ryan said.

Keiko glanced around the walk-in closet. "Yes. Clearly, she fled quickly. She had not planned on us finding her."

Ryan went back into the bedroom. He looked around for any photos or personal items in the room. "There's no pictures of herself," Ryan said. "So, we don't know what she looks like. And we don't know what her last name is. I assume your CSI people will dust for prints and gather trace evidence to get her DNA?"

"Yes, John."

Ryan and Keiko and the SWAT man searched the large apartment for several more hours, trying to find any clue as to where Nikita had gone.

But they found none.

Chapter 65

Osaka, Japan

Nikita paced the living room of the safe house like a caged tiger. Her brain was on overdrive as she tried to process the enormity of what had happened.

Somehow her operation in Tokyo had been discovered. It was not clear to her how it had happened, but obviously she had underestimated the American detective.

Nikita stopped pacing, went to the liquor cabinet in the room and poured herself a large glass of *sake*, which she drank down in one long pull. It was her fourth drink and the usual warm buzz the liquor gave her was absent today.

She was wearing a simple long-sleeved blouse and casual slacks. In her haste packing, she had not had time to take any of her beautiful kimonos with her. Instead, she had taken casual clothing and shoes.

Nikita went back to pacing the living room, which unlike the one in her magnificent penthouse in Tokyo, was small and drab.

The safe house itself, which was in a suburb of Osaka, was tiny and plain. It consisted of a small living room, a tiny office, her miniscule bedroom, two bathrooms, and a bunk room for the operatives. She had not planned on ever having to flee Tokyo, and had set up this house in the unlikely event her operation would be discovered.

Nikita shook her head slowly, realizing she should have planned better. She realized now she should have set up a more expansive operations center in Osaka. Clearly the house she was in now would not work. The place was not outfitted with computers, nor any other technology, and the house was way too small to function properly.

It would take time and money to outfit this place and make it fully operational. Although she had the money, she had another, bigger problem to deal with. It was only a matter of time before her boss called her and assigned her a new project.

Clearly, she would have to tell him what happened. But she dreaded that. The man paid her extremely well but demanded results. Fast results, not excuses.

Just then Hans Kruger came into the room.

"What the hell do you want?" she yelled.

He held his palms in front of him. "Sorry to disturb you. But I wanted to give you an update on how things were going."

She took a long breath and let it out slowly to calm herself. Then she slumped onto one of the lumpy couches in the room. "Go ahead. I'm sorry to snap at you, but I'm in a horrible mood."

He sat across from her. "Understandable. Besides myself, there are only five operatives left. I put them up at a hotel nearby."

"What happened to the others?"

"When we fled Tokyo, only five agreed to come to Osaka. I think the firefight and the police raiding our building scared the others."

Nikita tilted her head. "Did you offer them more money to come?"

"Of course. But that didn't work. Four of our operatives were killed in the firefight. That scared the rest most of all."

Nikita mulled that over. "Do you have any good news for me? I could use it."

He shook his head. "No."

She ground her teeth and almost told Kruger to go to hell. But she said nothing, knowing that would be unproductive. She needed him now more than ever. He was her smartest operative. She would need his expertise even more now, since the group was so small.

"I'm giving you a raise," she said, her voice calm.

"Really?"

"Yes. I'm doubling your pay, starting now."

"Thank you, Nikita."

She pointed at the front door. "Now get out of the house. I need to make an important phone call, and I need privacy."

Kruger stood. "As you wish."

The man left and closed the door behind him. She heard him locking it from the outside, then she heard his car drive away.

Nikita took her encrypted phone out of her pants pocket and stared at it, knowing the call would be difficult. But it was unavoidable.

She pressed the numbers she had memorized long ago.

When her boss answered, she said, "It's Nikita."

"I am so glad you called," he replied. "In fact, I was just thinking about you."

"You have a new assignment for me?"

"No, my dear Nikita. I was thinking about our personal relationship."

His words sent a chill down her spine.

The last time the two had been together, it had been dreadful. The sexual things he had demanded from her had made her feel dirty. Afterwards, she had taken three showers to make herself feel clean. She had hated the sex, but most of all, she hated that he was fully in control.

"I'm calling about a problem I'm having," she said. "I needed to make you aware of it."

"What kind of problem?"

"Somehow, the police have learned about my operation in Tokyo."

"How is that possible?" he said, his voice stern. "You have been so careful."

"Yes, that's true. But still, it's happened."

"Are you still in Tokyo now?"

"No. I'm at a new location. A safe house in Osaka."

"Do you have everything there to continue the operation? I have identified some new targets that need that need to be eliminated."

Nikita glanced around the small, plain living room. "No, not really."

"I have a solution for you. The perfect solution."

"What's that?" she said.

"You can come here. To my location. I have plenty of room for you and your team."

Nikita ground her teeth, and bile rose up her throat. She hated the idea. Loathed it, in fact. If she was based at his location, he would have access to her all the time.

"I don't know," she said, hesitantly.

"I insist, Nikita. You will love it."

Nikita's thoughts raced as she tried to come up with an alternate plan. After another tortured moment, she realized she had no other option.

"Say yes," he said, his voice gruff.

"Yes. I agree."

"Excellent. I will begin to prepare for your arrival."

Chapter 66

Tokyo, Japan

J.T. Ryan and Keiko Kanata were now at the small restaurant of the Wakana Hotel, the inn where he was staying. After finishing up at the Tokama building, she had driven them to the inn in her tiny Suzuki sedan.

Keiko was drinking *sake* and Ryan was sipping Sapporo beer. It had been a long day, and they were trying to unwind over a few drinks.

Keiko held up her glass and clinked it with his beer mug. "To a good day. We made a lot of progress, John. Thanks to you."

"I would feel a hell of a lot better if we had found the ringleader."

"That will come. I am sure of it."

"You sound confident, Keiko."

She gave him a small smile. "I am. We make a good team."

"You're right. We do make a good team."

Just then her cell phone rang and she took it out of her pocket. Then she listened for a moment and spoke rapidly in Japanese. Several minutes later she hung up the call.

Keiko's face lit up in excitement. "That call was from the lead technician of the Tokyo police. In one of the computers we found at the Tokama building, they located a photo and the name of the ringleader, Nikita."

Ryan's hope surged. "That's great! Who is she?"

"Her full name is Nikita Nakano, and she's listed as the owner of the Tokama Import Export Company. Our tech man is texting me her photo."

Her cell phone buzzed, and she opened the text. Then Keiko gave him her phone.

A beautiful Japanese woman was shown on the screen. It was difficult to tell Nikita's age, but she was gorgeous, with long, straight black hair and piercing and intelligent black eyes.

Ryan placed the phone on the table. "Now that we have this," he said, "we can start tracking down her whereabouts."

"My tech man is already working on that," Keiko said. "He does not think we will find her right away, but soon."

"Great," he said. "We should celebrate. Let's order a new round of drinks." He motioned to the waitress, held up two fingers, and she went into the kitchen to get another round.

"And I need to eat something also," Ryan said. "I'm starved."

"I can order for us, John."

"Good idea. But I don't want any Japanese food. I've had enough squid, ramen noodles, and *tempura* to last me a lifetime."

Keiko laughed. "What would you like then?"

"I'd love a hamburger and French fries. But they're not on the menu. I checked last time we were here."

"I think they will make it," she said, "if I ask them nicely."

The waitress came back and served them a fresh round of drinks.

Then Keiko spoke to her in Japanese.

The waitress kept shaking her head, and repeating the word *Ie*, which Ryan knew was 'no' in Japanese.

After another long moment of argument, Keiko pulled out her police badge and showed it to the other woman.

The waitress's eyes got big, and she finally nodded and said, *Hai*, which is 'yes'.

The waitress went back to the kitchen.

"I tried being nice," Keiko said. "But since that did not work, I told her I was a police officer and would send food inspectors to visit this restaurant if she didn't make the American food you wanted."

Ryan laughed. "Good for you."

Fifteen minutes later they were served hamburgers and French fries. To his surprise, the food was excellent.

They finished eating and then ordered another round of drinks.

When they were done, she said, "I am feeling a little woozy from all the *sake*. The drive to my apartment is an hour long. I need to rest a bit before I leave."

"No problem, Keiko. I'll pay the bill, and we can go up to my room. You can rest there until you're okay to drive. How does that sound?"

"Yes, that would be good."

Ryan paid the bill, and they went up to his hotel room. The room was small and was furnished with only a bed, a desk, and two chairs.

Keiko sat down on one of the chairs and Ryan sat on the other.

She lowered her gaze to the floor. "I need to be honest with you, John."

"About what?"

She looked up at him. "I was not totally honest with you at the restaurant. I am not woozy. I just wanted to … spend more time with you …."

Ryan studied her pretty face. She was an adorable looking young woman. She was wearing black slacks, a black jacket and a white blouse.

She blushed. "You are staring at me."

"I'm sorry. You're very attractive."

"You really think so?"

"I do, Keiko."

"Can I ask you something?"

"Of course."

"I asked you one time if there was a Mrs. Ryan and you said yes, there is, and she was your mother."

Ryan laughed. "Yeah, I remember."

"You were joking around then, but I need to know. Are you married?"

"No."

"Are you engaged?"

"No."

"Are you involved seriously with a woman, John?"

Ryan thought about Amanda Johansen and the beautiful time they had spent together in Amsterdam.

"I was with a lovely woman last month. But she lives far away from me. And to tell you the truth, I don't know if anything will come from that."

Keiko nodded. "I am glad you are not attached."

"Why is that?"

She lowered her gaze. "I like you. A lot. I hope we can become close."

"Are you sure about this, Keiko?"

"Yes."

Ryan pulled his chair next to her and put his arm around her. She was beautiful but also tiny and fragile.

She rested her head on his brawny chest, and he gently stroked her long, black hair. It felt good.

"When we first met," he said, "I noticed you were attractive right away, but you look so young. How old are you?"

"Twenty-five."

Ryan smiled. "I thought you were eighteen, at most."

She giggled. "We Asian women always look young to Western men. It's our doll-like faces, so I am told."

He continued gently stroking her hair and she pressed herself against him tightly. He felt himself becoming very aroused.

"I have to ask you something," he said, "and it's important."

"What?"

"Do you have any experience?"

"What do you mean, John?"

"You know, have you been intimate … with a man before? I don't want to take your innocence away."

She rubbed his chest with her dainty hand. "Yes. A little. I was with one man before."

"Are you still together?"

"Oh no. He left me, right after, you know, we did it."

"I bet that was difficult for you," he said.

"Yes, John. I cared for him. Very much. I thought we would be together for a long time. Maybe forever."

He held her closer, and she felt wonderful in his arms.

She looked up at him. "Will you kiss me, please."

Ryan leaned in and pressed his lips to hers and she kissed him back hungrily. They kissed for a long time, and it felt wonderful to him. Clearly it was great for her also.

When they broke off the kiss a moment later, they were both breathing heavy.

Ryan caressed her cheek gently. "You're so beautiful. But you're such a small woman. I don't want to hurt you in any way."

Her eyes were shiny with anticipation. "I am not as fragile as I look, John."

"You're sure about this?"

"Yes, very sure."

They kissed again, and then he carried her to the bed.

Chapter 67

Tokyo, Japan

It was dim in the hotel room, but J.T. Ryan could still see well enough to observe Keiko's lovely nude body. The young woman was lying on her side next to him on the bed. She was still asleep.

It had been a beautiful night for both of them.

Ryan lightly traced his hand over her face and then smoothed down her long, lustrous black hair.

Just then her eyelids fluttered open, and she smiled.

He kissed her gently and she returned the kiss.

"Are you hungry?" he said. "We can call the restaurant downstairs and have them make breakfast."

Keiko grinned and kissed him hard. When they broke the kiss, she said, "I am hungry for something else."

Ryan laughed. "For being a small woman, you have a big appetite."

She laughed also.

Just then her cell phone rang, and she grabbed it from the nightstand.

Keiko listened for a moment then replied in rapid Japanese.

Turning off the call, she said. "The tech people found her."

"Nikita Nakano?"

"Yes. They tracked her down to Osaka. That is a city about 300 miles southwest of Tokyo."

"How did they track her down?"

"She boarded a flight to there, then she rented a car at the airport in Osaka."

"Where is she now?"

"The Osaka police are trying to trace her whereabouts from the rental car's GPS. They should locate her soon."

"That's great news, Keiko. We should go to Osaka right away."

"Yes, we should."

"How long to get there?" he said.

"An hour by plane, or we can take the Shinkansen Bullet Train. That would take 2 ½ hours."

"Okay. Let's get dressed and we'll go."

Chapter 68

Osaka, Japan

Nikita was pacing the small living room of the safe house, her thoughts still in overdrive. She hated the idea of leaving Osaka and going to her boss's location but hadn't been able to come up with a better solution.

Clearly staying here in the safe house was going to be impossible. Without computer equipment and with such limited space, running a far-flung operation was going to be beyond difficult.

Just then she heard the wail of police cars, and by the level of the sound, she could tell it was far away.

But the howl got louder, and she raced to her bedroom, and quickly threw some clothes in an overnight bag.

Then she sprinted out of the home, not bothering to lock the door.

Chapter 69

Osaka, Japan

The Osaka police car drove onto the driveaway of the small home and stopped.

Keiko Kanata thanked the driver, a uniformed cop, and she and J.T. Ryan climbed out of the car.

There was a Toyota SUV parked in the driveway and Keiko pointed to it. "Nikita rented that SUV at the airport. But she left it here. The police who searched her home a few hours ago told me they found no one in the house."

"She's one step ahead of us," Ryan stated, shaking his head slowly.

"That is true, John. She is a smart woman."

"Deadly and smart."

There was a uniformed police officer posted at the front of the home and Keiko held up her shield for him to inspect.

Then she and Ryan entered the small house.

He glanced around the tiny living room. "This is nothing like her luxurious apartment in Tokyo. This looks like a safe house to me."

"I agree."

They searched the rest of the dwelling and came back to the living room. They had found no clues to her current whereabouts.

"How do we find her now?" Keiko asked.

"I don't know. She could have gone anywhere."

Chapter 70

Beijing, China

Nikita was waiting in the lobby of the China Film Group (CFG) headquarters building. She had been there many times before and was a familiar face at the CFG.

Nikita had been waiting in the lobby for half an hour, but she was used to the wait. She knew her boss always made his guests wait before meeting him. It was another way for him to maintain control.

Soon after the elevator opened, and a young Chinese woman stepped out. As usual, she was dressed in her PLA military uniform.

Nikita stood and shook hands with her. "It is good to see you again, Colonel Liu."

"And I you, Nikita." Colonel Liu had been General Zhang's assistant in all the years Nikita had known him.

Liu led the other woman to the elevator, and they took it to the top floor of the CFG building.

Then Nikita was shown into General Zhang's office. Since he was chairman of the China Film Group (CFG), the largest film company in China, General Zhang's office was lavishly furnished. It had a breathtaking view of Beijing's downtown skyline.

General Zhang Wei was seated behind his desk. As usual, he was wearing his People's Liberation Army military uniform. He stood, walked around his desk, and grinned widely.

"It is so good to see you, my dear Nikita."

She plastered a fake smile on her face. "It's great to see you also."

He was an obese man, with heavy jowls and a fleshy face, but his perfectly tailored uniform hid most of his grossly overweight body.

Zhang hugged her and she almost recoiled from his embrace, then forced herself to hug him back.

He motioned toward the conference table in the room. "Let us sit there. Would you like something to drink or eat? I can have Liu bring it to you."

"No, I'm good."

Zhang sat at the head of the table, and she took a chair close by.

"From our phone conversation," he said, interlacing his fat fingers on the table, "I understand the authorities in Japan learned of your operation?"

"That's right, General."

He pursed his fleshy lips. "How did it happen? You have been so careful, and so successful for such a long time."

Nikita shrugged. "It's unclear. The important thing is they did. I had no option but to leave Tokyo."

He nodded. "Of course. Well, since we talked, I've arranged for your operation to be based here, in Beijing."

"Here, in the CFG building?"

He gave her one of his sharklike grins, which had no humor in it. "No, not here. I must maintain plausible deniability for your operation."

"I understand, General."

She noticed the obese man's face was sweating, something else that repulsed her about him. Even though it was extremely cool in his office, the man was always perspiring.

He took out a handkerchief and mopped his brow. Then he spent the next ten minutes describing the facilities he had set up for her operation. When he was done, he asked, "How many of your operatives did you bring with you?"

"Six. Hans Kruger and five others."

"That is all, Nikita? But you had many more."

"That's true. But some were killed during the police raid, and the others didn't want to come to China."

"You will have to hire more," he said.

"Of course."

She had always wondered something about the operation, and since she was going to be located in China, decided to ask it now.

"It was never clear to me," Nikita said, "the purpose of the operation. I know you wanted movie people eliminated. The reason for that was never clear."

General Zhang wiped his brow with the handkerchief again. "I never told you, since it was not important for you to know. But since you are here, you will find out eventually."

There was a laptop computer on the conference table, and he powered it up and turned the screen so she could see it. Then he opened a computer file labeled: China Film Group.

The file showed a diagram. The top box of the diagram was the Chinese Communist Party. The box below that was the Central Propaganda Department, and beneath that was the China Film Group. The diagram was very detailed after that, and she stopped reading it.

"As you can see on the chart," Zhang said, "the CFG reports to the Propaganda Department, who ultimately reports to the CCP. You may not be aware of this, but the Chinese Communist Party controls every major policy decision in China. Many years ago, the CCP decided that it was important to shape public opinion around the world. The end goal of all of this to make China the dominant world power, replacing the United States."

He gave her another one of his sharklike grins. "China is a communist country, so the CCP can tell Chinese citizens what to do, and what to say, and by indoctrination, what to think."

He placed his fleshy hands flat on the table. "But beyond that, what the CCP wants, and what I also want, is to shape people's thinking worldwide, especially in America. And what better way to do that than create movies that showcase Communist China in a positive way?"

Nikita was now beginning to understand what it was all about.

The general wiped his brow again. "Since the China Film Group has tremendous financial resources, all of which are provided by the CCP, we finance many American films. And we have for many, many

226

years. Of the hundred highest-grossing American films released between 2014 and 2018, we at the China Film Group financed 41 of them."

Nikita's eyes widened, now realizing the extent of Zhang's control over the movie business.

"And since we finance these films," the general continued, "we control the content. The Chinese people in the movies are always the heroes, and China is portrayed as a beautiful and honorable country."

"Since you have that much control," she asked, "why do you need my operation?"

He began perspiring again and he wiped his face with the handkerchief. "Unfortunately, Nikita, not everyone is greedy at the movie studios. There are still influential people that don't want to portray China as a bastion of truth and justice. These people have scruples, and they cling to the idea that America is a just and noble country."

"That's why these people have to be eliminated?" she asked.

"Exactly."

"I understand now." She considered this for a long moment. She didn't really care or understand geopolitics. All she cared about was money, and the power and freedom it gave her. In a strange way, she mused, she was just like the greedy Hollywood producers, willing, even eager, to do whatever it took to get wealthy, no matter what the consequences.

"Do you have any more questions, Nikita?"

"No. I get the full picture now."

"Good." He closed the computer file and turned off the laptop. Then he said, "Now that you will be working and living here in Beijing, it will give us more time together. It is something I have always wanted."

She had been dreading this part of the conversation.

But she knew it was only a matter of time before he brought it up.

"My dear Nikita," he said suggestively. "You are looking extremely ravishing today. It is difficult for me to keep my hands off you."

She swallowed hard, already recoiling from the thought of his fat, sweaty hands touching every inch of her body. Recoiling from the thought of him penetrating her. The idea repulsed her, but she forced herself to ignore it.

"Your assistant is pretty," Nikita said. "I'm surprised you don't use her for your sexual needs."

Zhang waved a hand in the air. "Yes, yes, she is adequate. And very willing. But she is no Nikita."

His eyes were bright with lust.

He picked up the handset of the phone that was resting on the table, and said, "Colonel Liu, hold my calls. And I don't want to be interrupted for any reason."

Zhang hung up the phone and swiveled his chair so that he faced Nikita.

"You know what I want," he said, with a leer.

She didn't move, but instead continued sitting in the chair, paralyzed by her tortured thoughts. She dreaded what was to come, although she had submitted to him many times before.

His cold grin turned dark, his face red and angry now.

Sweat continued to bead on his forehead, and she could smell the dank, acrid odor emanating from him. General Zhang hardly bathed, she knew, another thing she hated about him.

"You know what to do!" he commanded, his voice ice cold now. "Get on your knees, Nikita! Do it now!"

And she did.

Then he unzipped his pants.

Chapter 71

Tokyo, Japan

J.T. Ryan and Detective Keiko Kanata took the Shinkansen Bullet Train from Osaka to Tokyo, then she drove them from the train station to the Tokyo Police Department building on Kasamigaseki Avenue.

The two of them were having lunch now, at the building's cafeteria. They were seated at a booth toward the back, and since it was midafternoon, there were few cops eating at the time.

"What do you think we should do now?" Keiko asked.

Ryan stopped eating his ham sandwich, the only thing on the menu that looked appetizing. "We need to go back to the Tokama building and check out Nikita's apartment again."

She frowned. "We already did that before we went to Osaka. Why go back?"

"I feel like we missed something. Some evidence that might lead us to her whereabouts."

"What do you think we will find, John?"

"A clue would be good."

"Okay. After we eat, I will drive us over."

Ryan had been thinking about something on the train ride from Osaka, but had not brought it up, and neither had Keiko.

"What happened the other night was great," he said, keeping his voice low.

She gave him a shy smile. "It was. It was very special."

"I've given it a lot of thought, Keiko. And I want to apologize. I should have stopped myself from … making love to you."

"But why? You did not do anything wrong. I wanted it as much as you did. It was beautiful. I enjoyed it as much as you did, John."

"I know. It's just …."

He covered one of her dainty hands with one of his brawny ones. "After we solve this case, I'll go back home to the U.S. You know that, right?"

"Yes, I know."

"So, what we're doing is only going to be temporary. And that's not fair to you, Keiko."

She looked puzzled. "What do you mean?"

"I'm sure you want to get married eventually. Have children. Live here in Japan and raise your children here with your husband."

"Yes. My parents want that for me … and I want it too."

"I can't give you that. I'm an American and I love my country. I want to live there. Do you understand?"

She nodded and her eyes misted over. "I understand. It makes me sad, but I do understand."

"Anyway, I'm not the kind of man you want. I'm not really a good man. I kill people and hurt people for a living. It's what I've done my whole life."

She squeezed his hand. "The people you kill are evil. They need to be killed."

"Probably. But still. I can't give you the kind of life you want, long term."

She wiped a tear from her cheek, then lowered her head. She covered her face with her hands, and she sobbed quietly for a few minutes.

Eventually she raised her eyes and gazed at him. "I understand what you are saying. I do not like it, but I understand."

She was distraught, and he hated seeing her that way.

Grinning, he said, "I've got some new jokes. Would you like to hear them?"

She took out a handkerchief and she wiped away her tears. "Yes. I would like that."

"Okay," he said. "Do you know why you should borrow money from pessimists?"

"Why?"

"They don't expect it back."

She smiled a bit.

"I got another one, Keiko. I tried to be a taxi driver, but I quit. I didn't like people talking behind my back."

She grinned and he could tell she was feeling better.

Then Ryan said, "A bartender is just like a pharmacist with a limited inventory."

Keiko laughed. "You are funny."

"I have more if you like."

She squeezed his hand. "I am feeling better now. You can stop."

He grinned. "All right."

They finished eating and Ryan paid the bill.

Then they left the cafeteria and went down to the parking garage. Once again Ryan squeezed into her tiny Suzuki sedan, and she drove them to the Tokama Import Export building.

***

Ryan and Keiko spent two hours methodically searching Nikita Nakano's apartment on the penthouse floor of the building.

When they were done, Keiko shook her head. "We found nothing, John."

"I know. I was sure we'd find some clue to her current location."

"What should we do now?"

Ryan mulled this over for a long moment. "You brought your laptop with you?"

"Yes. It is in my messenger bag."

"And you downloaded the info your tech guys obtained from Nikita's operation to your computer?"

"That is right, John. But we already went through that information."

Ryan rubbed his jaw. "Maybe we missed something."

She looked doubtful, then shook her head. "I think it is a waste of time."

"Humor me."

She nodded. She went to her messenger bag, took out her laptop, and placed it on the dining room table. Then she powered it up and they sat in front of it and spent the next three hours laboriously reading the vast amounts of data that it contained.

They stopped for a few minutes, and she made them sandwiches in the sumptuous kitchen. They ate quietly and when they were done, they went back to her computer.

Several hours later, she yawned, obviously tired from the laborious and boring search.

"There is nothing here," she said, yawning again.

Ryan nodded. "You may be right. But I hate giving up." Then he said, "If you want to go and sleep for a while, go ahead. I'll continue to work on this."

"Are you sure?"

"Yeah. I'll be fine."

Keiko glanced around the living room, noticed the large sofa there. "I will take a nap in the living room."

"Why don't you sleep in the master bedroom. There's a king size bed there that would be more comfortable."

Keiko tilted her head. "And sleep in Nikita's bed?"

"Why not? She's not coming back. She's gone for good."

"All right. But you will wake me if you find something?"

Ryan smiled. "I will."

The young Japanese woman went into the bedroom and Ryan continued searching through the countless files on her computer.

After a couple of hours, he yawned, went to the kitchen and made himself a pot of coffee. He drank one cup, and refilled it, then went back to the laptop.

Then he pored over the endless files, as he sipped coffee. It was an exhausting process, tedious and boring work. People always thought being a PI was cool and sexy, like they show in the movies and TV. But at lot of PI work, he knew from experience, was just like this.

After drinking the whole pot of coffee, he made himself another pot and went back to the laptop.

Glancing at his watch, he noted it was 3:15 a.m. He yawned and almost gave up then, but pushed himself to continue.

At 4 a.m. he found a hidden file, a file that was buried behind several empty ones.

It was a travel schedule, with itineraries for trips Nikita Nakano had taken.

He glanced through the long list and noticed something interesting right away.

Many of the trips were to one location.

Beijing, China.

Why is that? he pondered. *What's in Beijing?*

Confused but also elated by what he had found, he raced into the bedroom and turned on the overhead light.

Keiko was stretched out on the bed, sleeping. She was still wearing her white blouse and gray slacks, and she was hugging the big pillow tightly. She looked adorable and he hated waking her up, but knew it was what she wanted.

Ryan sat on the edge of the bed and shook her gently. "Keiko, wake up."

Her eyelids fluttered open, and she yawned. "What is it ...."

"I found something," he said, grinning. "I found where she could have gone."

Keiko bolted up from the bed and sat up. "Where?"

"China."

She looked puzzled. "China? What's there?"

Ryan shook his head. "I don't know. But I found her travel itinerary for the last two years. She went to Beijing many, many times. In fact, most of her trips were to there."

Keiko grinned. "You did it, John."

"We did it." He smiled. "It was a team effort."

"Like Batman and Robin."

Ryan laughed. "Yeah, like that." Then he turned serious, as he considered the implications of his finding.

"China is a communist country," he said. "I can't just go there and track her down easily. The Chinese government controls everything there, including travel. I know you have to be issued a visa just to visit the country."

"That is true, John. And I cannot help you if you go there and get arrested. I may be a detective in the Tokyo police force, but that means nothing to the Chinese government. In fact, Japan and China see each other as enemies."

"I've heard that. Which leaves me with a big problem. What do I do next?"

She shook her head. "I do not know."

Chapter 72

Tokyo, Japan

Several days later Detective Keiko Kanata drove J.T. Ryan to Narita airport. She parked her tiny Suzuki at the curb of the departing flights terminal and they both climbed out.

After getting his bag from the trunk, they looked at each other, not sure what to say. On the drive to the airport, they barely spoke, both realizing they might not see each other again after today. He was flying back to Atlanta, recognizing there was nothing else he could learn in Japan.

Ryan gazed down at her.

Her beautiful face was marred by her sad eyes. He wrapped his muscular arms around her and held her close.

They said nothing for a long moment, enjoying the intimacy.

When they separated, she looked up at him with her pretty, but red-rimmed eyes.

"Kiss me, please," she whispered. "One last time."

He did and they held the gentle and loving kiss for a long time.

When they ended the kiss, she caressed his cheek.

"*Daisuki. Aishiteru,*" she whispered. It was a Japanese phrase he didn't understand.

"What does that mean, Keiko?"

She smiled, but it was a sad smile. "You can look it up. Now go, John Ryan. Or you will miss your plane."

Ryan picked up his bag and turned toward the terminal building. He strode toward it, weaving around the throngs of Japanese and the other travelers from around the world.

When he reached the double door to the building, he glanced back toward Keiko. She was still standing there by her car, waving. He could see the tears flowing down her cheeks.

Ryan was feeling the same emotions she was, and he almost ran back to her.

But he realized his time in Japan was over.

He waved back and went inside the terminal.

Chapter 73

Atlanta, Georgia

J.T. Ryan's flight from Tokyo to Atlanta lasted over 20 hours, which included a refueling stop in Los Angeles.

When he finally got back to his apartment in midtown at 8 a.m. local time, he was tired and ready for bed. But he was eager to get started on the case again. So instead of going to bed, he showered, shaved, and changed clothes. After making himself coffee and scrambled eggs for breakfast, he pulled out his phone and made a call.

"It's Ryan," he said, when GBI Agent Kelly O'Hara picked up.

"You're back," she said. "That's good. We've got a lot to discuss. Did you find out where Nikita Nakano is?"

"Yes and no."

"What the hell does that mean, Ryan?"

"I believe she's in China. Probably in Beijing. But getting to her and arresting her there is going to be difficult."

"China. You're right. Arresting her there won't be simple," she replied. "But we've got an additional problem to deal with."

"What's that, Kelly?"

"There's been another movie murder."

"You're kidding."

"I don't kid around about murder," she said, her voice stern. "You should know that by now."

"Yeah, you're right. Where did the killing take place?"

237

"Vancouver, Canada."

Ryan thought about that for a moment and recalled that many American movies were filmed in Canada. It was much cheaper than in the U.S.

"Okay, Kelly. I guess I'll be heading to Vancouver next."

"That's right."

"Now we know something for sure."

"What's that, Ryan?"

"Nikita may not be in Japan anymore, but her operation is still continuing."

Chapter 74

Vancouver, Canada

J.T. Ryan had caught a Delta flight from Atlanta to Vancouver that same day and checked into a hotel near the city's scenic waterfront.

Ryan had been to Vancouver several times before and had always enjoyed it. The beautiful city featured picturesque natural beauty and a bustling, vibrant urban setting. It was a great destination for tourists from around the world, with plenty of restaurants, parks, and attractions. Among the many notable sites were the Harbour Centre, Canada Place, the Vancouver Art Gallery, Granville Island, and Stanley Park.

After checking into the hotel, Ryan drove his rented Ford Mustang to Stanley Park, the site of the most recent murder.

Stanley Park, a 1000-acre wooded area only a few blocks from downtown, was a popular spot for locals and tourists. The park featured numerous hiking trails, fir and cedar trees, beaches, and wonderful views of the Vancouver harbor. Ryan had been there several times before and enjoyed the park's natural beauty.

Ryan had called ahead and arranged to meet the lead police detective at the park. The murder had taken place near a parking lot adjacent to a hiking trail.

He parked the Mustang and climbed out, immediately spotting the yellow crime scene tape roping off the hiking trail. There were numerous Vancouver PD vehicles parked in the lot, and Ryan approached one of the uniformed officers. After identifying himself, the cop pointed him toward a plainclothes man on the hiking trail.

Ryan went under the crime scene tape and approached the man.

"I'm J.T. Ryan," he said. "Are you Detective Miller?"

"I am." The detective was a tall, lean man in his fifties with salt and pepper hair.

The two men shook hands and Ryan said, "Thanks for agreeing to see me, Detective."

"Not a problem. In fact, I'm glad you're here. I could use the help."

Ryan glanced down at the gravel and dirt trail and spotted the white tape outlining where the body had been. There were splotches of dark red on the ground also.

"It all happened right here," Miller said.

"I understand the victim was an actress."

"That's right, Ryan. Her name was Diane Monroe. She was famous, so I'm told. I don't go to the movies much, but apparently, she had been in several popular films."

"And she was working on a film now?" Ryan said.

"Yes. The movie was being filmed right here in Vancouver. As you may know, the Canadian movie industry is huge. In 2023, it had a production value of $ 12 billion dollars, with half that money coming from U.S. filmmakers. It's a lot cheaper to make films in our country than in the U.S. That's why I'm glad you're here. I'm getting a lot of heat to solve this case and solve it fast."

"I understand," Ryan said. "Was the filming of this movie here in Stanley Park?"

"No. It was being filmed on Vancouver Island. The actress who was murdered was just jogging on the trail. The hotel she was staying at is nearby."

"How was she killed?"

"Bullet wounds. Two shots. One to the body and a second one to the head."

"Caliber?"

"The M.E. thinks 9 mil."

Ryan mulled this for a moment. "Do you know what kind of movie they were making?"

"Sure do. She was starring in a superhero film. She was playing the lead role. The film was a sequel to the *Supergirl* movies."

Ryan glanced around the whole area carefully, looking up at the streetlamps above the nearby parking lot. He spotted something right away.

"There's a security camera up there on the streetlamp. Did you get any video?"

"Yeah. We got lucky there. The CCTV camera picked up a man wearing a hoody walking toward the trail. This happened at the time of when the murder took place."

"Have you been able to identify the man?" Ryan asked.

Miller shook his head. "No. The video is grainy, and the hoodie hides part of his face."

"I'd like to see it."

"Sure. I'll pull it up on my laptop. It's in my police car."

The two men left the trail and went to the parking lot. The detective booted up his computer and opened the video file.

Ryan watched the grainy, black and white video for several minutes, until a man in a hoody appeared on the screen. As the detective had said, it was difficult to identify who the man was.

Then the man turned his face and Ryan realized who it was immediately.

Ryan pointed to the computer screen. "I know who that is. His name is Kruger. Hans Kruger. He's a German assassin. A man I've been chasing for quite a while. He's killed several people in the movie industry."

"You're sure?"

"One hundred per cent."

"How can you be so sure?"

"Because he almost killed me. I'd know that bastard anywhere."

Chapter 75

Beijing, China

Nikita felt dirty.

She always did, after meeting with her boss. She had already taken two scalding hot showers, trying to scrub off the disgusting way he made her feel.

Nikita hated the sexual way he used her, hated the horrible things he made her do, but most of all she hated that he was in control. But she had no choice, she realized. Her expensive lifestyle would end without his financial support.

After soaping up her body one last time, she rinsed in the intensely hot water for another long moment.

Then she stepped out of the shower and dried herself. She slipped into a terrycloth robe and padded out of the bathroom, barefoot.

Going into the luxurious living room of her new apartment, she went to the liquor cabinet and poured herself a glass of *sake*. She sipped it slowly, the alcohol soothing her nerves.

Nikita glanced around the sumptuous living room. Although it was not as luxurious as her penthouse in Tokyo, her new condo was almost as good.

General Zhang had been true to his word, finding her this new place to live and setting up a new operations center.

Still, she knew that long term, it would not work. She despised Zhang and was repulsed by the sexually degrading way he used her.

Nikita sat on the suede leather sofa, and as she continued sipping *sake*, she powered up her laptop, which was resting on the teak coffee table.

After logging on to her VPN, she went online and accessed her Swiss bank accounts.

She scrolled down the long list of assets, money she had accumulated over the years from her work as the operation center manager. There were many cash accounts, in a multitude of currencies. And there were also bonds and stocks of major companies from around the world.

Nikita grinned when she stared at the total value of her financial holdings.

She was close, she realized.

Very, very close.

If she could hold on for a bit longer, she could turn her dreams into reality.

Just then she heard the chime of her apartment ring.

Getting up, she went to the front door and checked the security feed from the hallway. Seeing who it was, she opened the door and let the man inside.

"I just got back from my trip," Hans Kruger said. "You said you wanted to see me when I returned." She noticed the muscular man was wearing a black shirt and black slacks, his usual attire.

She closed the door to the apartment and motioned toward the living room.

"Let's go in there," she said, and Kruger sat on one of the couches. Nikita went to the liquor cabinet and poured out two glasses of *sake*. After handing one of the goblets to him, she sat across from him.

"Tell me what happened," she ordered. "Did things go the way I planned?"

"Yes. Everything was perfect. The actress has been terminated."

"Any problems?"

Kruger shook his head. "None. I was in and out of Vancouver in two days."

She sipped the *sake*. "Good. I'll have more work for you soon."

"All right, Nikita. Whatever you need."

He gave her a long, up-and-down look, appraising what she was wearing.

Nikita was dressed in only her terrycloth bathrobe.

"If we're done with business," he said with a leer, "we could go on to something more pleasant."

She considered this for a few minutes, recalling the many pleasurable times she'd had with Kruger.

But she felt different now.

Ever since she had moved to Beijing and had been subjected to Zhang's constant carnal demands, her desire for sex had evaporated.

Nikita shook her head. "Not today, Kruger. Not today."

Chapter 76

GBI Headquarters
Decatur, Georgia

"After I met with the Vancouver PD detective," J.T. Ryan said, "I spent three days looking for Kruger. But I found nothing."

Agent Kelly O'Hara tapped her pen on her desk. "You think he cleared out right after he assassinated the actress?"

"I do."

Ryan and Kelly were sitting in her office. She was at her desk, and he was on one of the visitors' chairs.

"So where are we on the case?" she asked.

He considered this for a minute. "We know Nikita Nakano's operation is still ongoing. The latest murder proves that. Kruger is one of her top assassins. We also know Nakano is no longer in Japan, and most likely in China now."

Kelly frowned. "China's a big country. With a population of one and a half billion people. Trying to find her in a place that massive is like looking for a needle in a haystack."

He smiled. "It would take an ace detective to find her. Lucky for you, I'm working the case."

She let out a long breath. "I know you're good. But you're not that good."

"Yeah, I know. But since Nakano traveled to Beijing several times, I'm guessing she may have relocated to there."

Kelly tapped her desk again. "And we have another problem. China is a communist country. You can't just waltz in there and arrest her. Assuming you can find her in the first place."

Ryan laughed. "You make it sound impossible."

She gave him a stern look, then her expression softened, and she smiled. "All right, tough guy. Tell me how you'd go about doing it."

"First thing, Kelly, I need a visa. You can't go into China without it. I traveled there years ago and got my visa from the Chinese Embassy in Washington."

"How'd you get it?"

"I was traveling with a tour group. I was on vacation that time."

"But this time you're not traveling with a tour group, Ryan."

"That's a fact. I'll need some type of cover." Ryan smiled. "I could pose as a comic, doing standup."

She shook her head, suppressing a grin. "That would never work."

"Why is that?"

"Because your jokes aren't funny!"

"Ouch! Are they that bad?"

"Yes!"

They both laughed at that.

"Okay," he said. "You're right, that won't work. So, let's come up with another cover."

They thought about this for a minute, and Ryan finally said, "I got it."

"What is it?"

"I'm a pretty good photographer. I could say I'm putting together a book of my photos of China. So, I'd have to visit the major cities in the country to take the pictures."

She considered this for a while. "It could work. I'll find out the application process for your visa and get that started."

"Great."

Then Kelly said, "Where would you start your search, when you get to China?"

"I've been thinking about that. I figure since Beijing is the city that Nakano visited the most, I'd start there."

"Okay, Ryan. By the way, do you speak Mandarin? I know that's the major language they speak in China."

He grinned. "Oh, yeah. I'm fluent in Mandarin."

"Bullshit."

"Wo jiao Ryan," he said. *"Ni hao ma, Kelly?"*

She tilted her head. "What did you say?"

"My name is Ryan. How are you, Kelly?"

She gave him a long look, appraising his veracity. "I still think you're bullshitting me."

"Lao shi nin hao, ni hen you qi zhi," he said.

She looked puzzled. "And what does that mean?"

"It means you're a beautiful woman."

Kelly frowned.

"Cut that out," she said. "I'm supposed to be your boss, remember?"

He laughed. "All right, I'll cut it out. But what I said is still true."

She pointed toward her office door. "Get out of here. I have a lot of work to do. And I also need to get your visa to China."

Ryan stood and gave her a half-salute. "Yes, ma'am."

Chapter 77

Beijing, China

J.T. Ryan's visa to China came through a week later and he booked an Air China flight from Atlanta into PEK, Beijing's largest airport. The flight took over 15 hours, not including the layover in Los Angeles, so by the time he landed in Beijing, he was tired and jetlagged.

When the plane landed, he reset his watch, since Beijing is 13 hours ahead of Eastern Standard Time.

Ryan grabbed his carryon bag and deplaned the Airbus A350, along with the other passengers. When he reached the terminal building, he took his camera out of his bag and slung it over his shoulder. Since he was supposed to be a photographer, he thought carrying the Canon would be a nice touch, especially going through Customs.

He collected his other luggage at the baggage area and got in line for Passport Control and Customs.

When his turn came, he gave the agent on duty his passport and visa and the man inspected them carefully.

Ryan spoke in Chinese to the man, although he was not nearly as fluent as he had led Kelly to believe. He had a rudimentary knowledge of Mandarin, hopefully enough to get him through this trip.

Soon after, he finished at the airport and took a taxi to his hotel. As he had done in Japan, he had decided not to drive a rental.

Ryan checked into the same JW Marriot Hotel he had stayed at on his previous trip to China. It was clean and modern and centrally located on Jia Guo Road, in the Chaoyang District of the city.

When he got to his room, he booted up his laptop and got on the internet. Then he went to Baidu, China's search engine. Baidu is that country's version of Google.

He searched for Nikita Nakano and found seventeen women by that name living in Beijing. Three of the women had their photos online and Ryan was able to rule them out when he compared them to the picture he had of Nakano. The other fourteen he would have to investigate further to see if one of them was the criminal he was seeking.

That done, he decided to call Kelly O'Hara. Before he left for his trip, she was in the process of searching for Nakano using GBI sources.

Getting out his phone, he tapped in her number. Since it was 7 p.m. in Beijing, he knew it would be 7 a.m. in Atlanta.

When she answered, he said, "Good morning, Kelly. Hopefully I'm not waking you up."

"I'll have you know," Kelly replied, her voice curt, "that I've been at the office for an hour already."

Ryan laughed. "Yeah. I figured that."

"How was your flight to China?"

"Long and tiring. Listen, the reason I was calling was to find out if you'd learned anything about Nakano's whereabouts."

"I've been working on that," she said. "We can trace her leaving Tokyo on a Japan Air flight and arriving in Beijing. She was on the flight manifest. But after that, there's no record of her."

"None at all?"

"No. It's almost like she left the Beijing airport and then disappeared without a trace."

Ryan considered this for a moment. "That's hard to believe. Everyone leaves a digital footprint these days. Any phone records?"

"No. She must be using an encrypted cell phone."

Ryan had already deduced this. "I agree. Maybe the reason you can't track Nakano is because she changed her identity after she landed in China."

"You think she's going by another name?"

"It's possible, Kelly."

"That's not good. Not good at all. That's going to make it much more difficult to find her."

"True," he said. "Listen, I've been doing online searches for Nakano using Baidu, the Chinese search engine. There's seventeen women with that name in this city, but by their photos I ruled out three of them. I'll track down the other fourteen. I'm hoping one of them is the criminal."

"Okay. Listen, Ryan. Try not to get arrested in Beijing. China's a communist country and their laws are super strict, especially with foreigners."

"Is that a note of concern I'm hearing?" he said with a chuckle. "I didn't know you cared that much about me."

He could sense her grimacing on the other end.

"That's not it at all," she said in a stern voice. "I need your help solving this case. And I'd have a hell of time springing you out of a Chinese prison."

"Yeah, you're right."

"You need to be careful, Ryan. There's been plenty of foreigners thrown into communist gulags. Remember Otto Warmbier? He was the American tourist who was sentenced to 15 years of hard labor in North Korea. All he did was steal a poster from a hotel. In prison he went into a coma and subsequently died."

Ryan recalled that. "I remember."

"So, you'll be careful?"

"I will, Kelly."

"You're not armed, are you?"

"Of course not. I left my gun at home."

"Good."

They talked for several more minutes and then hung up.

Then Ryan went down to the Marriott's restaurant on the first floor and had dinner. Luckily the menu included plenty of American style food and he was able to eat a good meal. He also drank two Tsingtao beers, a tasty lager he'd had on his previous trip to China.

Then he went back to his room and went to bed. He was tired from his long flight.

***

Ryan got an early start on his search the next morning.

He took a taxi to his first destination, and once they were on their way, he was glad he'd decided not to drive. The population of Beijing is over 22 million people, and the streets and avenues are choked with cars, trucks, vans, motorcycles, mopeds, bicycles, and pedestrians. The blare of honking horns and sirens was clearly audible inside the taxi. It was a madhouse of activity, made worse by the heavy smog over the city. The smog, which is caused by industrial production in Beijing, hangs like a blanket of gray haze over the whole area. He noticed many of the residents wore masks.

Ryan's first destination was an apartment building in the Fengtai district of the city. Located in the southwest part of Beijing, it was a working-class neighborhood, by the looks of it. The building seemed rundown, an unlikely place for Nakano to live, Ryan thought. He had been to her luxury apartment in Tokyo, and knew the woman lived extravagantly. But then again, she may have chosen it because it was a great place to hide out.

The building was ten stories, with no elevator, and Ryan climbed the stairs to the ninth floor. When he got to that floor, he strode to the right apartment, passing several residents along the way. Since most Chinese are not tall, he towered over them.

Expecting her to react negatively when she saw him, he braced himself before knocking on the door. Since he was not armed, he had to rely only on his fists.

Ryan knocked on the door and it was answered by a short and stooped elderly woman with white hair.

He spoke to her in Mandarin and after only a moment knew she was not the right Nakano. He thanked her and left the building.

He called Talixo, the cab company he had been using, and they picked him up a few minutes later.

Next Ryan headed to Qianmen, an exclusive district of the city. He had been to Qianmen on his previous trip, and knew the area was upscale, exactly the kind of place Nakano would enjoy living in. The Forbidden City, Tiananmen Square and the Temple of Heaven are all located there. Qianmen combines Qing Dynasty architecture with stores of international clothing brands, beautiful hutongs, and expensive restaurants.

The address he was looking for turned out to be a twenty-story luxury condo building.

After paying the cab fare, he went inside the sumptuous lobby, which was decorated with historic Chinese paintings and wall coverings. The space featured marble floors.

He took the elevator to the top floor and stepped out.

There were only four apartments on the floor, and he found the right one immediately.

Tensing himself once again, he rang the chime.

The camera over the door whirred to life and he knew the occupant was checking him out.

A moment later the door opened partway.

A beautiful, dark-haired Asian woman stood there, wearing a beige linen suit. At first, he thought it was her, but quickly realized this woman was much older.

Ryan spoke in Mandarin, asking her if she was Nikita Nakano.

The woman smiled. In English she replied, "Yes, I am Nikita. By the way, your Chinese accent is atrocious."

"Is it that bad?"

The woman laughed. "Yes. It is. Are you American? You sound American."

"I am."

"And you are looking for Nikita Nakano? That is a common name in Asia."

Ryan smiled. "So I gather." He took out the photo he had of the criminal and showed it to the woman. "This is the person I'm looking for. Do you recognize her?"

She took the picture and scrutinized it closely. "I do not recognize her. She is very beautiful."

"So are you."

The woman grinned. "I can see you are quite the charmer. Unlucky for you, I am already married."

Ryan laughed. "Yes, it is unlucky for me."

He took the photo and put it back in his jacket pocket.

Then he thanked the woman and left the condo tower.

After getting another taxi, he continued his search.

Chapter 78

Beijing, China

Nikita stepped out of the shower and dried herself. She slipped into a terrycloth robe and padded out of the bathroom, barefoot.

Going into the luxurious living room of her new apartment, she went to the liquor cabinet and poured herself a glass of *sake*. She sipped it slowly, the alcohol soothing her nerves.

She had spent the afternoon servicing General Zhang, hating every second of it. She despised the odorous Zhang and was repulsed by the sexually degrading way he used her, hated the vile sexual things he made her do. She loathed the touch of his sweaty, meaty hands on her, and hated the stench of his vile body odor.

But most of all she hated that he was in control.

Nikita's hatred of Zhang was reaching a boiling point. The loathing was so overwhelming that it made it hard for her to breathe. She needed to reconsider her future and make certain General Zhang was no longer a part of it.

Her thoughts were already turning to finding a way out.

Soon, she mused, her thoughts dark and tortured, *I will come up with a solution*.

Chapter 79

Beijing, China

The last three days had been a total bust, J.T. Ryan realized, as he got out of the cab and went into the Marriott Hotel.

Ryan had been able to track down all the fourteen Nikita Nakanos in Beijing. Unfortunately, none of them had been the right one.

He was convinced now that the criminal had assumed a new name and a new identity. Finding her was going to be extremely difficult.

Ryan went into his hotel room and took out his cell phone. Hopefully Kelly O'Hara had had better luck on her end.

Just as he was about to dial her number, his phone buzzed.

"I think I found her!" Kelly said, almost shouting.

"You located Nakano?"

"Yes! I think so!"

"That's great, Kelly."

"Remember when we talked last time, we thought she might have changed her identity?"

"I remember."

"Well, she did," Kelly said. "I did a search of passports issued by the Japanese government over the last couple of years. Using our GBI facial recognition programs, I compared Nakano's photo to the photos on all of those newly issued passports."

Ryan's enthusiasm grew. "And you found a match?"

"I did! It turns out there was a Japanese passport issued two years ago to a woman from Tokyo. Her photo is identical to Nakano's picture. I figure she paid off the right people and was able to obtain this new fraudulent identity."

"What's her new identity, Kelly?"

"The new name she's using is Mei Wang. My guess is once Nakano got to Beijing, she used her new identity to live there."

"That's great work!" he exclaimed. "I could kiss you right now!"

"Cut that out, Ryan. I'm supposed to be your boss, remember?"

He laughed. "How could I forget? You remind me every time we talk."

She said nothing for a while. "Am I that bad?"

"Yes, you are," he said, his tone playful.

"All right. I'll try not to be so uptight."

Then Ryan thought of something else. "Were you able to find out where Mei Wang lives in Beijing?"

"Not yet. I'm still trying to track her down."

"Okay. Call me as soon as you do."

"I will, Ryan."

They spoke for several minutes, said goodbye, and then hung up.

Ryan felt great.

They were close now.

Very close to catching the mastermind responsible for all the killings.

Chapter 80

Beijing, China

Nikita had finally figured it all out.

It had taken her a solid week to come up with her plan and work out the details.

It would not be easy, and it would not be without risk, but after she had implemented it, she would finally be free from General Zhang's clutches.

She despised him. And she despised herself for submitting to his degradation.

By Tuesday morning, all her plans were in place.

She felt a sense of relief, knowing that after today she would be free at last.

Since her meeting with General Zhang was not until this afternoon, she realized she could take a few hours this morning and visit a place she had never been to before. Although she had been to Beijing numerous times over the last several years, all those visits were business related, and she hadn't had time to do any sightseeing.

So, this morning she left her luxury apartment and took a cab to Beijing's most treasured and famous attraction, the Forbidden City. Located in the very heart of Beijing, the Forbidden City is officially known as the Palace Museum. China's most magnificent architectural complex, the huge palace was completed in the year 1,420 A.D. The palace was home to 24 Chinese emperors who ruled China for nearly 500 years. The Imperial Court lived there until 1912. In 1949, the palace grounds were open to the public as a museum.

Nikita spent three hours there, along with hundreds of other visitors. She explored as much of the palace as possible, enjoying the amazing historic architecture. She viewed the Outer Court, the Gate of Supreme Harmony, the Marble Carriageway, the Hall of Supreme Harmony, and the Imperial Gardens. There was so much to see that she realized it would take days to fully explore the extensive palace grounds. It is said that the Forbidden City has 9,999 rooms in the complex. Many of these rooms are ornate and extravagantly decorated with marble and gold.

After three hours exploring the Forbidden City, Nikita had lunch at a restaurant on the palace grounds and then took a cab to the headquarters building of the China Film Group.

Nikita was very prompt and got there five minutes before the appointed time.

Nevertheless, Nikita was kept waiting in the lobby for an hour. As usual, her boss was making her wait, something he did with all his guests as a way of maintaining control.

Eventually the elevator opened, and Colonel Liu stepped out. The young Chinese woman was wearing her PLA military uniform. Nikita had never seen her in any other attire.

Nikita stood and they shook hands. "It is good to see you again, Colonel Liu."

"And I you, Nikita."

Liu led the other woman to the elevator, and they took it to the top floor of the CFG building.

Then Nikita was shown into General Zhang's lavishly furnished office.

General Zhang Wei was seated behind his desk. Like always, he was wearing his People's Liberation Army uniform. He stood, walked around his desk, and grinned widely.

"It is so good to see you, Nikita."

She plastered a phony smile on her face. "It's great to see you also."

Zhang hugged her and she almost recoiled from his embrace, then forced herself to hug him back.

258

He motioned toward the conference table in the room. "Let us sit there. Would you like something to eat or drink?"

"No, I just had lunch. I'm fine."

Zhang sat at the head of the table, and she took a chair close by.

He interlaced his fat fingers on the table. "Is everything running smoothly at your new operations center?"

"Yes, General. The office space you set up for us has been excellent."

"And you have all the computer equipment you need?"

She nodded. "Yes. Everything we needed has been provided."

He pursed his fleshy lips. "And your new apartment? Is it satisfactory?"

"It's quite beautiful."

Zhang beamed. "Excellent. I spared no expense. I wanted everything to be perfect for you."

She forced a phony smile. "It is, General. You have been very generous."

She noticed the obese man's face was sweating heavily, something else that repulsed her about him. Even though it was extremely cool in his office, the man was always perspiring.

He took out a handkerchief and mopped his brow.

There was a laptop computer on the conference table, and he powered it up and turned the screen so she could see it. Then he opened a computer file labeled: China Film Group.

Then he spent an hour describing the next operations he wanted her team to undertake. Zhang gave her the details of the three movie industry people that needed elimination.

When he was done, he said, "Any questions?"

"No, General. These assignments are clear cut. I have no questions."

"Excellent."

He closed the computer file. Then he said, "Now that we have concluded our business discussion, we can turn to more enjoyable matters."

She had been dreading this part of the conversation, but knew it was only a matter of time before he brought it up.

"My dear Nikita," he said with a leer. "You are looking extremely beautiful today. It is difficult to keep my hands off you."

She swallowed hard, already recoiling from the thought of his fat, sweaty hands touching her body. Cringing from the thought of him penetrating her.

The idea repulsed her, but she forced herself to ignore it. The only thing that made it bearable was knowing that today would be the last time.

His eyes were bright with lust.

He picked up the handset of the phone that was resting on the table, and said, "Colonel Liu, hold my calls. And I do not want to be interrupted for any reason."

Zhang hung up the phone and swiveled his chair so that he faced Nikita.

"You know what to do," he demanded.

She didn't move, but instead continued sitting in the chair, paralyzed by her tortured thoughts.

She dreaded what was to come.

Impatient with her, he scowled, his face red and angry.

Sweat continued to bead on his forehead, and she could smell the acrid stench emanating from him. Zhang hardly bathed, another thing she hated about him.

"You know what I want!" he ordered, his voice harsh. "Get on your knees, Nikita!"

And she did.

Then he unzipped his pants.

Nikita almost ran out of the room but forced herself to continue.

Zhang gave her one of his icy sharklike grins, anticipating the pleasure she was about to give him.

"Do it now!" he growled.

Still on her knees, she reached with her hand and took his cock out of his pants. Then she began massaging him, the way he liked.

The general moaned with pleasure and closed his eyes, obviously relishing the moment.

Then he opened his eyes.

With a sneer he said, "Use your mouth now, Nikita. You know what to do."

But instead of opening her mouth, Nikita pulled out the knife she had in her pocket and slashed it across the base of his cock. Once, twice, three times, as blood spurted out, drenching his pants.

Zhang screamed, a bloodcurdling shout that, had the room not been soundproofed, would have been heard outside the office.

As he looked down at himself, horror on his face, he kept shrieking. His eyes were wide with terror and agony.

She was still holding on to his bloody cutoff cock, gore dripping from it. She opened her hand, and his bloody body part fell to the floor.

Her heart was racing, but her thoughts were triumphant.

For the first time since coming into his office today, she felt good. In fact, she felt great.

Zhang's screams turned into gasps, his body convulsing as he bled out. Moments later his body sagged, his eyes rolled white, and his head lolled on his chest.

Nikita got up from her knees and checked the man's pulse. Zhang was dead.

Then she went to the bathroom that was adjacent to the office. She washed the blood off her hands and went back into the office.

Taking a flash drive out of her handbag, she went to the computer that was on the conference table. Then she downloaded the China Film Group files that were on the laptop to the flash drive. She didn't know if she would ever need the information that was on there, but it could be valuable to her in the future.

That done, she picked up her handbag and hung it over her shoulder.

Nikita left the general's office and closed the door behind her. She stopped at Colonel Liu's desk and said to her, "General Zhang does not want to be disturbed. He's taking a nap now. He'll call you when he wakes up."

Liu gave her a knowing smile. "I understand, Nikita."

Liu, Nikita knew, had submitted to the general's sexual needs many times and was used to his habits.

Then Nikita left the China Film Group building and took a cab to PEK, Beijing's largest airport.

Once she got there, she retrieved her luggage from the lockers at the airport. She had packed and put her bags there yesterday.

Then she went to the ticket counter and presented her boarding pass and passport.

Thirty minutes later she was on a plane heading out of China.

Chapter 81

Beijing, China

J.T. Ryan's phone buzzed, and he took it out of his pocket.

"I found her!" he heard Kelly O'Hara say excitedly.

"You found Nakano?"

"Yes! I found out where she lives under her new name, Mei Wang."

"That's great, Kelly."

Kelly gave him the address in Beijing, and they spoke for several minutes. Then she said, "I want you to be careful. That woman is a ruthless killer."

Ryan laughed. "Yes, mom. I'll be careful."

"Don't kid around."

"Sorry," he replied, turning serious now. "I promise I'll be careful."

"Thank you. Have you figured out how to approach her?"

"Yeah. I've been working on that for a few days."

"Okay, Ryan. Call me if you need anything."

"I will."

"And please do not get arrested," she said, concern in her voice. "I'm a law-enforcement officer in the U.S. That means nothing to the Chinese government. If you get imprisoned, I'm not sure I can get you out."

Ryan had already considered this. "I know, Kelly."

They talked for several more minutes, said goodbye and hung up.

Ryan was in his hotel room at the Marriott, and he went to his laptop and booted it up. Then he did an online search for the address

263

Kelly had given him. It turned out that Nakano's apartment was located in Chaoyang, an upscale district of Beijing. He pulled up a map of the city and saw the Marriott was not far away from that area.

As he had told Kelly on the phone, he had spent the last few days preparing. He was going to use a ruse he used before in order to access her apartment.

Ryan had been able to obtain a FedEx uniform and cap and began putting it on now.

When he was done, he picked up the empty FedEx box he had obtained at one of their locations and left his room.

He took the elevator to the first floor and exited the hotel.

Recalling the map he had pulled up, he began walking.

It was early evening, and he figured by the time he reached the address, Nakano would be home from work.

As usual, the crowded city was a madhouse of activity. The streets were full of vehicles and the sidewalks were jam-packed with pedestrians.

A half-hour later he reached the right apartment building, which turned out to be a luxury condo tower fifty stories high. The building was situated among other upscale, contemporary structures. He noticed the pedestrians on the sidewalks were all well-dressed.

Ryan went into the lobby of the building, which had a beautiful five-story high atrium. The floors were marble, and the walls were decorated with expensive looking modern art. The whole place smelled of money. Big money.

There was a concierge behind a desk in the lobby and Ryan approached him.

He raised the FedEx package he was holding and spoke to the concierge in Mandarin.

The concierge replied and gave him directions to the condo unit, which was located on the penthouse floor of the building.

Ryan reached the right floor a while later and found the right apartment. Like the lobby, the floors on this level were made of marble and the walls were decorated with expensive looking modern art.

When he stepped in front of the impressive ornate door of Nakano's condo, he rang the chime. He tensed, preparing himself for the fight that was to come. He knew she was a cold-blooded killer and would be well armed, while he had to rely of his fists and brute strength to overpower her.

He waited and when there was no answer, he rang the chime again. Nothing happened. The security camera above the door did not power on, nor were there any footfalls from inside the condo.

Realizing the woman was not at home, he took out his lock pick set and worked on the door mechanism. After a moment he heard a click, and he turned the knob.

Ryan slipped inside and closed the door behind him.

It was dim in the spacious, beautifully decorated foyer.

The large space to the right of him, a luxuriously furnished living room, was also dim.

Could Nakano be asleep? he wondered. It was too early in the evening for that, he thought. Still, it was a possibility.

Staying absolutely quiet, he crept into the other rooms of the condo, including the dining room, the sumptuous kitchen, an office, and several bedrooms. All the rooms were vacant. There was no one in the apartment, he realized.

Turning on some of the overhead lights, he searched each of the rooms thoroughly. In the room that had been converted into an office, he found no computers or phones. However, he did see wiring and connections to computer printers.

In the office he found some files which clearly showed he was in the right place. Nikita Nakano's name was on several documents and receipts.

Ryan went back to the master bedroom and inspected it carefully. He found no documents there, but he saw that many of the hangers in the closet were empty. Only a few pieces of clothing remained. Clearly Nakano had fled.

Going into the luxurious master bath, he found no women's makeup and no hair products or toothbrushes.

It was clear that Nakano was gone.

"Damn it!" he said, realizing the criminal had gotten away once again. His hands tightened into fists, and his heart pounded in his chest. He had been chasing Nakano for months, halfway across the world, and he still had nothing to show for it.

Ryan gulped in air, and let it out slowly, trying to control his rage, knowing anger would solve nothing.

Going into the sumptuous kitchen, he opened the massive refrigerator. He saw several bottles of *Nongfu Spring*, China's most popular bottled water, and he took one.

He sat at the granite topped kitchen table and opened the bottle. He sipped it slowly, trying to sort his thoughts.

Knowing he was at a dead end for now, he took out his phone and dialed a number he had memorized.

When Kelly O'Hara answered, he said, "It's me."

"Did you find Nakano?"

"I'm in her apartment now," he replied. "Most of her clothes are gone and there are no computers or phones here. Looks to me like she fled."

"You're kidding."

"I wish I was," he said, in a dejected tone.

"Do you think she went somewhere else in China?"

"I don't know. But I'm pretty sure she's not coming back to Beijing any time soon."

"Damn it! We were so close!"

"I know, Kelly."

"What do we do now?"

"I'll stay here in Beijing and keep looking for her. Maybe I can find some clue to her whereabouts."

"I'll work the case from my end. Maybe I can track her down."

"That's good," he replied without enthusiasm, his voice morose.

"You sound terrible. Are you okay?"

"I feel like crap."

"I know what you mean, Ryan. I feel the same way. This woman is so damn elusive. We get close, then she vanishes."

They talked for several more minutes, said goodbye, and he hung up.

Chapter 82

Beijing, China

J.T. Ryan spent the following week trying to track down Nakano in Beijing. He tried to trace her whereabouts, but he came up empty.

Nakano had vanished without a trace.

And Kelly had not had any success either.

Realizing he was at a dead end, Ryan booked a Delta flight back to Atlanta.

A day later he was home, dejected at his lack of success.

Chapter 83

GBI Headquarters
Decatur, Georgia

"I spent a week looking for Nakano," J.T. Ryan said. "But I found nothing."

Agent Kelly O'Hara tapped her pen on her desk. "Do you think she's still somewhere in China?"

"I don't know. She fled Beijing. I found no trace of her there. And she never returned to her apartment."

Ryan and Kelly were sitting in her office. She was at her desk, and he was in one of the visitors' chairs.

Kelly frowned. "Why did she flee Beijing? There's no way she could have known we were close to catching her."

"I agree, Kelly. It must have been something else."

"So where are we on the case?" she asked.

Ryan shrugged. "Nowhere good."

They went quiet for a long moment, then Kelly said, "There is one positive development."

"What's that?"

"There have been no movie murders in the last three weeks."

"Yeah, that's true," he said. "Up until now, the killings were happening on a weekly basis. It's possible we disrupted her operation."

"Then it's a win for us," she replied, tapping her pen on her desk again.

"I agree. But I still need to catch her and bring her to justice. Nakano is a brutal killer and needs to pay for her crimes."

"We'll find her," Kelly replied, with no enthusiasm. It was clear that Kelly was just as disappointed as he was.

"By the way, where is Marie Dubois?" he said. "The French assassin I arrested in Tokyo."

"Dubois testified to the Tokyo police, and they transferred her to us. She's now being held here in Georgia at McRae Women's Prison. After her trial, she'll serve her time at the Supermax Prison in Florence, Colorado."

"That's good. She needs to pay for her crimes."

"She does," Kelly said. Then she smiled. "I have something for you that should improve your mood."

"What is it?"

Kelly reached into a desk drawer and removed a key fob, which she placed on her desk. "This is the key to the Corvette you bought from the GBI impound garage."

Ryan grinned widely. "I'd forgotten all about that. With all my traveling, that car was the last thing on my mind."

She slid the keys toward him. "Your check cleared, so it's all yours."

Ryan took the keys and put them in his pocket. "Thanks, Kelly."

"You said the Corvette needed work," she said. "But can I get a ride in it when it's fixed up?"

"You bet! I'll take you to the Varsity and we can have lunch there."

She grimaced. "I can't believe you eat there. It's all greasy food."

He smiled. "Chili dogs and onion rings? It's great food."

She let out a long breath and shook her head slowly. "Men."

Ryan laughed. "If there's nothing else, I'll get going then."

"Okay. I'm still going to continue working on the case. I've got a boatload of other cases, but I want to solve the movie murders."

"So do I," he said.

Ryan stood, they said goodbye, and he left her office.

Chapter 84

Atlanta, Georgia

J.T. Ryan was in the underground garage of his apartment building. His red Corvette was parked next to his Chevy Tahoe.

Ryan had just changed the oil and filter on the Corvette, which was a top-of-the-line Stingray Coupe 3LT model. It was almost brand new, although it had been driven hard. The tires were worn and there was some damage to the bodywork. The only reason he'd been able to buy it from the GBI at a great price was because it needed a lot of work. But he loved cars, so for him it was a labor of love.

Ryan wiped his greasy hands with a rag, then closed the lid of the mid-engine compartment. Opening the driver's door, he climbed inside and examined the tan leather seats of the sports car. Luckily the interior of the Corvette was spotless, unlike the exterior.

He pressed the ignition button, and the powerful 495 HP motor rumbled to life. The engine needed a tune-up, something he was looking forward to doing.

Ryan turned off the motor and got out of the Corvette. He inspected the bodywork and tires. The Michelin Pilot Sport 4S high-performance tires would need replacement, and they would be expensive.

Just then his phone buzzed, and he took it out of his jeans' pocket.

"Hi, Ryan," Kelly O'Hara said when he answered.

"Well, if isn't my favorite GBI agent."

"How many GBI agents do you know?" she replied.

"Besides you, none."

"So how can I be your favorite?"

Ryan laughed. "Good point, Kelly. What's up? Have you learned something new on the case?"

"No. But I'm still working on it. I'm calling about something else."

"What is it?"

"I've been offered a promotion at the GBI," she said, her voice guarded.

"That's great, Kelly! I'm glad for you."

"I'm not sure I should take it."

"Why?"

"I don't really know. It's hard to explain."

Ryan considered this and said, "Listen, let me take you to dinner. We can talk about it then."

"If you're thinking of taking me to the Varsity, forget it."

Ryan laughed. "No, not there. Someplace nice."

"Okay. But this is a business dinner. It's not a date. You're still working for me, and we need to keep our relationship professional."

"Yes, ma'am," he replied, trying not to laugh. Then he said, "I'll pick you up at your house at seven tonight."

"Let me give you my address."

"You don't need to. I'll find it. I'm an ace detective, remember?"

"Do you ever stop joking around?"

He laughed. "No."

"See you at seven."

They said goodbye and they hung up.

Then Ryan went back to working on his Corvette. His next step was to wash and wax the sports car.

***

Kelly's home turned out to be a comfortable-looking two-story Craftsman style house in a middle-class neighborhood of Rockport, a suburb north of Atlanta. The house was bordered by a white picket fence and an American flag was hanging by the door.

Ryan drove his Corvette onto the driveway of the home and climbed out. He approached the entrance and was about to press the bell when the door opened, and Kelly walked out. The GBI agent was wearing a black skirt, a light blue blouse with a gray blazer and she looked amazing. Her long, auburn hair was pulled back in a ponytail.

After she locked the door to her house, they walked back to his car.

"Wow!" she said. "Your car looks really good now." She tilted her head. "I think I gave you too good a deal on it."

"I've been working on it," he replied. "It still needs a lot more TLC, but it's getting there."

He opened the passenger door for her, and she got in. Then he strode around to the other side and climbed in.

"Is this car like the one the PI on the TV show drives?" she asked.

"You mean Magnum PI? No, Magnum drives a Ferrari. This car's a lot less expensive than that."

"I don't know much about cars. I drive the SUV they issue to all GBI agents, and I'm happy with it."

Ryan fired up the Corvette and drove out of the neighborhood.

They reached the restaurant twenty minutes later.

"The Brookwood," she said. "I've never been here before. It's a classy place. I should have dressed up."

"You look great, Kelly."

"Thanks."

They went inside the restaurant and got a booth by the fireplace, which was roaring. The place was decorated in dark woods, brass lamps, and had an intimate, upscale vibe to it, the reason Ryan enjoyed it so much.

When the waiter came, Kelly ordered a glass of Cabernet and Ryan ordered a Heineken. He would have preferred a Coors, but the restaurant was too upmarket to stock that brand of beer.

The drinks came moments later, and he held up his glass. "I propose a toast, Kelly. To your new job."

She clinked her glass to his and said nothing.

"You don't seem too excited about this promotion," he said.

"I'm not."

"Why?"

She shrugged. "I like being a field agent. This promotion makes me a manager. I'd have other agents reporting to me."

"And that's a bad thing?"

She frowned. "I think what you do is exciting. Being a PI. If I become a manager, I'd be in the office a lot more. I wouldn't be in the field much at all."

"I can understand that. But still, it's a big deal for you. Right?"

"Yes."

"Would you make more money?"

"A lot more."

"And you'd get a nicer office?"

"Yes."

"Sounds to me like you should take it, Kelly."

"I guess you're right."

Ryan smiled. "My guess is one day you'll be in charge of the GBI."

She tilted her head. "You're such a bullshitter."

"I'm being totally serious about this. You're smart, savvy, and have good people skills. You've got everything it takes to go to the top."

She gave him a long gaze as if trying to judge his truthfulness. Finally, she said, "Okay, I can see you're not joking around."

Ryan took a sip of his beer. "Let me ask you something. If you don't take this promotion, who will get the job?"

"Another one of the agents. A male GBI agent."

"What's he like?"

She scowled. "He's a real jerk. He thinks he's a lot smarter than he really is."

"So, you wouldn't like working for him, would you?"

"I'd hate it."

"There's your answer, Kelly."

She sipped her Cabernet and mulled this over for a moment. "You make a lot of sense, Ryan."

"So, you'll take the new job?"

She smiled for the first time that evening. "Yes, I am going to take it."

"That's great." He raised his glass, and they clinked again.

"Thank you, Ryan. For helping me work through this."

"No problem. That's what friends are for."

Kelly looked pensive. "I think I told you this before, but I was married years ago," she said her voice low and sad. "I got a divorce. I found out my husband was cheating on me. It was an ugly divorce. Ever since then, I've been gun shy about men."

"I remember you telling me that."

"You're the first guy I've had dinner with, in a romantic kind of place like this."

"I'm honored," he replied.

"Is that another one of your bullshit lines?"

He shook his head. "Not at all. I'm being totally honest. You're an amazing, highly intelligent, and beautiful woman."

She blushed a little and looked down at the table. "Thank you for that. But I'm too skittish to, you know ...."

"To what?"

She looked up at him. "The thing men and women do, when they like each other a lot ...."

Ryan covered one of her hands with his. "I understand, Kelly. And that's fine."

"So, we can be friends?" she said, her voice earnest. "Without doing it?"

"Of course we can."

"Thank you, Ryan."

He smiled. "You know, you can call me J.T."

"I know." She paused, then said, "But if I call you by your last name, it keeps our relationship professional, right?"

"It does."

The waiter came back and gave them the menus.

She pored over it for a long time. "What's good here?"

"Everything."

"There's so much here and all of it sounds good."

274

"Would you like me to order for both of us, Kelly?"

"Yes, please."

The waiter came back, and he ordered the almond crusted trout for Kelly and the New York strip for himself.

The food came a while later and she tasted it.

"This is delicious," she said.

"I knew you'd like it."

She grinned. "You've brought other women here, haven't you."

"Yes. But only the very special ones."

She blushed. "Stop that. We're only friends, remember?"

Ryan laughed. "I know."

When they finished dinner, and the waiter had cleared their plates, she said, "When the bill comes, I want to pay for it."

Ryan shook his head. "Oh, no you won't. I've never let a woman pay before and I'm not starting now."

She frowned. "You're kind of a male chauvinist, you know that?"

"That may be true. But I'm paying and that's that."

Her frown eventually evaporated. "All right. Have it your way." She went quiet a moment, then in a low voice said, "You're such a gentleman. That's nice."

"I'm glad you think so."

After Ryan had paid the bill, he drove them back to her house in Rockport. He pulled onto her driveway and shut off the Corvette.

"I'd invite you in," Kelly said, "but I've had a lot of wine tonight. I don't trust myself."

"I understand," he replied.

"Really?"

"Yes, really."

She gave him a long look. "You're so different than every other man I've ever known. Most guys would get mad, or argumentative and try to talk me into ... you know ...."

"I know."

She leaned toward him and kissed him on the cheek.

Surprised, he said, "What was that for?"

She smiled. "For being so understanding. For being my friend."

Then she climbed out of the sports car and went into her house, waving at him before she closed the door.

Chapter 85

Reykjavik, Iceland

The country of Iceland is a Nordic island nation located north of Europe, between the North Atlantic Ocean and the Artic Ocean. It's a sparsely populated nation, with only 400,000 residents. Its official language is Icelandic, although many of the people there speak English.

Geologically, Iceland is on a rift between tectonic plates, the reason the interior of the country is dominated by waterfalls, geysers, snow-topped mountains, and glaciers. Its wild and scenic landscape makes it a popular destination for tourists from around the world. The Gullfoss waterfalls, the geothermal waters of the Blue Lagoon, and the Vatnajokull glaciers are some of the most magnificent natural wonders on earth.

Nearly all the country's population lives in the coastal areas of the island. In fact, almost all the towns are close to Ring Road, the highway that follows the coast and encircles the nation.

The settlement of Iceland began in 847 A.D., when Norwegians immigrated to the island. In the 13th century, the island became a territory of Norway. Then in 1814, Iceland became a part of Denmark. After World War II, the island declared its independence and turned into a sovereign nation.

Reykjavik is the largest city in Iceland and its capital. The city is the center of the country's economy and government activity. It's also the hub of most cultural events and has a population of 145,000. Most of the high-end restaurants, hotels, clubs, and museums are located in the city. Harpa Hall, the ultra-modern glass and steel concert hall, is located on the waterfront of the city, and is Reykjavik's most iconic landmark.

Nikita was in Reykjavik now.

After fleeing China, she had taken flights to several different countries, under assumed names, trying to conceal her final destination.

Nikita knew that the murder of General Zhang would enrage the CCP and make them hungry for revenge. And she also knew the leaders of the Communist Party of China were smart, devious, and evil.

But then, she mused, *so am I.*

And after a month living in Iceland, she was confident she had escaped the clutches of the CCP.

Nikita was in the bathroom of her penthouse condo now. Staring at her reflection in the mirror, she continued combing her hair.

Her biggest regret was having to cut her long, beautiful raven hair. Her hair was short now and dyed a blonde color.

She could not alter her Asian features, but the new hair color and length made her appear much different than before.

Done in the bathroom, she went into the spacious living room, which had a spectacular view of the city's waterfront and harbor. Although her new home was not as luxurious as her beloved condo in Tokyo, it suited her needs for now. She planned on buying a large estate in the outskirts of the city, once she was completely sure no one had tracked her to Iceland.

Nikita went to her liquor cabinet and poured herself a large tumbler of *sake*.

Sitting on her plush leather sofa, she powered up her laptop, which was resting on the glass coffee table.

After logging on to her VPN, she went online and accessed her Swiss bank accounts.

She scrolled down the long list of assets, money she had accumulated over the years from her work as the operation center manager. There were cash accounts, in a multitude of currencies.

And there were also bonds and stocks of major companies from around the world.

Nikita grinned when she stared at the total value of her financial holdings.

Life is good, she mused, taking a long sip of *sake*.

Life is very good.

Chapter 86

Atlanta, Georgia

J.T. Ryan was in his office in midtown, scanning his email.

After that, he stood up from his desk and refilled his cup from the coffee maker. He also took a chocolate donut from the Krispy Kreme box he had bought earlier.

Then Ryan began reviewing the pending cases he was working on. Since no new leads had developed on the movie murders case, he had moved on to his other clients.

Just then he heard a knock at his door.

Ryan opened a desk drawer and placed his hand on the handgun inside. In his line of work, it was good to be cautious.

"Come in," he said.

His office door opened, and Kelly O'Hara entered. The attractive redhead with the piercing green eyes was wearing a sophisticated gray business suit with a white blouse.

"You're looking very stylish today," Ryan said with a grin. "Your promotion to supervisory agent seems to suit you well."

Kelly smiled and sat on one of the visitors' chairs fronting his desk. "Thank you. I'm starting to get used to the new job."

"How do you like it so far?"

She waved her hand in the air. "It's more paperwork, and more meetings, and less time in the field. But the money's good, and the idea of being a boss is growing on me. I never thought I'd enjoy being in charge, but it does have a lot of advantages."

"I'm glad for you, Kelly."

She tilted her head. "Thank you for giving me the advice to take it."

"That's what friends are for."

Then he pointed to his coffee maker. "Want a cup? I just brewed some this morning."

She made a face. "No, thanks. I'll pass. I've had your sludge before."

Ryan laughed. "Okay. How about some donuts?"

"You trying to make me fat?"

He gave her an up and down look, taking in her slender and curvaceous figure. "I don't think you have anything to worry about."

"Maybe so, but I'll still pass on the donuts."

"So, is this is a social call?" he said. "If it's not business, I can take you to lunch at the Varsity."

Kelly shook her head. "No, this isn't a social call. It's business."

"What's up?"

"The movie murders case we've been working on for a while. There have been no new killings in over a month. But at the same time, we haven't had a lead either. The ringleader, Nikita Nakano, vanished after she flew out of Beijing."

Ryan shook his head slowly, angry with that situation. "Yeah. I've moved on to my other cases, but I still need to find her and put her behind bars."

"Me too. After my promotion, I got a boatload of new cases to work on. But I've never given up on Nakano."

"So, what's new, Kelly?"

"I've kept researching her background, and I learned that over the last couple of years, she was issued several passports under different aliases."

"She's a smart criminal," Ryan said.

"True. So, I was able to track her down from the time she flew out of Beijing. It appears she flew to Canada and then to Spain, and then Norway, all under different names. I traced her using facial recognition software."

"That's great, Kelly. Good work. So, she's in Norway now?"

Kelly shook her head. "No. She left there and went to a different country."

"Where?"

"Iceland."

Ryan considered this a moment. "That's interesting. But it makes sense. Iceland is a remote place. Not many people go there, or even know it exists."

"I agree, Ryan. It would be a great place to hide out. She went to Reykjavik, the main city in Iceland."

"Looks like I'll be heading there next. I'll check the airline schedules and see what I can get."

"You ever been there?" she asked.

"Yeah. Once before, working on a case years ago."

"Do you speak Icelandic?"

"No. Didn't need to. Most everybody there speaks English."

"Okay. By the way, before I came here, I checked the gun laws in Iceland. They're strict, like the rest of Europe. I suggest you leave your weapon at home."

Ryan let out a long breath. "Yeah, I know. I'm not happy about it, but I'll play by their rules."

Kelly pulled a sheet of paper from her suit jacket and handed it to Ryan.

"This is a list of names that Nakano used on her different passports," she said. "As you can see, it's a long list."

Ryan scanned the list. "This woman is evil but also highly intelligent. She may be going by another name now that's not on this list. I'll have to track her down by her photograph."

"Sounds good, Ryan. How soon can you get started?"

"Right away."

Kelly looked at the tall stack of folders on his desk and pointed at them. "Are those the other cases you're working on?"

"They are."

"So, my case takes priority?"

Ryan nodded. "Of course. I want to catch this criminal. And I have another reason."

"What's that?"

"We're friends, Kelly. Your cases go to the front of the line."

"Thanks."

"No thanks needed."

Kelly reached into her pocket and took out a laminated card which she placed on his desk.

Ryan picked it up and read it. It was a GBI identification badge with his name and title of Consultant.

"Now that I'm a supervisory agent at the GBI," she said, "I can do things I couldn't before. You're now officially a contractor for the Georgia Bureau of Investigation."

Ryan grinned and pocketed the ID card. "This may come in handy, if I get in trouble with the law."

"True. But do me a favor."

"What's that?"

"Try not to get arrested. Iceland is a foreign country."

Ryan laughed. "I'll do my best. But I make no promises."

She shook her head slowly, then smiled. "You're impossible, sometimes."

"Yeah, but I'm also charming and witty. By the way, I've got a couple of new jokes if you'd like to hear them."

Kelly stood. "As tempting as that sounds, I've got to get back to my office. I've got a lot of work to do."

"Okay, Kelly."

Then she left his office, and Ryan went to his laptop to check airline schedules to Iceland.

Chapter 87

Reykjavik, Iceland

After researching the flight schedules, J.T. Ryan realized there were no direct flights into Reykjavik from Atlanta. But he did find an overnight KLM flight into Oslo, Norway, which connected to an SAS flight into Reykjavik's Keflavík airport.

At the airport's Avis car rental place, the agent recommended he go with a four-wheel drive vehicle, since it had snowed the previous day. It was December now and Iceland was turning bitter cold.

Once Ryan left the terminal building and strode toward his rented Range Rover, he was glad he had brought a heavy coat, since it was 5 degrees Fahrenheit outside.

He placed his bag in the back seat and started up the vehicle. Then he drove out of the airport complex and headed towards the city center, which was 30 miles away.

Once he got into Reykjavik, he checked into a hotel he had stayed at previously, the Hilton Reykjavik Nordica.

After checking in, he showered and changed clothes and ate at the hotel restaurant. He had been able to sleep on the flight over, so he was rested and eager to start working on the case.

From experience as a private investigator, Ryan knew bars were a great place to learn information. So he went into the tavern at the hotel, which was located on the first floor, adjacent to the lobby.

The place was large and empty of patrons, so he went to the long, wooden bar and sat on one of the stools.

The barmaid, a young woman in her twenties came over. She had a plain face and mousy brunette hair. She wore a black apron over her gray shirt and slacks.

"What would you like to drink?" she said, in accented English.

"What's the best Icelandic beer?"

"Ulfur."

"I'll have that. On tap, if you have it."

She nodded, went to the tap and poured a large glass, which she placed in front of him.

He read her name tag, which said, *Susan.*

Ryan smiled. "Is Susan your real name?"

She shook her head. "No. It is Adalbjorg. But it is too hard for the tourists to pronounce. So, I decided to go by Susan, and ever since then, my tips have been much bigger."

Ryan waved a hand in the air. "Where is everybody? This is a big hotel – this bar should be packed at this time of the day."

"The tour bus took most of them to the Blue Lagoon. It is the city's major attraction. You know what that is?"

"Sure. The geothermal spa. I went there last time I was in Reykjavik."

She placed a bowl of nuts in front of him and he nibbled on a few as he sipped his beer.

"How long have you worked here?" he said, to make conversation. Since the woman was a local, he figured she might be a good source of information.

She shook her head slowly. "Too long. But there is not much industry in Iceland. Most of the jobs here at tied to tourism." She gave him a tired smile. "I am hoping to find a rich husband, so I can quit this job."

He grinned. "For a good-looking woman like you, that shouldn't be hard."

"Thanks for the compliment. But I stare at the mirror every day. I am nothing to look at."

"I think every woman is beautiful," he said. "Each in their own way."

She cocked her head as if trying to determine if he was joking. She must have sensed that he was being honest, because she nodded. "Maybe you are right, mister."

Ryan extended his hand. "I'm John Ryan, by the way. It's nice to meet you, Susan."

She shook his hand. "Good to meet you, John. Are you a tourist?"

"No. Actually I'm a private investigator." He reached in his pocket, took out one of his business cards and handed it to her.

She glanced at it. "You are from Atlanta? You are a long way from home."

"I am. I'm working on a case. I'm looking for someone. Maybe you can help me find her."

Ryan took out his wallet, removed 200 Kronas and placed the bills on the top of the bar. "And I'm willing to pay for it."

Susan's eyes opened wide. "That is a lot of money."

"It's yours if can help me."

"Sure! I would be glad to." Then she grinned. "This is cool. Like being a spy, right?"

Ryan laughed. "Yeah. Something like that." He slipped the photo of Nikita Nakano out of his jacket and handed it to her. "This is the woman I'm looking for. Her real name is Nikita Nakano, but she goes by a long list of aliases."

Susan studied the picture closely. "She is very pretty."

"She is. But she's a criminal."

"Really?"

"Yes. Have you ever seen her?"

Susan shook her head. "No."

Ryan pushed the Kronas toward the barmaid. "You can keep the money. Ask around. Talk to your friends here in town. If you can get me a lead, I'll pay you more."

"Really?"

"Yes, really."

Susan took the money and stuffed it into her apron. "Would you like another beer, John?"

"I would." Then he glanced around the bar and saw that it was still empty of patrons. "And I'll buy you one, if you'd like. Doesn't look like you're going to be busy any time soon."

"That would be nice." She went to the tap and poured out two glasses of beer and came back.

The photo of Nikita was still on top of the bar, and she glanced at it. "Can I keep this picture?"

"Of course. I've got plenty more."

"You said this Nikita woman is a criminal. Is she dangerous?"

"Very. So don't approach her. If you see her, just call me. I don't want to see you get hurt."

"All right."

Susan took a sip of beer. "Your card says you're *J.T. Ryan*. What's the T. stand for?"

Ryan smiled. "Terrific."

"That was a joke, right?"

"Yes."

"You are not like a lot of the Americans we get here."

"What are they like?"

"They are all in a rush to see this and that, and take photos, and then go to another part of Iceland, and take more photos and post them on social media. Are you on social media, John?"

Ryan shook his head. "No. I don't really like it. I'm only on there if I'm trying to solve a case."

"I am not on social media either." She took another sip of beer, then munched on some peanuts. "I will ask around about the woman you are looking for. I know a lot of people in Reykjavik. I have lived here my whole life."

"How do you like it?"

She frowned. "I do not, really. I am tired of living here. It is a small place. Sometimes I feel trapped living here."

Ryan mulled this over for a moment. "Have you ever thought of moving to the U.S.?"

Her eyes lit up. "Oh, yes! I would love to move there."

"What's stopping you?"

She shook her head. "Money. I make just enough to buy groceries and pay my rent."

"I'll tell you what, Susan. If you can help me solve this case, maybe I can help you get to the United States. How does that sound?"

She gave him a skeptical look. "Are you serious, John? Or are you joking around?"

"I'm totally serious."

Susan picked up the photo of Nikita Nakano and stared at it intently. "I will work on this. Like I said before, I know a lot of people here."

Chapter 88

Reykjavik, Iceland

J.T. Ryan had spent three days in the city, looking for Nikita Nakano. But he found nothing. He had shown her photo to countless people, and no one recognized her. He'd also spent time with the local Reykjavik police, who seemed clueless as to her whereabouts.

Clearly the woman had changed her name, or appearance, or even worse, she had moved on to another country. This last possibility really bothered Ryan, because if it was true, he would be at a dead end.

On the fourth day of his stay, Ryan got in his rented Range Rover and started it up, eager to begin his search again.

Just then his cell phone buzzed, and he took it out of his coat pocket.

"It is Susan!" he heard the woman say in an excited tone. "I may have found her!"

"That's great," Ryan replied. "Where are you now?"

"At the same place I am always at. The bar at the Hilton."

"Good. I'm right outside the hotel now. I'll come back in."

He hung up and turned off the Range Rover. Then he climbed out and zipped up his coat. It had snowed heavily the night before and he trudged over the snow on the parking lot toward the building. It was bitter cold outside, and he missed Atlanta's good weather.

Ryan went in the building and then into the tavern on the first floor. Like the last time he had been there, the place was empty. He assumed the tourists were all on sightseeing trips.

Susan was behind the wooden bar, wiping it down. The young brunette was wearing a black apron over a white shirt and gray slacks.

Susan smiled. "I think I may have found her."

"Where is she?" he said, sitting at one of the stools in front of the bar.

"You said you would pay more?"

"I did." Ryan unzipped his coat, removed his wallet and took out 200 Kronas, which he placed on top of the bar.

"Ever since we met," Susan said, "I have been talking to people I know, including my relatives here in the city. A cousin of mine thinks he may know who she is."

"Who's your cousin?"

She looked at the money. "Can I have it?"

Ryan pushed the Kronas toward her, and she stuffed them in her apron. "My cousin is named Andri Olafur. He works at a realty company here in the city. He thinks he may know who she is."

"Okay, Susan. Where do I find him?"

"The realty office is by the town square, not far from the Hallgrimskirkja Church. Do you know where that is?"

"I do. I've been in town for three days so I'm familiar with the area."

Susan gave him the address and he thanked her and went back to his Range Rover. He found the realty office soon after, which turned out to be an old wooden two-story house that had been renovated to accommodate a business. It was located on Frikirkjuvegur Street, overlooking Tjornin Lake. Like most structures in Reykjavik, the building was painted in bright colors.

Ryan parked his vehicle on the street and went inside. There was only one person in the small office, and he approached him.

"I'm John Ryan," he said to the young man. "Are you Andri Olafur?"

The young man stood up from his desk. "Yes, I am."

"Susan sent me," Ryan said.

"Yes, yes, she told me about you. You are looking for the Asian woman. Is that right?"

"That's right." Ryan took out the photo of Nikita Nakano and showed it to the man. "Is this her?"

Andri Olafur stared at the picture carefully. "I believe it is her. But she looks different than in this photo. Now she has blonde hair, cut short."

"Where can I find her?"

Olafur grinned. "Information is not free."

Ryan had been expecting this. He took out his wallet and pulled out two hundred Kronas. He didn't hand it to the man, but instead said, "If you're bullshitting me, I won't be a happy man."

Ryan closed his fist and held it in front of the man's face. "And you don't want to see me when I'm angry."

Olafur's eyes opened wide. He raised his palms in front of him. "No, it is true. I have dealt with this Asian woman. She just looks different than in the photo."

"All right," Ryan said, giving him the cash. "Now where do I find her?"

The young man wrote on a notepad, tore out the sheet and handed it to Ryan. "She lives in a luxury condo close to the waterfront. The address is there."

"Did you sell it to her?"

The young man shook his head. "No. She is leasing it now, but she told me she wants to buy a bigger place in a few months."

"Okay. Do not contact her. She's a dangerous criminal. Do you understand?"

The young man nodded. "Yes. Are you going to arrest her?"

"Yes. That's my plan."

Ryan thanked the man and left the realty office.

Chapter 89

Reykjavik, Iceland

J.T. Ryan went back to the Range Rover and climbed inside. Then he mulled over what to do. He considered contacting the Reykjavik police before going after Nakano, but knew the criminal was wealthy and could have paid off people in the police department. Ryan didn't think that was the case here, but he also knew greed is one of mankind's strongest motivators.

Deciding to go after her on his own, he fired up the vehicle and drove toward the waterfront. Parking in the municipal lot on Girgsgata Street, he continued on foot. The young realty agent had told him the building Nakano lived in was close to Harpa Hall, the ultra-modern glass and steel concert hall. The Harpa was easy to find, since it's the city's most iconic building.

Ryan walked for two blocks and spotted the five-story condo building soon after. The place looked upscale, and he went into the lobby. Marble floors and high-end furnishings decorated the space.

Ryan bypassed the elevators and took the stairs to the top floor.

The realty agent had said she lived on that floor, so he strode down the richly carpeted corridor until he located the right unit.

He noticed the security camera above the impressive teak door right away, so he kept on walking, as he tried to formulate the best way to approach her.

Ryan had spotted two security guards in the lobby, along with CCTV cameras in the corridors, so he knew security in the building was sophisticated. But he needed to maintain the element of surprise as long as possible.

Knowing that if he broke into, or forced himself into the apartment, he would be detected, he needed to come up with a better approach.

Going back down to the lobby, he noticed there was a café there selling newspapers, coffee, and sundry items. He purchased a coffee and a newspaper and sat on one of the lounging sofas close to the elevators.

Then he pretended to read the paper as he sipped coffee, while keeping watch on the elevator doors. He figured the woman would eventually come out or go in the elevators. It could be a long wait, he knew, but right now it was his best way of catching her.

After two boring hours of nothing happening, he almost gave up. Glancing at his watch, he decided to wait another hour.

Soon after, the elevator doors opened, and a slender Asian woman stepped out. She was wearing a heavy coat and boots, obviously dressed for outdoor weather.

The woman was attractive and had short blonde hair, and at first, he didn't recognize her. But her beautiful Asian features were unmistakable – the woman was Nikita Nakano.

Ryan watched as she strode past him and headed toward the building's parking garage, which was adjacent to the lobby.

He folded his newspaper and stood, following her at a discreet distance. He went through the glass doors leading to the garage and watched as she climbed into a white Cadillac Escalade.

After a quick glance around to ensure there were no security guards nearby, Ryan sprinted to the Escalade. Then he flung open the passenger door and jumped inside, slamming the door shut behind him.

Nakano's eyes bulged in shock, but she recovered quickly, and she reached into her purse. She pulled out a Glock pistol and pointed it at his face.

"Get the fuck out!" she screamed. "Or you die now!"

Ryan grabbed the gun and wrestled it away from her.

"If this is a robbery," she snarled, "you'll be disappointed. I have no cash in my purse." It was clear she hadn't recognized him.

Ryan racked the slide on the pistol and leveled it at her. "This isn't a robbery, Nakano."

She seemed confused. "My name's not Nakano." Then her expression changed from confusion to rage.

"You, bastard!" she yelled. "How the hell did you find me, Ryan?"

"Does it matter how? The only thing that's important is I'm here." He pressed the muzzle of the gun to her forehead. "If you don't follow my instructions, you're a dead woman. Understand?"

Nakano's eyes widened. "Yes! Yes, I understand ...."

"Good."

"Please ... put down the gun ... it could go off ...."

Ryan grinned, despite the tenseness of the situation. "We can only hope."

"Please, Ryan."

He pulled the pistol away from her face, but kept it trained on her.

"What happens ... now ...." she said, her voice shaky.

"We need to have a long conversation," he said. "Then I call the police and you'll be arrested."

She stared at him and by her expression it was clear she was thinking furiously how to outsmart him.

"Let's go back up to my apartment," she said her voice calmer now. "We can talk there."

Ryan thought that through, realized he couldn't keep her in the car much longer. One of the guards on patrol would walk by and see what was going on, and all hell would break loose.

"All right, Nakano. We'll do that. The gun will be in my pocket. One false move from you and you die. Understood?"

She nodded. "I understand."

"Give me your key fob for the vehicle."

She reached in her purse, took out the fob, and he pocketed it.

Then he said, "I'll go out of the car, open your door and we'll walk side by side. Then we'll go upstairs."

Ryan exited the Escalade and escorted her back into the lobby, and then into the elevator.

They went up to her floor and she let them into her apartment. When they were inside, she turned off the alarm system.

Ryan pulled the gun out of his coat pocket and held it at his side. "Is there anyone else here, in your apartment?"

"No. I live alone," she said.

"Okay. Let's go in the living room so we can have our talk. But remember, if you try anything, you're dead. You're a cold-blooded assassin, so I won't hesitate to kill you."

"I'm not going to try to trick you, Ryan. I'm not stupid." Then she said, "Can I take off my coat?"

"Go ahead."

She removed her coat and rested it on one of the plush leather sofas. He glanced around the luxurious room, noticed the expensive artwork on the walls and high-end glass and chrome furnishings.

"Sit down, Nakano."

"Can I have a drink first? I need to calm my nerves."

He motioned with the pistol. "Do it. But no false moves."

"You want a drink? I have *sake* and bourbon."

Ryan shook his head. "No."

She poured out a tall glass of liquor and sat on one of the sofas in the room.

Ryan took off his coat and sat on a couch opposite hers. He held the Glock at his side.

She took a sip of her drink. "What happens now, Ryan?"

"I want you to tell me everything about your operation."

"And after that?"

"Then I call the Reykjavik police and have you arrested."

Nakano took another sip, then said, "I'm a wealthy woman. Very wealthy. I'll pay you a lot of money to let me go."

"Forget it. I'm not for sale."

She smiled. "Everyone has a price. What's yours? A million dollars? You can have it. I can wire you the money right now."

"I said forget it. You're wasting your time."

A self-satisfied smile crossed her lips. "Two million, then. How does that sound?"

"No deal."

She studied him for a long moment, then she smiled seductively. "Maybe I can interest you in another way."

The gorgeous Asian woman was wearing a low-cut white dress, and she pulled the hem up to show a lot of her beautiful legs. Then she spread her legs slowly, so he could see everything she had to offer. It was clear she was not wearing underwear.

He stared at her, becoming aroused. She was one of the most desirable women he had ever met.

Nakano grinned fiercely.

"See something you like?" she whispered. Clearly, she was enjoying herself. "You can have me and two million dollars."

Ryan tore his eyes away from her body and looked up at her face. "I said no, Nakano."

The Asian woman frowned, then glared. She crossed her legs and pulled the hem of her dress over them.

Nakano folded her arms in front of her. "Tell me something, Ryan. When we were in the car earlier, why did you grab my gun? Weren't you afraid I'd shoot you?"

"I figured you didn't have a round in the chamber. And I was right. When I racked the slide, no bullet ejected."

She glared. "How'd you figure it out?"

"Easy. Glocks don't have external safeties, so most people who carry that type of gun are worried it'll go off accidentally if they have a bullet in the chamber."

She nodded. "I'll remember that for next time."

"There won't be a next time, Nakano. You're going to prison for the rest of your life."

The woman shook her head. "No way. I'm not talking. I'm not going to incriminate myself. You're only assuming I'm a killer. You have no evidence."

"We don't need your testimony. We've got someone else who's already testified to the District Attorney."

"Who?"

"Remember Marie Dubois?"

She frowned. "You've arrested her?"

"Yes. With Dubois's testimony and with the financial records we've been able to obtain about your operation, we've got you cold for murder and conspiracy to murder on a long list of people."

She glared at him, and said nothing for a long moment, as if trying to decide what to do.

"Can I have another drink?" she said.

"You're stalling, Nakano. Tell me everything about your operation."

"Please, Ryan. Let me get another drink. It may be my last before I go to prison."

He motioned with the pistol. "Okay. But no false moves, or you die now."

"I understand." She stood, went to the liquor cabinet and poured herself a tall glass of *sake*. He watched her carefully as she took a sip of the drink and sat back down.

Ryan pointed the Glock at her face. "Drop the knife."

"What knife?"

"The small knife you got from the cabinet and is hidden in your palm now."

Nakano scowled. "You bastard!"

"Do it!"

She dropped the knife, and it fell to the carpeted floor.

"It's obvious I can't trust you. Get on the floor, Nakano, face down."

"Are you going to fuck me?" she screeched. "I'm not going to let you do that, you bastard!"

"Don't flatter yourself, bitch. Now get on the floor!"

She grimaced but did as she was told.

Ryan pulled out plastic cuffs and tied her hands behind her back. When he was done, he grabbed one of her arms and pulled her up, then pushed her on to the sofa.

He sat back down on the opposite couch, holding the gun at his side.

"What happens to me after I'm arrested?" she asked, her face clouded with fear now. It was the first time today that she looked worried.

"You'll go to prison for the rest of your life. You may even get the death penalty. That'll be up to the prosecutors and the judge."

She said nothing, the color drained from her face.

"I don't want to die, Ryan. And I don't want to spend the rest of my life in prison."

"You should have thought of that before you took up a life of crime."

She fought a sense of panic, then said, "What if I were to give you something extremely valuable. If I did that, could I get a lighter sentence?"

"You've already offered me money and sex, and I said no to both."

Nakano shook her head. "Something more valuable than that. I can give you everything. The people who hired me, the people who paid me to carry out the movie murders."

Ryan had always wondered why the murders were taking place. He and Kelly had never been able to figure that part out.

"By your expression, Ryan, I can see you're interested."

"Maybe I am. But my guess is you're giving me a boatload of bullshit."

"No! It's true! And I have all the proof. I have a flash drive with all the information about the operation."

"Where's the flash drive?" he said, still suspicious.

"In a safe in my bedroom."

"All right. For the moment, I believe you. Let's go get this flash drive."

"Not so fast, Ryan. I want to make a deal. I give you the flash drive and explain the whole operation, and I get a reduced sentence. No death penalty and no life in prison."

"Fine. I'll talk to the D.A. and tell them you cooperated. I'll do everything I can to get you a reduced sentence." He paused, then said, "How do you know I'll keep my word? I could be lying to you."

She sneered. "Because you're a man of principle. You proved you can't be bought off. You turned down two million dollars and sex with me. Anybody who does that will keep their word."

Ryan nodded. "That makes sense."

"So do we have a deal?"

"Yes, if the information proves to be true."

"It is! I guarantee it."

"Get up, Nakano. We'll go get your flash drive." He motioned with the pistol. "But if you try to escape, you're a dead woman."

She let out a long breath. "Yeah, I know."

They went into her luxurious bedroom, and she gave him the combination to her safe.

Ryan opened it and removed the flash drive that was inside. He noticed there was a stack of passports from different countries in the safe, along with bundles of U.S. dollars, Euros, and Icelandic Kronas.

Ryan pocketed the flash drive, and they returned to the living room and sat down on opposite sofas. Ryan held the pistol at his side.

"Okay, Nakano, start talking. And leave nothing out."

The Asian woman began describing the operation and was done an hour later.

Ryan was stunned by what he had heard.

"So, all of the movie murders were ordered by this General Zhang?" he said.

"Yes."

"And he's the Chairman of the China Film Group?"

"Yes. But he's dead now."

"How did that come about?"

She flashed an evil grin. "I killed that bastard! He made me his sex slave and I hated it. So, I cut off his cock and he bled out."

By the intense way she said this it was clear it was true.

"So, who runs the China Film Group now?"

"Probably his house cunt, his assistant Colonel Liu."

"Tell me again about the China Film Group. You said they're part of the Chinese government?"

"Yes. The China Film Group is the largest movie production company in China. It is owned and operated by the Central Propaganda Department of the Chinese Communist Party. As you probably know, the CCP controls all major decisions that rule the country. The ultimate decision maker in the CCP is the President of Communist China."

She paused, then continued. "The China Film Group is a state monopoly that not only makes films but also distributes them. It also owns all the movie theaters in China and many of the movie theaters around the world. In addition to this, the China Film Group controls which films American studios can show in the country of China. And since China is such a huge market, American film companies are eager to tailor their movies to what China dictates."

"I'm starting to understand, Nakano. Keep going."

"As I mentioned before," she said, "the Chinese Communist Party controls every major policy decision in China. Many years ago, the CCP decided that it was important to shape public opinion around the world. The end goal of all of this to make China the dominant world power, replacing the United States."

"I get it. Tell me more."

"Since the China Film Group has tremendous financial resources," she said, "all of which are provided by the CCP, they finance many American films. And they have for many, many years. Of the hundred highest-grossing American films released between 2014 and 2018, the China Film Group financed 41 of them."

"You're kidding."

"No, it's true," she said. "General Zhang told me all about this, and the information on the flash drive proves it."

"I didn't realize the scope of this whole thing," he said.

"And since the China Film Group finances these films," she continued, "they control the content. The Chinese people in the movies are always the heroes, and China is portrayed as a beautiful and honorable country."

"Since the China Film Group has that much control," he asked, "why did they need your operation? Why do they want movie people murdered?"

"Not everyone is greedy at the American movie studios," Nakano said. "There are still influential people that don't want to portray China as a bastion of truth and justice. These people have scruples, and they cling to the idea that America is a just and noble country."

"That's why these people have to be eliminated?" he asked.

"Exactly."

"I understand now," he replied. The magnitude of the Chinese Communist plot to take over American film making was massive.

"What I can't figure out, Nakano, is why you ran the operation out of Japan and not China. And you yourself are Japanese, not Chinese."

"General Zhang explained that to me," she said. "He called it 'Plausible Deniability'. So, if my operation in Japan was ever exposed, the general and the China Film Group would not be complicit. They would deny any involvement in the murders."

It was all making sense to Ryan now. "But why did you leave Japan?"

She shook her head and glared at him. "Because of you, you bastard! You were getting too close to finding me. So, I fled to China and set up shop there."

"You were always one step ahead of me, Nakano. I almost got you in Tokyo, and then in Beijing. By the time I found where you lived in China, you had already fled."

The Asian woman let out a long breath and her shoulders slumped. "I figured no one would locate me here in Iceland."

"We almost didn't. Lucky for us, we knew what you looked like, because you kept changing your name to a long list of aliases."

She grimaced. "I thought that by changing my hair color and cutting it short, I'd be able to evade capture."

"When I saw you in the lobby of this building, you almost fooled me. At first, I didn't recognize it was you. But you're such a beautiful woman, I figured it out."

"Tell me something, Ryan."

"What?"

"Do you think I look better as a blonde or with raven hair?"

"What does it matter now, Nakano?"

"I'm a vain woman. Humor me."

"You're gorgeous with your long, black hair. It complements your Asian features. You're still good looking as a blonde, but it makes you look cheap."

She nodded. "Yeah. I think so too. I hate the blonde look."

"Don't worry, when they put you in prison, your blonde dye job will wear off."

She scowled. "Don't remind me, you bastard." She paused a moment, then said, "I've told you everything. I've given you all the proof in the flash drive. Is our deal still good? You'll talk to the prosecutors?"

"Yes, I give you my word."

"Thank you. So, what happens now?"

"I call the Reykjavik police, and they'll come here and arrest you. Then you'll extradited and flown to the United States. There you'll be tried for murder and conspiracy to murder."

She said nothing for a long moment. Then she flashed a seductive grin. "My offer still stands. You can fuck me and get the two million dollars. It's not too late."

Ryan laughed. "I got to say, you do have a lot of hutzpah, lady. You're a cold-blooded killer, but you're also a gutsy and intelligent woman."

Her smile remained. "So, the answer is still no?"

"That's right, Nakano. The answer is no."

Chapter 90

GBI Headquarters
Decatur, Georgia

"What did you find on the flash drive I got from Nakano?" J.T. Ryan asked.

Agent Kelly O'Hara reached in a drawer, took out the drive and placed it on her desk. "I've spent hours reading all the information on there. And I've done research on the people and organizations that are listed. It's all true, Ryan. Everything Nakano told you is true."

"I had a feeling it was. Nakano is a cold-blooded killer, but I had the sense she was being honest about this."

Ryan and Kelly were sitting in her office. She was at her desk, and he was in one of the visitors' chairs.

"I did research on the China Film Group," Kelly said. "And they have been financing American movies for a long time. Which gave the Chinese Communist government a lot of leverage to control the content of the films."

Ryan considered this a moment. "What about Nakano's operation to murder people in the film business. Have you been able to track down who was paying for it?"

"I have. Nakano's Tokyo operation was funded by the China Film Group. The payments are clearly listed on the flash drive, and I was able to track down the bank transfers."

"Great work, Kelly."

"Thanks. But you did all the heavy lifting. You were the one who found Nakano, arrested her and got the information."

"Where is she now?" he asked.

"She's being held at McRae Women's Prison, in Helena, Georgia. After her trial and conviction, she'll serve her time at the Supermax Prison in Florence, Colorado. There's also the possibility she'll get the death sentence."

"I promised Nakano I'd talk to the prosecutors, try to get her a better prison cell, if nothing else."

"You'll get your chance, Ryan."

She picked up the flash drive and held it up. "The question I have, now that we have all this information about the China Film Group, what do we do with it? Clearly, they're a threat to the United States. Their Communist propaganda is indoctrinating Americans through movies all the time."

"I've given that a lot of thought, Kelly. And I think I've come up with a plan."

"I'm listening."

"Remember the first movie murder we worked on, a while back? It involved the actress who was killed in Rome. The film was being made by Genesis Films, the movie studio here in Atlanta."

"Of course I remember. So, what do you propose to do?"

"I need you to talk to the chairman of Genesis," he said, "and have him hire me as a producer for a little while, as a cover. Can you that?"

Kelly tapped her pen on her desk. "Sure, I'd be glad to."

"Once I'm 'working' for Genesis, I'll set up a meeting with the China Film Group, ostensibly to get financing for a movie Genesis is planning to make."

"Okay, that sounds plausible. What are you going to do when you meet with the Chinese?"

Ryan picked up the flash drive that was on her desk. "I'll make a copy of this and give it to them. Tell them we'll expose their murderous plot to the whole world unless they shut down their operation."

Kelly said nothing for a moment. "It'll be dangerous. They might kill you right then and there."

"Yeah. I thought about that. It's a chance I'm willing to take."

Kelly shook her head. "I can't let you do this. It's too dangerous. The CCP is a ruthless government."

"Can you think of any other way to take down the China Film Group?"

"No."

"Then I've got to do it, Kelly."

She shook her head again. "No."

"Why not?"

She looked away from him, clearly not wanting to meet his gaze. "I don't want you to get killed, that's why ... I ...."

"This is what I do for a living, Kelly."

She finally met his eyes. She was blushing a bit. "I know. Still ...."

"You need to leave your personal feelings out of it," he said. "You know my approach will work."

After a moment, she nodded. "All right. I'm not happy about it, but I don't see any other option."

"Thank you."

"Who will you meet with, at the China Film Group?"

"Nakano told me she killed the person who was running it, a man by the name of General Zhang. I want to meet with whoever took his place."

"When I was doing the research, the new chairman is a woman by the name of Colonel Liu. She's an officer in the People's Liberation Army."

"I remember that name, Kelly. Nakano said she was Zhang's assistant."

"I'll call the chairman of the Genesis Film company today and have him put you on his payroll. Then he can arrange a meeting with you and Colonel Liu. When do you want to go?"

"As soon as possible."

Chapter 91

Beijing, China

J.T. Ryan was waiting in the lobby of the China Film Group headquarters building.

Ryan had been waiting in the lobby for an hour past his appointment time. He figured the new chairman of the company made all her guests wait, as a way of maintaining control.

Soon after the elevator opened, and a young Chinese man stepped out. He was wearing a PLA military uniform.

"I am Captain Chen," the young man said to Ryan. "If you follow me, I will take you to see Colonel Liu."

They took the elevator to the top floor of the CFG building.

Then Ryan was shown into Colonel Liu's office. It had a great view of Beijing's downtown skyline.

Colonel Liu stood up from her desk, went around it and shook hands with Ryan. Then she went back to her desk, and he sat in one of the chairs fronting it.

"Would you like some tea or coffee, Mr. Ryan?" the colonel said. "I can have my assistant get it for you."

"No, I'm good," he replied. He noticed the colonel was an attractive Chinese woman in her mid-thirties. She was wearing a military uniform.

"To be honest with you, Mr. Ryan, I was surprised to get a call from Genesis Films to arrange this meeting. Genesis has been reluctant to accept financing from us in the past."

"I'm aware of that, Colonel. In fact, I'm very familiar with the threats the China Film Group has made to Genesis. And not just threats, but actual acts of violence, including murder."

Liu's eyes widened and she sat up straight in her chair. "I do not know what you are talking about."

Ryan removed a flash drive from his pocket and placed it on the colonel's desk. "What's on this drive will refresh your memory."

Liu stared at the drive but didn't pick it up. "What's that?"

"It's a detailed account of the China Film Group's involvement and funding of an operation. An operation that intimidates and murders movie people not willing to do the CCP's bidding."

Liu scowled. "If this is an absurd American joke, it is not funny."

Then she pointed at her office door. "Get out of my office! Now! Or I'll have you arrested."

"I'll leave when I'm done talking. Ever heard of a Japanese woman named Nikita Nakano?"

At the mention of Nakano's name, Liu's expression changed from a scowl to uncertainty.

"Nakano," Ryan continued, "was paid by the China Film Group to kill people in the film business who could not be intimidated or bought off."

The colonel stabbed her index finger toward his face. "That is a lie!"

"The proof is all there, on this flash drive, Colonel. Including bank account transfers, and the names of everyone involved in this operation. In fact, your name is mentioned many times along with General Zhang's. Clearly you and the general were involved in this murderous criminal conspiracy. By the way, you should know that we've arrested Nikita Nakano. She has cooperated and is willing to testify. She's currently in a U.S. prison."

Liu's scowl disappeared and was replaced by a frown.

She said nothing for a long moment, then she pressed a button on her desk.

Almost instantly, the office door opened and four uniformed soldiers rushed inside. All of them were armed with AK-47 rifles.

"Arrest this man!" Liu shouted at them in Mandarin.

A chill went down Ryan's spine, recalling what Kelly had said to him before he left for China. He visualized dying in a grim, filthy, dungeon-like prison.

"Before you arrest me," he said, "you need to know that I'm working for a U.S. law-enforcement agency. We've made many copies of this flash drive. If I don't return safely to the United States, the information will be shared with every news outlet in the world. You need to think about that before you lock me up."

Liu's eyes widened.

She went quiet, her face a jumble of emotions. Clearly, she was trying to process what was happening.

After a minute, she spoke in Mandarin to the four soldiers in the room. "You can leave now," she said. "Do not arrest him."

They gave her a questioning look, then nodded and left the office, closing the door behind them.

"What is it you really want, Mr. Ryan?" Liu said, her voice shaky.

"All of it must stop. The murders, the intimidation, the coercion. The takeover of American movies must end. Now."

"I will have to speak with my superiors," she said. "They will decide what to do."

"And who would that be?"

"The China Film Group is owned by the Central Propaganda Department of the Chinese Communist Party. It will be up to the CCP to decide."

"All right," he replied. "I've said what I needed to say. Can I go now?"

She flashed him a look of intense hatred and her hands formed into fists.

Then she let out a long breath and her shoulders sagged a bit. "Yes, Mr. Ryan. You can go now. But never return to China. If you do, you will be killed immediately. Do you understand?"

"I do," he replied, relieved he would not die today.

Then he stood and left her office.

Chapter 92

Atlanta, Georgia

J.T. Ryan was in his apartment, drinking scotch and listening to classical music. The composition playing on the stereo was his favorite, Brahms Intermezzo in A Major.

Just then there was a knock at his door. He unholstered his Desert Eagle and peered through the spyhole. Seeing who it was, he opened the door.

Kelly O'Hara stood there, and when she saw the pistol in his hand, she held up her palms. "It's just me, Ryan. You can put that away."

Ryan let her inside and closed the door behind her, then holstered the Desert Eagle.

"Sorry, Kelly. Ever since I got back from China, I've been edgy."

She tilted her head. "That's understandable. You were lucky to make it out of there alive."

"Yeah. I keep thinking a platoon of Chinese Communist goons is going to break down my door and blow me away."

Kelly grinned. "We'll, you'll be happy to know that I've got good news on that front."

"Really?"

"Yeah. That's why I'm here, to tell you all about it. But I could use a drink first."

He held up the tumbler of scotch he was drinking. "Want one of these? It's scotch whiskey."

She shook her head. "I never drink the hard stuff. But I'll take a beer."

"Sure. Let's go in the kitchen and I'll get us a couple."

Kelly followed Ryan into the kitchen, and she sat at the dinette table, while he got two bottles of Guinness from the fridge. He uncapped them, handed one to her and sat down across from her.

Ryan noticed the attractive redhead was wearing a stylish blue business suit, a light gray silk blouse, and heels. She had a leather messenger bag over one shoulder.

Kelly held her Guinness up in the air. "Cheers."

He clinked his bottle to hers and said, *"Ganbei"*.

"What's that mean, Ryan?"

"It's Mandarin Chinese for *Cheers*."

The young woman took a sip of the stout beer, then set the bottle down on the table.

"So, let me tell you the good news!" she said, excitedly. "Ever since you got back from your trip, I've been monitoring news reports from China, and in particular, the Chinese movie business." She grinned widely. "And today I found out something amazing."

"What is it, Kelly?"

"The China Film Group has ceased operations. All their employees have been laid off. And their headquarters building in Beijing has been shuttered."

Ryan smiled, overjoyed at the news. "That's great!"

"I know! We won, Ryan! We won."

"I could kiss you right now!"

She blushed a bright shade of red and looked down at the table. "Please, don't," she said in a low voice. "If you do, I'm not sure I can control myself …."

"I'm sorry, Kelly. I didn't mean to make you uncomfortable."

She raised her eyes and met his gaze. "It's okay. I'm just not ready for anything right now."

She covered one of his hands with her palm. "I hope you understand …."

"I do."

He took a long pull of his Guinness.

"So, tell me more about what happened in China," he said. "What about the person I met with, the boss of the China Film Group. Her name is Colonel Liu."

Kelly shook her head. "Her name was in the news also. Apparently, Colonel Liu was killed in a car accident in Beijing. A truck crashed into her car. Her body was found in the wreckage."

"Sounds suspicious," he said.

"I though so too. I figure the CCP murdered Liu and staged the accident to cover up the killing." She paused, then said, "There was another dead body found in Liu's car – a German man named Hans Kruger."

Ryan mulled over everything Kelly had just told him.

"It looks like," he said, "the Chinese Communist Party was afraid this whole movie murder conspiracy would become public knowledge and decided to get ahead of it by shutting down the China Film Group. And by getting rid of all the people there."

"You're right," she said.

"Any other news, Kelly?"

"Yeah. And this news is closer to home."

"What is it?"

Kelly took a sip of her beer. "You remember me telling you that Nikita Nakano was being held at McRae Women's Prison until her trial?"

"Yes."

"Well, yesterday the guards found her dead body. One of the other inmates shived her in the back. Nakano had ten stab wounds and bled out."

Ryan let out a long breath. "I'm thinking the CCP arranged the murder. Dead people tell no tales."

"Yeah. I thought the same thing."

Then Kelly opened the leather satchel she had brought with her, took out a check and handed it to him.

Ryan glanced at it, saw the check was made out to him for a large sum of money. "What's this for?"

"A bonus. For a job well done. The GBI would have never solved this case without your help."

Ryan grinned. "Thanks, Kelly. I appreciate it. This'll come in handy to buy engine parts and new tires for my Corvette."

Then he paused and thought about something else. "There's someone else who deserves recognition."

"Who's that, Ryan?"

"When I was in Iceland, a young woman there was helpful in locating Nakano. Her name is Susan Olafur and she's a barmaid at the Hilton Hotel in Reykjavik. I know she was interested in moving to the U.S. It would be great if you could get her an American work permit and help her find a job in the U.S."

"Consider it done, Ryan."

"Thank you."

"By the way," Kelly said, "now that you're done with the movie murders case, what do you plan on doing?"

"It's been a tough couple of months. I'm thinking of going on vacation for a while."

"Understandable," she replied.

Then she reached into her bag and took out a manila folder, which she handed to him.

"When you get back from vacation," she said, "this is the case I could use some help with."

Ryan scanned the file. It was an intriguing murder mystery, full of conspiracy and betrayal. It involved very rich and very powerful people. It was exactly the kind of case he enjoyed working on.

"I'll take it," he said. "In fact, I'll start working on it right away."

"What about your vacation?"

Ryan grinned. "The vacation can wait."

END

About the Author

Lee Gimenez is the award-winning author of 20 books. He is best known for his highly acclaimed J.T. Ryan mystery thrillers. Lee was a Finalist for the Author Academy Award, and many of his books were Featured Novels of the International Thriller Writers Association. They include The FBI MURDERS, KILLSHOT, TRIPWIRE, FBI CODE RED, CROSSFIRE, The MEDIA MURDERS, SKYFLASH, KILLING WEST, and The WASHINGTON ULTIMATUM. Lee is a multi-year nominee for the Georgia Author of the Year Award and is a U.S. Army veteran. His books are available at Amazon and many other bookstores.

All of Lee Gimenez's novels are available at Amazon and other bookstores worldwide.

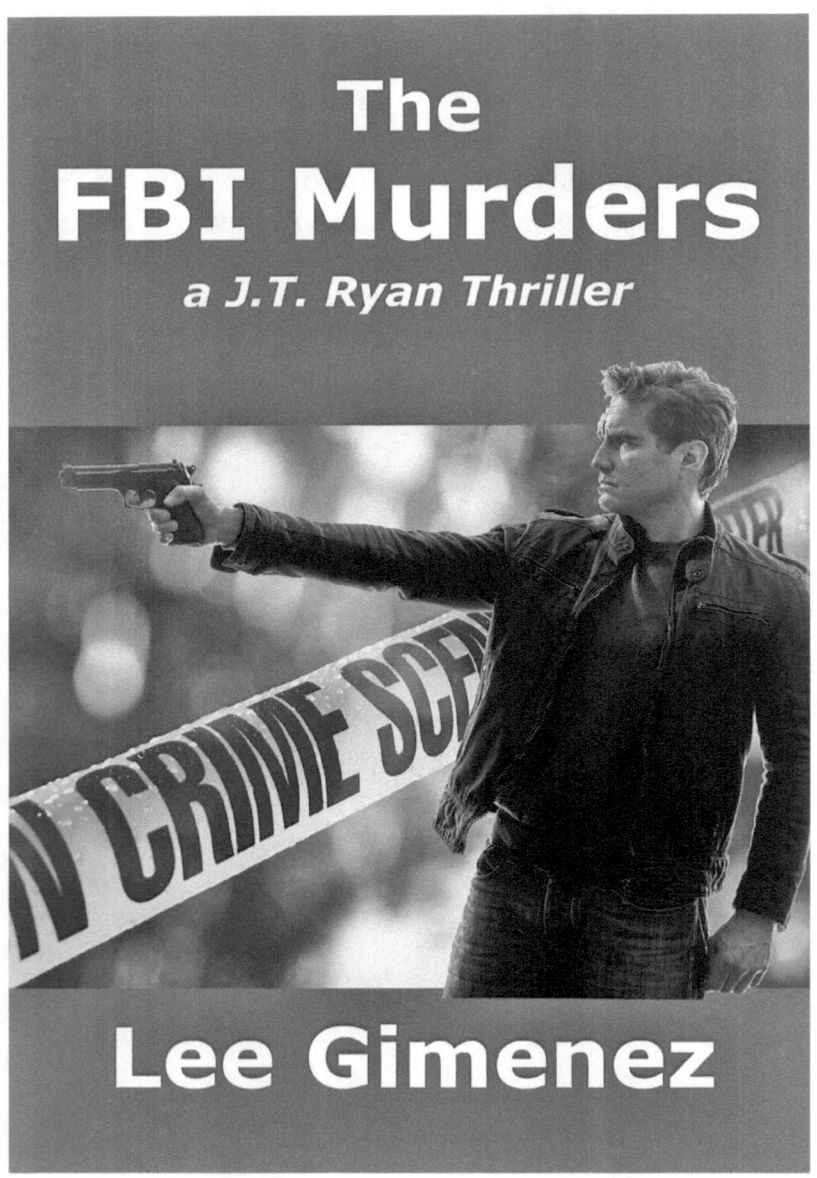

The
SIGMA
CONSPIRACY
a J.T. Ryan Thriller

Lee Gimenez

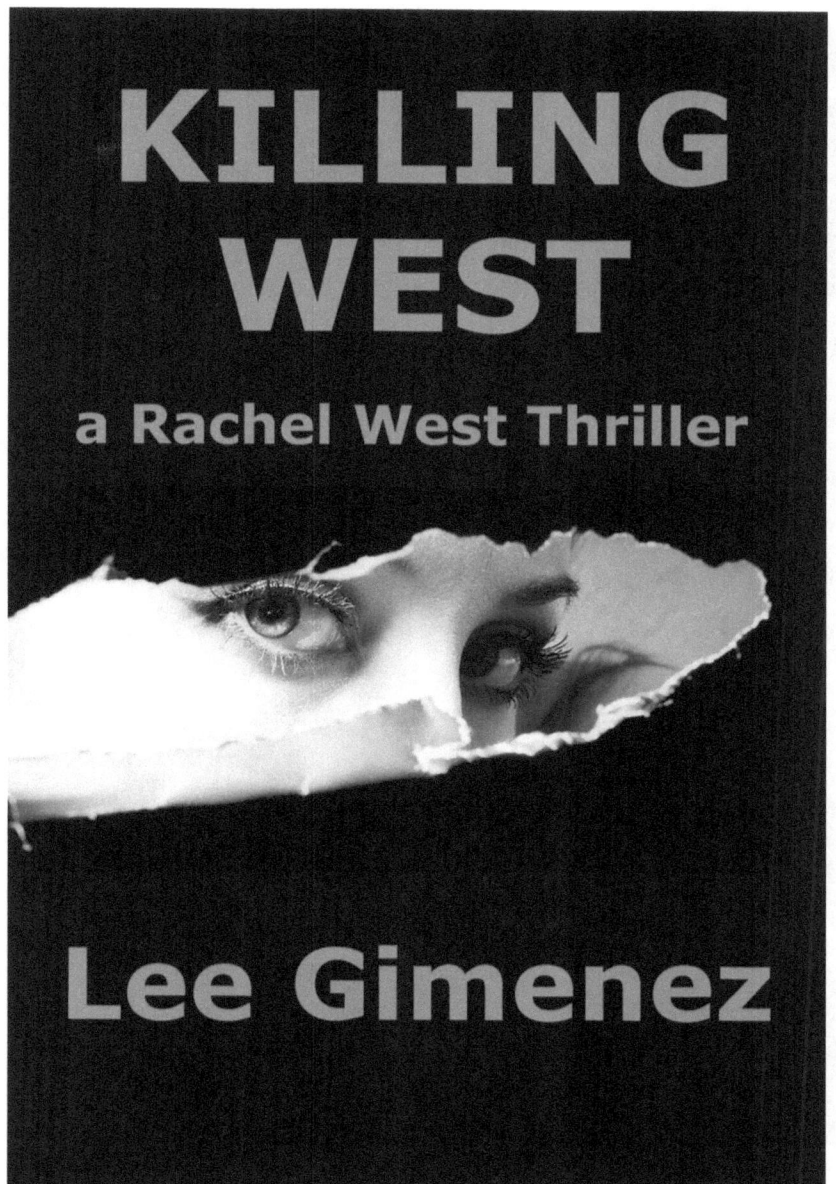

The
Washington
Ultimatum
Lee Gimenez